When
to
Cry Uncle

When
to
Cry Uncle

A NOVEL

PEGGY AYLESWORTH NOVOTNY

ISBN E-book: 979-8-9889356-0-5
ISBN Paperback: 989-8-9889356-1-2

To the memory of my loving parents and to my
wonderful children and grandchildren.

When
to
Cry Uncle

CHAPTER 1

A New Hire

According to Alfred, Lord Tennyson, "Tis better to have loved and lost than never to have loved at all." I get that, Al, but just how many times is a person supposed to lose before she throws in the towel? Such was my dilemma last summer during one of the craziest weeks of my life. I wasn't looking for romance. In fact, I'd sworn off entirely after the collapse of my second marriage. When an exceptional chance for romance swept into my life, decisions loomed large. My memory of that week remains vivid, so I've written an account to remind myself of the lessons it provided. I hope my recollections will be useful for readers who are forced to snatch clarity from the jaws of indecision. For the outcome to make some sort of sense, I'd better start at the beginning.

It was the week of the Fourth of July, and my special guests were due at the inn the next day. I was waiting in line at the grocery store deli and reviewing my shopping list when I heard someone sniffling behind me. The sound was coming from directly behind my head, so I thought it must be from an adult and not a child. I wondered why an adult would stand there sniffling without blowing their nose. The sniffling persisted and was becoming irritating.

I wanted to turn around and look but didn't want to appear rude. I needed a reason besides outright nosiness to sneak a peek at the sniffler. I rifled through my purse, which was wedged under dark rye bread in the child seat of my cart, and pulled out a tissue. The wadded tissue smelled like stale perfume and mints, but it was better than what the sniffler was using, which was nothing apparently.

Out of the corner of my eye, I glimpsed a woman with puffy eyes and tears running down her cheeks. I recognized her vaguely but couldn't remember why. She was fortyish with light brown shoulder-length hair. Even at a glance, I could tell she was crying and not sniffling from a head cold or allergies. I had to make a quick decision about whether or not to offer her the tissue. In doing so, I would also have to acknowledge that she was having an issue. Was I ready to offer words of concern and consolation? I wasn't sure. It can be annoying to receive unsolicited concern, and I thought she must have enough problems without a stranger prying into her life. She probably wanted to pick up some potato salad and scoot home.

"Do you think I could possibly use your tissue?" the sniffler asked.

"Oh, of course," I said, shaking the tissue to make it less wadded. I had no choice now. We had spoken, so I had to acknowledge her condition. "Are you alright? Can I help?" I suddenly envisioned myself cooking and cleaning for her and her seven children, who were homeless because their house burned down and her no-good husband had deserted them.

"No thanks. I've just had a bad day," she said. "I didn't know I was going to start crying like this in the grocery store. It's embarrassing, but I need a few things." She blew her nose long and hard.

"Would you like to go ahead of me? I'm not in a hurry," I said. My remark wasn't exactly true because I had several things to take care of at the inn. "Just here to pick up some odds and ends."

"I don't want to hold you up," she replied.

"No, really, it's fine," I said. "I think you should go ahead."

When the deli lady asked, "Who's next, please?" the sniffler placed her order. If she had seven children, they were small eaters with good taste. She ordered a half pound of imported ham, a half-pound of crab salad, and a quarter-pound of marinated olives—the latter ruling out most kids.

"I think I know you," said the sniffler, dabbing her eyes. "Do you have a child at Noblesville High School?"

"I did last year. My daughter is a freshman at Ball State now."

The sniffler's eyes began to clear as I placed my order for a pound of thin-sliced rare roast beef and a quarter pound of crumbled blue cheese.

"Were you in the Drama Boosters Club?" she asked. "I think I met you at one of the meetings."

"Yes, I went to some of those meetings," I said. "I remember you now. Do you have a child in drama?"

Her eyes filled with tears again, and her bottom lip shook as she whispered, "I was there for my ex-husband's son, Teddy. He was a freshman last year. I don't get to see him much now that his dad and I are divorced."

"I'm sorry," I said. "I didn't mean to make you cry again." The deli lady handed me the blue cheese.

"I've told myself to get a grip," she said. She leaned in as though wanting to share a secret. "I don't know why I don't listen to myself." Other customers were rolling their eyes since we were holding up the line.

The deli lady held up a slice of roast beef. "Thin enough?" she asked.

"A little thinner, please," I replied. I turned to the sniffler. "Sometimes crying sneaks up on a person. It comes out of nowhere.

There probably isn't anybody in this line or in the whole store who hasn't had a sneak attack of crying sometime."

The deli lady finished my order, and I made room for it in my cart. Since the sniffler and I were finished at the deli, a decision arose. Should I offer another wadded tissue and say so long or should I keep talking with her? If she was crying over the breakup of her marriage, did I really want to know about it? Could I stand hearing a story that might hit close to my own bones? I had a sudden urge to ditch my cart along with the rare roast beef and blue cheese and break for the automatic doors. On the other hand, how could I turn my back on her? I pushed my cart alongside hers and nodded in the direction of the salad bar. She followed me.

"Are you gonna be alright?" I asked.

"I think so," she said, unconvincingly.

"Okay, look, whatever is the matter, things will get better; I'm sure of it. It feels terrible now, but time will help." My words were so dismissive. I only assumed she was crying about her divorce. What if she was crying about a sick child or parent or somebody in the military in some God-forsaken country?

"I'm okay, really. Thanks," she said. She pushed her cart away from mine and headed toward frozen food.

I went back to the deli to pick up the mozzarella I'd forgotten. A few minutes later, as I hit the snacks aisle, I saw the sniffler staring as if transfixed on pretzel rods. I'd rounded the corner so hurriedly that there was no turning back. She didn't move or even blink. I tried not to stare, but I couldn't help it. It would be like not watching a motionless lizard. I pretended to read the nutritional facts on a bag of pork rinds while keeping her in my sight. No movement. I knew she was in trouble, so I pushed my cart to hers.

"Would you like to get a cup of something with me?" I asked. "The coffee bar has a raspberry cream latte to die for."

"I don't want to hold you up," she said. "I'm sure you have other things to do."

"Nah," I said. But I was churning inside because I should have been at the inn freshening bathrooms, making beds, and excavating my refrigerator.

We pushed our carts to the coffee bar. She ordered the latte; I ordered espresso with a few drops of crème de cacao since I'd be up late anyway.

"I don't want to pry," I said. "We could sit here and not even talk if you'd like. It just upsets me seeing someone cry like that, and I thought . . . well, maybe it would help to talk. Anyway, the latte alone might cheer you up. It's a happy potion." Again, I felt dismissive, but I was struggling for words. "By the way, my name is Jill Merrick. I live on Allisonville Road a little north of here."

"Teri Bennett," she said, softly. "I got my second divorce about six months ago, and I'm still a mess. I thought Jerry and I were so right. Things were really good between us until his first wife tried to get him back, at least it seemed like she was trying. She used every trick in the book, but he couldn't see it. It was a nightmare. I think he still loved me when we divorced, but he was confused. She used Teddy to get to him all the time. I couldn't take it. I was afraid he'd go back to her. I saw the rice pudding at the deli and remembered how much Jerry loves it. That's all it takes to set me off."

"Sounds like Jerry didn't give you much reassurance," I said. "I mean, it wasn't your fault he let her mess up your marriage."

"I'm the one who messed it up. I didn't trust him. I drove him right back to her. Played right into her hands. When he found out I'd put a tail on him, it finished everything."

"A tail?" I asked. "Wasn't it enough that he had horns and a pitchfork?" Teri didn't laugh. "Just out of curiosity, where did you find somebody in Noblesville to tail your husband?"

"My sister's husband's brother is a detective in Indianapolis. He helped me hire a guy. My sister thought it was a great idea. Turns out it wasn't, but I was so jealous that I couldn't see straight. The guy wasn't very good, either. Jerry called me one day and said my private eye was a fast food junky. I asked him what he was talking about, and he said the guy kept leaving trash in the parking lot next to his office. He was tired of cleaning up after him."

"What did you say?"

"What could I say? I denied it."

We sat in silence for a few awkward moments. After draining her latte, Teri said, "Love makes a person do stupid things."

"Can't argue with that," I said. "Do you mind if I ask why you hired the guy? What did you think your husband was doing?"

Teri rolled her eyes. "I had it stuck in my head that Jerry still cared for her. I didn't have proof, but she kept making excuses to see him. He fell for it every time."

"Okay, it's been six months since your divorce," I said. "Has he gone back to her?"

"Well, that's the weird thing about it; he hasn't. I have friends who have seen them together, but they don't act like they're together—you know, a couple I mean."

"Huh," I said. We sat in silence again. "How 'bout another latte? My treat."

"No thanks," Teri said. "It was nice of you to stop and talk to me. There aren't many people who would do that. Nobody helps strangers anymore. We're all afraid of each other. Do you mind if I ask about you? You said you live north of here on Allisonville Road. Whereabouts?"

"I own the Bray Farm Bed and Breakfast Inn just after you pass Connor Prairie Homestead."

"You're kidding," Teri said. "I've always wanted to see the inside of that place. It's so pretty and so big. You own that?"

"You should have to clean it. If you think it looks big from the outside, come over and dust sometime."

"Bray. Bray. There are a million Brays in Hamilton County, aren't there?"

"The Brays have lived around Noblesville since dirt," I said. I hoped to avoid a lengthier discussion of my oak-like family tree. "I grew up on that farm, inherited it from my parents, Buck and Mona. When Mother and Daddy died, I turned the house into a bed and breakfast. I love the place, but it's a lot of work."

"Are you booked most of the time?"

"Yeah, we stay pretty busy. Holidays are nuts. I go all out with Christmas trees and lights. Summer's busy, too, though. People visit Connor Prairie, the state fair, and other fun stuff and they stay at my place."

"Who takes care of all those flowers?"

"You're looking at her, but I hire summer help. Bonnie Tubman has helped me for several summers. Maybe you know Bonnie. She teaches English at the high school. Sad to say, I've just lost her because of her arthritis, so I'm looking for someone else."

"Does she live with Stuart Tubman on Division Road?"

"Yeah," I said. I chuckled at Teri's question as if the ultra-conservative Bonnie and Stu were shacked up. "She's been married to Stu for thirty years. Do you know Stu?"

"I know his voice on the phone. I know him like I know most of the people around here who don't have city water. I work for Wren Water Softener Company. You know, the 'tweet yourself to soft water' people."

"Oh, my goodness," I said. "You work for Bud and Billy Wren? They're crazy. I went to high school with them. They were both in my graduating class. Bud's older than Billy, but he failed once or twice. He was wild and still scares the hell out of me. He drove the loudest cars and picked fights with everybody. The moron even picked fights with girls."

"I know," Teri said, slumping a bit. "That's why I divorced him."

"Oh, geez," I said. "I'm sorry. I didn't mean … well, Bud was really good in shop class. He was good with . . . uh . . . motors. Everybody said so."

"It's okay," Teri said. She cracked a resigned smile. "Bud is crazy. I stayed at 'tweet yourself' because they pay pretty well. Bud and I don't speak much. Actually, we get along better now than when we were married. I take the orders for water conditioners and he installs. It works out okay."

"That's good," I said. The knot in my stomach tightened as I thought of all the things not getting done at the inn. "Well, I should get my groceries home."

"Is the inn full now?"

"I don't have any guests right now. My daughters are coming home for a week. They'll be here tomorrow evening. I saved a couple of weeks this year for them, and the Fourth of July week is one. My younger daughter, Lauren, and her friend will be here. My older daughter, Stephanie, and her husband are coming, too. Can't wait to see them."

"So, Lauren is the freshman at Ball State and Stephanie is … ?"

"She's working on a PhD in history at IU. Her husband, Robert, is an English professor there."

"Wow. They all sound so smart."

"Well, I'm proud of them."

"You're single?"

"I'm divorced, too," I said. I had no intention of saying more on that topic. I was the designated rescuer at the moment, and it would stay that way. "You okay now?" I asked. I slid to the edge of my chair and gathered my things.

"Yeah, I'll be alright. Thanks again." Then, in the manner of an old friend, Teri said, "May I ask you one more thing? Would you consider letting me help with your gardens?"

"Really?" I asked. "You want to help me?" I panicked slightly imagining the disaster that was sure to follow a spur-of-the-moment hire. "Are you a gardener? I mean, it's hard work, and I need somebody who can work on their own."

"I won't lie to you," Teri said. "I've never done much gardening, but I'd love to try. I learn fast, and I'm very dependable. I haven't missed a day at 'tweet yourself' for ages. I'd have to work part-time, of course, because of my job, but I could help after work and weekends."

Teri's honesty and the fact that I was desperate for help made her offer appealing. "Well, okay, we could give it a try," I said. I suddenly remembered the summer when I hired my neighbor's son for yard work and barn chores. Uncle Mort and I mostly found Stevie Catzwell napping or smoking offensive-smelling concoctions in the barn. Firing Stevie placed a figurative fence between me and the Catzwells that was still entrenched.

"I can use help right away," I said. "Can you start soon?"

"I don't have anything to do tomorrow afternoon," Teri replied.

"Tomorrow is Sunday. Do you want to wait until a weekday?"

"No, I'd love to start tomorrow, if that's alright."

"Do you think we could give it a trial period? You may not like the work."

Teri gave me a little smile indicating that she knew a trial period would protect me, too. "Sure, that's a good idea," she said. "I'm so excited! I feel a lot better now." She gave me a sweet hug that left me feeling I had known her for much longer than fifteen minutes.

We firmed up the details and went separate ways. I double-checked my grocery list: eggplant, crab meat, mozzarella, fresh garlic, chicken breasts, ciabatta bread, a couple of favorite wines, etc., etc. It was all there.

As I drove home, I wondered what Buck Bray would have said to me for hiring someone as spontaneously as I'd hired Teri Bennett. In zero to fifteen minutes, I'd gone from not knowing her to hiring her to tend my lovely gardens. I couldn't dwell on that; I had groceries in need of refrigeration and an inn to freshen up.

CHAPTER 2

Give Me Strength

I stayed in bed that Sunday morning to gather my thoughts about the week ahead. My noisy guinea fowl scratched at the ground beneath my bedroom window as they do most mornings about seven o'clock. The long legs I'd inherited from Buck ached from house and garden work. I'd recently turned fifty years old, and the option of leaping out of bed was fading.

It wasn't just my legs that held me back. I needed extra time to get my head right for the week. I had to chat with myself about how I'd be with Lauren and Stephanie. I promised myself that I wouldn't ask Lauren about boys she dated at Ball State, and under no circumstances would I say a word to Stephanie on the subject of her getting pregnant. No matter how much the girls baited me, I wouldn't take the bait.

It was great to lounge in the quiet with no guests bumping around the inn and no reason to make a big country breakfast, so I dozed a little longer. By seven-thirty, the July sun was already duking it out with the central air unit. I wondered if Uncle Mort had gathered eggs and fed the chickens, chores he often left to me. I looked out the window to see if he'd let the chickens out of the coop and into the surrounding pen. No chickens. Apparently, I'd be adding that chore to my morning to-do list.

I fell back onto the pillow and closed my eyes, but they kept popping open. Though I was excited about the week ahead, my excitement was tinged with apprehension. I anticipated an emotionally hectic time as always when my girls share the same space.

Stephanie and Robert had breezed home toward the end of IU's spring semester, but they stayed with Robert's parents in Indianapolis and were completely preoccupied. Stephanie was working on her dissertation, and Robert had a research project underway. Lauren and her roommate, Chickie Stampler, had breezed home for a couple of days at Easter, but they were always on the go.

The quiet in the house was delicious. I lay in my trusty four-poster bed, the one Buck and Mona bought for me on my tenth birthday. It's the bed I came home to on college breaks and the one Phil and I slept in when visiting home. Stephanie and Lauren would jump on the bed until Mona bribed them off with ice cream or brownies. I still love the big soft bed. I stared at my feet wondering if I should paint my toenails since the girls paint theirs. It was delightful to have a morning to contemplate toenails.

Did I really think my plans for the week would stick? I could only guess how the week would unfold. I knew I would serve dinner around seven o'clock that evening if everyone arrived as planned. Tomorrow, we would all have breakfast at Eddie's Café on the square in Noblesville. After breakfast, we'd watch the Noblesville Fourth of July parade and cheer for Rita and Pink on their spirited palominos. We'd take in sidewalk sales uptown and have dinner on Pink and Rita's pontoon boat in the evening. If we could get through those events without incident, I'd let the rest of the week sort itself out.

The guinea fowl were back under my window like feathered alarm clocks pecking the seconds away in the grass. My poor Rhode Island Reds were still in the coop, but I wanted one more moment of blissful silence. The only sounds were my breath and the comforting whoosh of cool air streaming through the air ducts.

My thoughts drifted back to my toenails and to Rita, who had dropped a small fortune in nail salons. Rita, my best friend, moved from Kentucky to Indiana with her family at the beginning of our sophomore year of high school. Though we're very different in temperament, we became inseparable buddies. She is a force, well-fixed, opinionated, and the center of her own universe. But we've ridden out life's storms together and are as close as any sisters. I tell her my innermost thoughts—some that I wouldn't dare share with my daughters. Whether or not I ask for her opinion, she delivers it unvarnished but with love. I do the same for her.

I began thinking in realistic terms. Soon, Stephanie, Lauren, Chickie, and Rita would collide center stage in the little drama of my life. The thought made me bolt upright. I threw back the sheets, hit the shower, jumped into a pair of jeans, and adjusted my attitude. I would soon be with the people I love most in the world. I would make the most of it.

The chickens nearly stampeded as I opened the coop door, egg basket in hand. They raced into the sunshine, ruffling their feathers in indignation at my tardiness. Reds are beautiful, and I never get tired of watching them. There are bosses, boss's toadies, tattletales, quiet and faithful workers, challengers to the rule, and former challengers living in wounded resignation. Since I only keep chickens for the eggs and not to hatch chicks, roosters are of little use. Besides, I don't like roosters' personalities—bullies by nature.

As I entered the coop and untied the feed sack, I heard Uncle Mort's unmistakable chuckle as he peered into the coop. "Thought about lettin' you sleep this mornin'," he said, "but then I thought, nah, why should she sleep when I have to git up? A little late, ain'tcha?"

"Morning," I said. "I needed some extra peace and quiet with the girls coming home tonight."

"Oh, lord, I forgot they was comin'. What time they gittin' here?"

"I told them I'd have dinner ready about seven o'clock," I said, while collecting pretty brown eggs from the nests. "Hope you'll join us."

"Maybe. Did you notice I took out the one they've all been peckin' at? I took her over to my place for a while until her feathers grow back. They would've pecked 'er clean here."

"What would I do without you?" I replied. "I've been so busy the last few days, I forgot about the poor thing. Thanks." I reached under a broody hen who lunged at my hand with lightning speed. Undaunted, I moved back in for her eggs. "Corn looks good."

"Yup, not bad, but we can use s'more rain. Can't git too much rain this time o' year. They used to say corn should be knee-high by the Fourth of July. We like it shoulder high now, ya know."

Without a doubt, that was the millionth time I'd heard Mort debunk the "knee-high by the Fourth of July" adage. Mentioning corn to him in May, June, and July leads to labyrinthian musings about days gone by on the Indiana farm, just as it had with his best friend, my father. I wasn't in the mood for talk of a better world in yesteryear. For good or for bad, this was my world now, so I had to make the most of it.

"Do ya remember Harlowe Barnes is comin' on Friday?" Mort asked.

"Harlowe Barnes has the personality of a stump," I replied.

"Didn't know personality counts for shearin' sheep. If you're so picky, I'll give you the phone book. We'll see how many shearers you find." Score one for Mort.

I continued plundering nests and asked, "Is the hay ready to cut?"

"Gonna cut it tomorrow."

"On the Fourth of July? Why don't you wait a day and come to the parade with us? Rita and Pink invited us to dinner on the pontoon. It'll be fun."

"I'm not 'bout to set sail with Pink Restin so he can try to sell me a truck all day. Nor am I gonna listen to Miss High and Mighty blabbin'. Besides, rain's in the forecast. Gotta cut it tomorrow." He inspected my basket of eggs and re-tied the feed sack to improve upon my work.

Mort and I both knew my invitation was purely a courtesy. He hadn't attended the Noblesville Fourth of July parade since he played the trumpet in the high school marching band in the late 1950s. Though Rita and her husband, Pink, were my dearest friends, Mort would only take them in small doses.

"I need to tell you something," I said, reluctantly. "I hired someone yesterday to help with the gardens. Bonnie's arthritis has gotten the best of her, and I need somebody. I met a woman who wants to help. She's from Noblesville; her name is Teri."

"Okay," Mort replied. We stepped outside the coop and into the sunny chicken pen. "You're the boss here. I don't need to know." I breathed a sigh of relief when he didn't ask if my new hire knew something about gardening. He climbed into his pickup and drove down the lane connecting our farms.

I walked from the chicken pen to the vegetable garden, hooked the basket of eggs on a fence post, pet my little calico cat, and surveyed the farms. My sheep and Mort's cattle were grazing. The corn and soybeans were flourishing, the chickens were scratching at the earth, the sky was clear, the guinea fowl were making their rounds, and the gardens were thriving in the July sauna. Everything felt right, and it made me happy. Like a sculptor chipping away unwanted shards, I'd chipped away chaos in my life until I made order and a pleasant little world called the Bray Farm Bed and Breakfast Inn where I was mistress.

I pulled weeds here and there and harvested basil and thyme for dinner. I clipped a bunch of lavender to place in the bedrooms that would once again be Stephanie and Lauren's, if only for the week. The lavender would help them sleep peacefully.

CHAPTER 3

Flowers vs. Weeds

It was late afternoon when I finally placed the lavender on nightstands in each guest room. A glare from a car shot through a window. Teri Bennett had arrived, so I hustled to the kitchen door to greet her. "I'm here and ready to learn," she said. "I wasn't sure what to wear, so I put on these old cut-offs. Should I have dressed better?"

"Yes. I'd like you to go home and put on white linen slacks, a flouncy blouse, and a hat with ribbons. That's what I wear in the garden."

"Oh," she said, pivoting to go back out the door.

"No, no. I'm joking," I said. I pulled her gently back into the kitchen. "You're dressed just right. How about a nickel tour of the inn before we check out the gardens?"

Teri pried off her tennis shoes in an instinctive show of courtesy. The nickel tour became a twenty-five-cent tour as she asked questions about my antiques and poked politely around the inn's guest rooms and adjoining bathrooms. "Wow, what a beautiful place," she said. "Was it this beautiful when you were growing up?"

"My mother loved antiques. She inherited most of the pieces from her family. She was an only child like me and a little spoiled, I think. She was fussy about the house. Daddy was very down to earth and liked things comfy, so it was always a tug o' war between them. The house was smaller when I was a kid. I remodeled the kitchen and added the south wing guest rooms when I decided to try the B and B. I didn't always know what I was doing, but it's worked out."

"Your kitchen is so big," said Teri. She ran her fingers over the Viking stove that took me two years to pay off. "If I liked to cook, I'd invest in one of these, but I hate cooking. Jerry didn't ask me to cook much. He loves Chinese takeout more than anything else, anyway, so we ordered from Benny's Hunan House of China all the time. Jerry always got a bag of fortune cookies, and we'd pick out the ones we liked. He was so sweet that way."

Changing the topic, I said, "My girls will be here pretty soon. Let's take a walk in the gardens and get you started."

"I'm sorry for talking about Jerry so much," Teri said. "Just tell me to be quiet when I do that."

"Okay," I said with a wink.

The hottest part of the day had passed, but the July sun was still putting up a fight. Teri and I strolled through the gardens and I narrated. "My perennial flowers are mostly along the lane and driveway. I have Asiatic lilies, dahlias, rudbeckia, bee balm, coneflowers, and sedum. Straight ahead is my little formal garden with mostly boxwoods and flowering shrubs. The roses over the trellis were planted by my folks when I was little. I can't remember a time when they weren't there. My father loved roses. There are about fifty rose bushes scattered around the place; some were planted by my grandmother Bray, but Daddy planted most of them. Over there you can see the area where I grow veggies. I like to serve my guests fresh herbs and vegetables. What I don't serve to guests, we sell at the farmer's market in town. The kitchen herb garden is next to the porch. I over-planted this spring, and now it's gotten away from me."

"Excuse me for interrupting, but did you say 'we'?" asked Teri.

"Did I?"

"You said, 'We sell veggies at the farmer's market.' Does somebody else live here with you?"

"Oh, I haven't told you about Mort. Mort Linderman owns the farm next to mine."

"I know Mr. Linderman," said Teri. "I mean, I know his voice. He's been a 'tweet yourself' customer for ages. He gives Bud and Billy a run for their money. Billy calls him an old character. Bud calls him . . . well, other things."

"Yeah, a great old character," I said. "He's my rock. He and Daddy were farming partners. I've always called him Uncle Mort. His wife's name was Geneva; she was Aunt Geneva to me. I miss her almost as much as I miss my mother. I was like a big sister to their two boys, but they're so wrapped up being important businessmen now that they hardly come home. Mort takes our herbs and vegetables to the farmer's market in town. It's not a thriving business, but he gets a kick out of talking to everybody and haggling with customers. He knows every person over seventy-five in town. By the way, do you know anything about herbs?"

"Not much, really. Is sassafras an herb? My aunt made sassafras tea. I pretended to drink it but spit it out when she wasn't looking. Made me feel sick."

"Sassafras is a root, but the jury is still out on whether it's safe to drink as tea." I wasn't sure where to begin schooling Teri on herbs. "For the moment, I'll just stand here and point to things. This is thyme. Sage is over there. I have a ton of rosemary; it's over there.

Here's parsley. The mint over there is about to take over the world; now that makes great tea."

The noisy guinea fowl appeared suddenly and stared at us before proceeding with their movable feast. "The gang's here to tell me it's six o'clock," I said. "This is their last stop before roosting."

"Are they little turkeys?" asked Teri.

"Guinea fowl," I said, chuckling. "They lay beautiful small eggs and are good to eat, a little tough maybe if you cook them too fast. I mostly keep them around to eat bugs and ticks."

"Do you kill them yourself?"

"Oh, no, I take them and the chickens to a processing plant in Lebanon. I'm not a pioneer woman or anything." I led Teri first to my garden shed for a basket, gloves, and wide-brimmed hat and then to the long line of perennials growing along the lane leading to the inn. "For tonight, I'll just ask you to pull weeds in these perennial beds. We'll worry about the herb beds another time."

"How do I know which ones are weeds?" asked Teri. She looked bewildered.

Buck Bray's specter appeared leaning on a hoe and rolling his eyes. Not wanting to seem impatient with Teri, I smiled. Then I took a deep breath and launched into *Flowers vs. Weeds, 101*. Dinner would be late.

CHAPTER 4

Hello Professor Milner

I decided to keep dinner simple since it's impossible to cook anything complicated with people vying for attention and standing in the way. I planned grilled chicken sandwiches with tomatoes, basil, and mozzarella cheese. I'd made sour cream cheesecake with raspberry drizzle for dessert and planned Champagne mojitos as a chaser.

Lauren and Chickie arrived around seven o'clock looking tan and radiant like people returning from a Caribbean cruise instead of scholarly shut-ins. Lauren looked radiant with her marvelous mane of nut-brown hair and meticulous eye makeup. Chickie, with her perfectly trimmed short auburn pageboy, wore her shirt collar standing up confidently like she had the world by the tail. Completing their first year at college made them seem more grown up.

As we shuffled their bags from the car to the inn, Lauren said, "Chickie and I think we should have the blue room this time. Stephanie and Robert had it last time, and it's our turn. It has the best view and the biggest bathroom. Why should they get it every time? Could we have it this time, please?" So much for grown up.

As the girls settled in, I poured lemonade for us on the screen porch. By now, the porch, which is on the east side of the inn, was cooling off and throwing shadows on the herb garden and rose trellis. I could see the top of Teri's head bobbing up and down as she yanked what I hoped were weeds along the lane.

"Who's that, Mom?" asked Lauren. She and Chickie settled on the porch swing and reached for the lemonade.

"That's Teri Bennett. She's a very sweet person that I just met. She'll be helping me with the gardens this summer."

"Did you fire Mrs. Tubman?" asked Lauren.

"No, of course I didn't fire her. She's having a bad time with her arthritis, so she had to quit at least for a while."

"Remember when Raymond Tubman asked you out, Lauren?" Chickie said. "We had to do some quick thinking to get you out of that one. Raymond was so weird. Remember how he stared at you in Algebra? I always wanted to tell him that there's medicine for pimples."

"Okay, Chickie," I interrupted. "The Tubmans are friends of ours."

"I'm glad to be home, Mom," Lauren said. "I'm not sure summer school was a good idea. I probably should have taken the summer off and worked at Eddie's. Studying in the summer is harder than I thought."

"I can't help noticing you're both quite tan," I said. "You are going to classes, aren't you?" I wasn't certain that I wanted the answer.

"I love the inn, Mrs. Merrick," said Chickie. "It's so cozy, and your flowers are amazing. Thanks for letting me stay this week." Chickie's diversionary tactic was annoying. She might just as well have said that Halley's comet was streaking past. But since the girls had just arrived, I was willing to let the topic of classes and grades drop for the moment.

"You're welcome," I replied. "We're going to have a great week. I've planned some good food and there's plenty to do. Tomorrow we can go to the parade. Rita and Pink will be in full regalia, and we don't want to miss that. They've invited us for dinner on the pontoon, and then we can go to Symphony on the Prairie. Noblesville is having sidewalk days, too, so we might find some good stuff. There's a summer festival in Lafayette on Friday and Saturday, and Rita told me about a horse show at the fairgrounds this week. Sound like fun?"

"We have to tell you something, Mom, and please don't be mad about it," said Lauren. I held my breath and shot a suspicious look in her direction.

"What is it?" I asked.

"Well, Mr. Silvio called us a few months ago and asked if we wanted to be in *Much Ado About Nothing* in his Shakespeare in the Park series. The parts are so good; we couldn't say no. I'm playing Hero, and Chickie is Beatrice."

Oddly, my first reaction was neither surprise nor anger but rather a sense of congratulations to Mr. Silvio, the girls' high school drama teacher, for excellent type-casting. As Hero, Lauren could swoon better than Sarah Bernhardt. As Beatrice, Chickie wouldn't have to act at all. "And you didn't think to mention this to me," I said.

"I told my parents right away," said Chickie. "I don't know why Lauren made such a big deal out of telling you, Mrs. Merrick. Now that we're in college, I think we should just tell our parents the truth about what we're doing. What's the big deal, anyway?"

"When is this play," I asked, "and when does your second summer session start? How will you pull it off?"

"It's all set," said Lauren. "The timing is perfect. The play runs next weekend, and we're off this week. We'll have to rehearse every night. Mr. Silvio invited us to his house tonight. We've been working on the lines, so it's just blocking now."

"Oh, really. How nice," I said. "Guess it never occurred to you to share this news with me?"

"I knew you'd want us to spend time with you this week, Mom, and I didn't know how to tell you. I tried a couple of times, but . . . well, I'm sorry."

"Mrs. Merrick, Craig Deluca is playing Signior Benedick," Chickie interjected, "and this is our big chance with him."

"Who's Craig Deluca?" I asked.

"He's this hot guy who goes to IU," Chickie said. "He's making a name for himself at the IU drama school. He's from Indianapolis. He's about seven feet tall with shoulders like this and a voice that could melt butta."

"How do you know him, Lauren?" I asked.

"Everybody in theatre around Indianapolis knows him," Chickie answered. "Mr. Silvio introduced us to him at Christmas. Oh, he's yummy."

"So, it doesn't matter which one of you hooks him?" I asked. Hiding my smirk was impossible.

"Chickie likes him more than I do," said Lauren. "Really, he's not a god or anything."

Clasping her hand as if in prayer, Chickie said, "No, just a demigod."

"So," I said, "I guess this means you'll be occupied with rehearsals this week, and we should plan to see *Much Ado About Nothing*. I'm sure Steph and Robert will want to go, and I'll invite Rita and Pink and Mort. It'll be great to see you guys on stage again. Just wish you'd told me before this."

Silence settled in as we sipped lemonade, and I came to grips with altered plans. A late afternoon breeze threaded its way through the roses bringing a heavenly scent. Lauren and Chickie chattered on. I sat back in my rocking chair listening and trying to remember what it was like to be as carefree and confident as the two of them. I couldn't remember that far back.

"Mrs. Merrick, would you mind if I call you Jill now?" asked Chickie, abruptly.

"What?" I said, shaking off my reverie.

"Now that I'm in college, I'd like to call other adults by their first name. Would you mind?"

I searched Lauren's face to see if she was embarrassed by Chickie's request. From her expression I could tell they were in cahoots, and she was probably planning to ask Chickie's parents the same irritating question. "I'll get back to you on that," I said. "I favor the status quo for now."

"No problem. But I'm ready for adults to see me as an equal," said Chickie.

I withheld the remark on the tip of my tongue. Why start the week on a sour note? Maybe it was good that Lauren and Chickie would be occupied all week. Maybe it would keep me from strangling one of them. Maybe I should call Mr. Silvio and thank him for taking them off my hands. Maybe I should channel Shakespeare and thank him for writing plays.

Stephanie and Robert's Jeep wheeled up the lane and halted in the driveway. The front doors of the Jeep opened almost before it stopped. Lauren, Chickie, and I formed a welcome committee. Stephanie and Robert hopped out quickly for hugs. Then a third person emerged from the back seat.

"Mom, I'm sure you remember Lawrence Milner, Robert's uncle," said Stephanie. "You met him at our wedding."

"Oh yes, of course," I said. A man who looked like Robert Redford in his prime shook my hand.

"It's nice to see you again, Jill," said Lawrence. His baritone voice hung in the air like an intoxicating vapor. "It was kind of you to invite me. What a great place. I promise to stay out of the way this week. I'm working on a book, so I'll be happily attached to my laptop and no trouble."

"We're delighted to have you here," I said. I smiled to hide my surprise and disappointment in my elder daughter, who had also found it necessary to keep me in the dark.

"Robert and Steph talk about the inn all the time," said Lawrence, "so I talked them into asking for an invitation." He pulled luggage from the Jeep. "Sure hope you didn't mind."

"Of course not," I said. "I was delighted to invite you." I blushed and couldn't look directly into the eyes of such a duped man. "And I'm sure you remember Lauren, Stephanie's sister, and her friend, Chickie Stampler."

"Oh, yes," said Lawrence. He shook Lauren's hand and studied her face. "You've grown up in the past couple of years. It's a pleasure to see you, Lauren, and to meet you . . . eh . . . Chickie?"

"Yes, Uncle, I forgot to warn you," said Robert. "We'll have to put up with Tweedledee and Tweedledumber all week. They may look harmless, but they'll have you reaching for arsenic by Wednesday."

"Don't worry about us," said Chickie. "Shakespeare called and begged us to work for him this week. He has starring roles for us. You won't get to see us as much as you'd like. Poor you."

"Now, would that be William Shakespeare or his cousin, Gus Shakespeare, the horse thief?" asked Robert.

"Time out," I said. "You have all week to squabble. Better pace yourselves. Let's get you settled."

As Robert, Lawrence, Chickie, and Lauren sprinted ahead with the bags, I held Stephanie back for the inevitable chat, "It seems that Lawrence isn't the only person Robert failed to warn."

"I'm so sorry, Mom," said Stephanie. "I told Robert that he should ask you since Lawrence is his uncle, but he thought I had asked. When we stopped for gas, we realized that neither of us had asked you. I feel terrible about this. I hope you don't mind. Uncle Lawrence is such a gentleman. He'll probably stay in his room all week writing his book."

"I don't want him to stay in his room," I said, "but you should have let me know. It's a whole week, and he may not enjoy anything I've planned. He may be totally bored, and everything could get weird."

"No, Mom, really," said Stephanie, "Uncle Lawrence will be so happy here, and you'll like him. He's been a bachelor for years, so he's good at taking care of himself. You should see how tidy he keeps his house."

"It's a good thing I have plenty of guest rooms," I said.

"Speaking of guest rooms," said Stephanie, "you did save the blue room for Robert and me, didn't you?"

CHAPTER 5

Abandoned in Good Company

The choice of guest rooms was made easier with the appearance of Lawrence. Since he was our guest that week, he lodged in the blue room. Lauren and Chickie had the good grace to mutter about it in low tones. As everyone settled in, I rushed around in a panic. There would now be nine people besides me at the dinner table: Lauren, Chickie, Stephanie, Robert, Lawrence, Rita, Pink, Mort, and Teri, too, if she wanted to stay. The menu seemed like a good idea when I dreamt it up, but I didn't know if Lawrence would like it. He might be a vegetarian or a picky foodie. Well, with my large pantry, I could surely find something he'd like.

I'd almost forgotten about poor Teri Bennett, who was still in the lane pulling weeds—or flowers. I dashed out the kitchen door, across the porch, and down the steps. Pink and Rita had arrived and were unloading their horses. Teri was watching them, spellbound.

"Where in the hell can a guy find some buckets around here?" roared Pink. "Our babies have been ridin' for hours, and we gotta get 'em some water."

I hustled to my garden shed for buckets, rigged the hose, and began helping Rhondo and Big Dude to water. After customary hugs and kisses, I introduced Pink and Rita to Teri. She couldn't keep her eyes off the magnificent, if slightly fat, palominos. Pink kept a tight grip on the lead ropes.

"May I touch one of them," Teri asked, extending her hand gingerly.

"Sure, darlin'," said Rita. "Big Dude's a little steadier than my baby, Rhondo, so step up to his head and give him some love. You can kiss him if you want. I kiss 'em all the time, don't I, big lover!" She pursed her lips and hugged Big Dude's neck affectionately.

"I didn't know you were bringing the horses over tonight," I said. "Should we put them in the barn while we eat?"

"Jill, darlin', you have to go easy on us," said Pink.

"We can't stay for dinner, Little Pie Dough," said Rita. "We've been on the road all day takin' the babies to the farrier in Bloomin'ton. We've got to get 'em home and ready for the parade in the mornin'. They haven't had their saunas yet. We're just stoppin' to apologize in person. I'm sorry, Honey Bun. I'm sure you have somethin' very nice planned for dinner, too."

"Now, Jilly, don't be mad at us," Pink said. "The babies had to have new shoes. We meant to leave for Bloomington at the crack of dawn, but a big sale came down at the dealership, and I couldn't leave 'til noon."

"Well, I'm disappointed," I said. I stroked Big Dude's velvety muzzle and tried not to be overly dramatic. "I was counting on all of us being together tonight. Mort is even joining us, and that took a lot of convincing."

By this time, the setting sun was ablaze, and the powerful scents of horses, freshly cut hay, herbs, and warm earth encircled us. Lauren, Chickie, Stephanie, Robert, and Lawrence soon joined us. They were also mesmerized by the horses. There were hugs and kisses all around, and I introduced Teri. I also introduced my unexpected guest to Pink and Rita. "This is Lawrence Milner, Robert's uncle. I'm sure you met Lawrence at Steph and Robert's wedding."

"Oh, sure. Hello, Mr. Milner," said Rita. She shook Lawrence's hand and stared at him for so long that it became awkward.

"Lawrence is staying with us this week," I announced. "He says he's going to be writing a book, but we're going to distract him and make him have some fun."

"The horses are really something," said Lawrence. "They must take a lot of time and attention. I hear you'll be in the parade tomorrow."

With his usual bluster, Pink said, "We stable 'em up in Kokomo. Rita's not exactly the type to shovel shit, and I own a car dealership; so, we can't see 'em every day. We ride as much as we can. I grew up with horses. Can't imagine life without 'em. They're a big expense, but we figure it's worth it."

"Tell us about yourself, Mr. Milner," said Rita. "What do you do?"

"I teach history at IU. Been there about fifteen years."

"And you write books, huh?" said Rita. "This book you're writin' now, what's it 'bout?"

"The New Deal."

"I know all about new deals," said Pink. "I can give you a great new deal on a pickup truck right now!" Rita rolled her eyes while everyone else laughed.

"Jilly," said Rita, "I need to borrow some hedge clippers, and I need 'em tonight. Let's walk to the shed so I don't forget 'em." She pulled on my arm excitedly.

As we walked toward the garden shed, Pink shouted, "What the hell do you need hedge clippers for, Darlin'? You don't know how to use 'em."

Rita pulled me into the shed. She had a look on her face like a ten-year-old girl bursting to tell a big fat secret. "Jilly, that man is staying at your house all week? Are you kiddin' me? He's gorgeous! I don't remember meetin' him at Steph's weddin'. Was he under a table or somethin'? How are you gonna entertain him? And why didn't you tell me he was comin'?"

"I didn't know he was coming," I said. "He thinks Steph and Robert asked me, but the knuckleheads forgot. So, now he's here, and I have to figure it out. Don't embarrass me by staring at him. All I know is that any man that good looking has an interesting past." I pulled some clippers off the shelf. "No hurry to return these."

Rita recoiled as if the clippers were a snake. "What would I want with those dirty things, Honey?" she asked.

We rejoined the group, and luckily the hedge clippers were forgotten. The sun was making a final curtain call as fireworks began popping in the sky in all directions. Fireflies lit the gardens and fields. Pink and Rita loaded Big Dude and Rhondo into the trailer, gave more kisses, and pulled away. As I waved goodbye, I had an urge to go home with them. Then I looked at my beautiful daughters in the fading summer light and knew they needed me where I was.

In Indiana, as the summer sun sinks and evening brings blessed relief from the heat, mosquitoes rise like hellhounds. Five at a time, they drain your blood. As we slapped them off and made our way inside the inn, Teri signaled for a word with me. "I'm going home now, Jill. Thanks for letting me work in your garden today. I hope I didn't pull up the wrong plants."

"No, it's I who must thank you," I said. "This isn't how I wanted your first day to go, but things got so hectic. I hope you'll stay for dinner."

"I'm tired and dirty. I think I'll just go home if that's okay. I hope you'll let me come back." Teri looked sad.

"Are you okay?" I asked.

"Oh, yeah," she said. Her eyes welled with tears. "I've been thinking about Jerry and feeling sorry for myself. You have such a wonderful family. I'll never have that."

"Teri, believe me, my life has not been perfect," I said. "I'll tell you a few things about myself sometime."

Mort's pickup truck pulled into the driveway and my heart sank. I'd barely started dinner, and he's not a patient man. I introduced him to Teri and moments later found myself interrupting their conversation about water softeners and crazy Bud Wren. "I'm sorry, Uncle Mort," I said. "Dinner will be late. There's been so much going on." I swatted a mosquito on the back of my neck.

"It's okay, Jillian," said Mort. "I've been balin' hay over at Catzwell's, and I'm done in. Have to take a rain check." Normally, I would have pleaded with him to stay, but with his short fuse and the present chaos, I was relieved.

"We'll miss you," I said, somewhat insincerely.

As I watched Mort and Teri's vehicles pulling away, I remembered that Lauren and Chickie would soon be leaving for a rehearsal at Mr. Silvio's. I suddenly feared that Robert and Stephanie might also abandon me and I'd be alone with Lawrence. What would I say? What would we do? I was sure they wouldn't leave so soon.

Stephanie met me at the kitchen door. "Mom, do you have a plan for dinner," she asked, "or should Robert and I run out for something?"

"Chickie and I are leaving in thirty minutes," Lauren announced. "We can grab some food on the way."

"Absolutely not," I insisted. "We're making dinner together." I paused momentarily and beheld Lauren, Stephanie, Robert, and Chickie's faces. They had no idea how often I thought of them each day. I was delighted to be with them and glad Lawrence had joined our family circle for the week.

The ingredients were all in my possession: chicken cutlets, olive oil, lemons, fresh thyme, garlic cloves, tomatoes, ciabatta rolls, mozzarella cheese and fresh basil. Lawrence tied an apron around his neck and waist. It brushed his thick sandy hair and knocked his perfect haircut slightly out of place. The stray hairs and ill-fitting apron did nothing to diminish his good looks. It was obvious that he was comfortable in the kitchen.

After setting the table, Lauren and Chickie pulled out their *Much Ado* scripts. Chickie thrust hers at Robert. "Here," she said. "You be Benedick."

"Which act?" he asked.

"There!" she said, stabbing the script with her finger.

With the diction of a Shakespearean actor, Robert began Signior Benedick's lines: "If Signior Leonato be her father, she would not have his head on her shoulders for all Messina, as like him as she is."

Chickie recited, "I wonder that you will still be talking, Signior Benedict, nobody marks you." She was delighted to spar with Robert in the guise of Beatrice.

"What, my Lady Disdain? Are you yet living?" Robert returned fire.

"Is it possible disdain should die while she hath such meet food to feed it as Signior Benedick? Courtesy itself must convert to disdain if you come in her presence." Chickie's sharp retort matched her perfectly memorized lines.

"Then courtesy is a turncoat," Robert read. "But it is certain I am loved of all ladies, only you excepted; and I would I could find in my heart that I had not a hard heart, for truly I love none."

Hearing Robert and Chickie bicker was old hat, but bickering in the language of Shakespeare was new and amusing. Before I knew it, the chicken cutlets were on fire. I pulled them off the grill holding back swear words for Lawrence's sake. I brushed the top half of the ciabatta rolls with olive oil, and Lawrence placed them methodically on the grill top.

"A dear happiness to women," Chickie continued. "They would else have been troubled with a pernicious suitor. I thank God and my cold blood I am of your humor for that. I had rather hear my dog bark than a man swear he loves me."

"Don't worry," said Robert, dropping the Benedick persona. "You'll never hear that."

"I don't even hear your nasty words, Robert. Please read the lines as they're written," Chickie said. Lawrence, Stephanie, and I chuckled at the silliness.

"I had planned Champagne mojitos," I said, "but since we're short on time, we'll have to make do with the Champagne on its own. Any objections?" I took a bottle from the fridge and passed it along with a corkscrew to Lawrence, ignoring that he might object to alcohol. He took the bottle, stepped to the sink, and uncorked it effortlessly.

Stephanie sprang to my stemware cabinet and plopped six Champagne glasses on the table perfectly in time for Lawrence's approach with the fizzing bottle. "To each of us," said Robert, "and to being together and even to you, Lady Disdain." He raised his glass and nodded to us all. "Something tells me this is going to be a week to remember."

"Speaking of remembering, where were we?" Chickie asked. "Oh, yeah, right here." She stabbed Robert's script with her finger again.

Robert picked up a sandwich with one hand, took a huge bite, and dismissed Chickie with the other hand saying, "I would my horse had the speed of your tongue and so good a continuer, but keep your way, i' God's name, I have done."

Chickie stuffed the last bit of her sandwich into her mouth. "You always end with a jade's trick," she said. "I know you of old."

"What's a jade, anyway?" asked Lauren.

"It's something about a horse," said Chickie. "We've gotta go. I know you'll all miss us. Thank you for dinner, Jill; it was delicious."

"Jill?" Stephanie and Robert questioned in unison.

"I don't even call you Jill," Robert said. "Do you mean Lady Disdain can call you by your first name? What impertinence."

"She asked, and I told her I'd think about it," I said. "I did not give her permission." I gave Chickie the evil eye.

"Dinner was lovely, Mom. Thanks," said Lauren, heading for the door. "Don't wait up for us."

"Lovely? Dinner was lovely," Stephanie repeated mockingly. "Who is she trying to impress?"

"She's trying to grow up, Steph," I said. "Give her a break."

"They're so grown up that they ran out of here without doing dishes," said Robert.

"Robert and I will clean up and you and Uncle Lawrence can relax," said Stephanie.

"That's nice, but I'm used to doing dishes," said Lawrence.

"What's the rush?" I asked. "Let's polish off the Champagne and have some coffee and dessert on the porch. We're on vacation, remember? It's a beautiful night. Anyway, I'd like your opinion on the dessert. I'm working up a few new recipes for guests, and I have high hopes for the cheesecake."

Stephanie squirmed in her chair and looked at Robert. "That sounds great, Mom," she said, "but something's sort of come up. We got a call from Steve and Katie Moore that some of the old gang is meeting at the reservoir tonight. Steve borrowed some fancy boat from his boss, and it sounds like a really good time. We haven't seen any of them for ages. I hope you understand. We'll have the rest of the week together; I promise."

My heart raced and my palms got clammy. That which was foretold had come to pass. The entire group was jumping ship. Entertaining people was routine for me. I had successfully established the inn by offering easy-going hospitality, good food, and impeccable accommodations. I'd been looking forward to a week, no matter how chaotic, with family and friends. Now, against my will, I was back in hostess mode. This wouldn't have bothered me as much if my remaining guest had been more run-of-the-mill, but Lawrence Milner was not run-of-the-mill. So, I was trapped. If I objected too much, Lawrence might feel burdensome. It wasn't his fault that my daughter and son-in-law were absent-minded.

"Well, this isn't what I expected," I said, "but I know you want to see your friends. I'll take you up on doing the dishes before you go. And remember we're having breakfast at Eddie's at nine o'clock sharp in the morning. The parade starts at ten."

I felt like a blushing schoolgirl with Lawrence and hated the feeling. I was reminded of my high school days when I sat next to Howie Leonard in typing class. Howie was the most handsome senior at Noblesville High School. He was smooth and so well-mannered that every girl in school wanted a date with him. We thought he'd come from another planet. I couldn't make eye contact with Howie when he asked to borrow my Whiteout or how to spell a word. He was different from the other boys. Howie freaked me out.

As ridiculous as it seemed, Lawrence was freaking me out, too. I was a middle-aged woman with grown daughters. I ran a business and had been married twice. The idea that a handsome face could be so unnerving didn't make sense.

"Jill," Lawrence said, softly, "please don't feel like you have to entertain me. I'd planned to work on my book tonight, so I'll make myself scarce."

I composed myself. "Looks like I've been abandoned," I said. "I'll be disappointed to eat dessert alone. I hope you'll stay, Lawrence. It's a lovely night."

"Well, if you don't mind spending a few minutes with a boring old professor, I'm a sucker for dessert. And summer evenings like this are rare." Lawrence and I made our way onto the porch and into rocking chairs.

Stephanie and Robert soon stepped onto the porch, made sheepish goodbyes, and drove off in the last remnants of daylight.

CHAPTER 6

Indiana Soulmates

The weather was rare indeed. It was the kind of evening that people in chilly climates ache for in January. Crickets sang their summer songs. Fireworks continued to pop near and far. Moths and bats circled the light above the barnyard. The sky was clear, and a full moon was beginning to bathe the gardens in a silvery light.

I had a taste for espresso with dessert even if it meant insomnia. Lawrence happily complied. We sipped and stared into the fading light beyond the porch for a few moments without speaking. It was surreal sitting there with a man I barely knew and listening to him breathe, sip, chew, and clink his fork on the plate. For weeks, I'd looked forward to gathering on the porch with people I knew well. I'd spent many summer nights on the porch with my mother and father, boyfriends, girlfriends, and husbands. I told myself to relax and enjoy the moment for what it was—whatever it was.

Lawrence broke the silence, "This is just what I needed, Jill." He sat back in his chair and relaxed. My tiny four-letter name sounded melodic coming from him.

"I'm glad," I said. I kicked off my shoes and tucked one leg under me in the rocking chair. "So, did you grow up in Martinsville like Robert? It's pretty country down there."

"Yeah, I did. It's a good place to be from. I grew up on a small farm just south of Martinsville. My brother, Robert's dad, is ten years older than me, and it was just the two of us with our parents, so we both grew up like only children."

"Do you still have the farm?"

"My brother and his family live on the farm. I help him with planting and harvesting when I can. It's not exactly a money-maker, but he won't give it up. I enjoy the work."

"So, what did boys do for entertainment in Martinsville when you were growing up?" My question felt ridiculous since I was quite certain of the answer.

"Nothing very exciting," Lawrence said. "I baled a lot of hay, learned to fix broken-down corn pickers, went to school, and played basketball like a zillion Indiana boys. Basketball was a big deal for me. Had to leave it behind when I went to college."

"Were you as good as Jimmy in *Hoosiers*? Were you the guy that made all the big plays?"

"No, I was the steady, dependable kid. I could hit the basket but wasn't the star."

"I loved Gene Hackman in that movie. He took everybody's insults and just kept going. Barbara Hershey was terrible to him. He shouldn't have fallen in love with her."

"Yeah, great movie," Lawrence said. He didn't pick up on the conversational thread about *Hoosiers*, so I dropped it. I rocked in my chair, but that made me feel like a nervous granny, so I stopped.

I held up my long-snouted espresso pot. "More?" I asked.

"Better not. I'll be awake all night. I'm looking forward to getting into that great fluffy bed of yours. Uh, I mean, you know what I mean. The bed looks very comfortable." Blood rose in my neck and face. I was glad for the dim light. Lawrence laughed, so I laughed. His laugh was more like a growl from the back of his throat than a hearty laugh. He struck me as a worldly man who plays it close to the vest. No belly laughing.

"Do you like it in Bloomington?" I asked.

"I enjoy Bloomington. You can be a perpetual student in that town." There was sure to be a long story behind Lawrence's comment, but I thought it best not to pry.

"I suppose you have a special area of teaching and research."

"Twentieth Century American mainly."

"Where did you get your degrees?"

"Undergrad Wabash College, master's Wisconsin State, PhD Ohio State." Lawrence gave a self-effacing smile. "Been a history nerd all my life."

"You don't look like a nerd, Lawrence." I wanted to say that he looked like a great big hunk, but I refrained.

"Now, may I ask you a couple of questions, Jill?"

"Oh, lord," I said. "I suppose so, as long as there are no quizzes on the New Deal or the Second World War or Watergate."

"You're safe. Stephanie and Robert have told me a lot about you, but after seeing your place, a few things don't add up. I can't imagine how one person takes care of all this."

"You were supposed to meet my dear Dutch uncle and neighbor, Mort Linderman, at dinner, but he begged off. Mort and my father farmed together and were best friends. Mort farms my land and helps with just about anything I need. His place is on the other side of the woods. I hire help with the gardens and have a cleaning service. I do the cooking and pretty much everything else. The work never ends, but I knew what I was getting into when I opened the inn."

"Well, I'd take my hat off to you if I was wearing one. You're an amazing person."

"Oh, not really. I've been lucky in many ways."

Without a crescendo, the sound of chickens squawking bloody murder broke the stillness like a train whistle. I jumped to my feet, scrambled for my shoes, and bolted for the screen door. "I forgot to shut up the chickens!" I blurted.

"Do you think they're getting away?" Lawrence asked. I would have found his question hilarious and schooled him on chicken behavior if time had allowed. There wasn't time to discuss how chickens don't run away from home on purpose.

With Lawrence at my heels, I grabbed a flashlight from the garden shed. As we approached the outer pen, the flashlight caught the glowing eyes of a four-legged creature darting from the open door of the coop. Racing for a closer look, we could see a fox with a limp hen in its jaws.

"Where's your gun?" Lawrence yelled.

"I don't use guns!" I snapped.

The fox was trapped in the outer pen and searching frantically for an escape route. I waved my arms and threw rocks at the fence, hoping the hen would be dropped. Lawrence dashed toward the fox as if to snatch the hen away.

"No. Stop!" I yelled. "Never mind! It could be rabid. Don't go near it!"

"Don't you want the chicken?" he yelled. I didn't know whether to be sick to my stomach about the kill or to laugh at Lawrence's heroics.

"Not enough to risk it," I said. The fox found a tunnel and slid under the fence with its prize. It darted down the path toward Mort's house and into the woods. Lawrence and I watched helplessly. Using the flashlight, I located the tunnel under the fence.

"Let's check the flock," I said. Inside the coop, the remaining hens were perched disdainfully. "I failed them, and they can't wait to tell Mort in the morning."

"You're kidding, right?"

"Half kidding," I said. "Mort knows every animal on both farms. He'll take roll in the morning and find out. I'll call him first thing."

"So, you don't own a gun?"

"I said I don't use guns. My first husband owned shotguns. Mort keeps them at his place. I hate guns." We headed to the inn aided by the yard light, the moonlight, and my flickering flashlight. "I take it you didn't raise chickens on your farm."

"Nah, just corn, wheat, and soybeans."

As we reached the porch, Lawrence's gait slowed. He turned and sat on the top step. "Do you mind if I sit here for a minute and look at the stars?" he asked. I joined him, and we looked skyward. A few wispy clouds drifted between us and the bright moon. Stars were visible now and the air was fragrant. Evidently, both of our lives were steeped in rural Indiana. Our Hoosier bond replaced words. There was the Wabash and the White, hills in the south, flat land in the north, corn and soybeans everywhere, county fairs, down-to-earth people, fall pumpkins, the Indy 500, majestic Brown County, basketball, hot summers, grey winters, tornadoes, rhubarb pie, picnics, porches, and little parades with big hopes.

Lawrence folded his arms and rested the back of his head on the screen door. His breathing made no sound. I thought of the poor dead hen as well as the dead perennials which likely festooned the fence along the lane. A mosquito bit my neck, and Lawrence slapped one on the side of his face. "We'd better go in or the kids will find our bloodless bodies when they get home," I said.

Lawrence insisted on helping me tidy the kitchen. I introduced him to my extensive linen closet and luxury soap collection. He selected Crabtree and Evelyn soap. Good choice, I thought. We said goodnight.

As I climbed into bed and listened to the whoosh of cooling air through the vent, the house felt different because Lawrence was in it. I had fallen asleep on a hundred nights when strangers filled the guest rooms, but this was different. It was unnerving and yet comforting. Now, if my other house guests arrived home safely, all would be well. I had learned to stop waiting up for my daughters at night. I slept unusually well until morning.

CHAPTER 7

Hero In A Tree

The big day had arrived—July 4. I awoke early and thought of my mother, Mona Bray, who was born on the Fourth of July. As far back as I could remember, she'd put on a huge spread of food for family, neighbors, and friends after the parade. She'd bake a big birthday cake for herself with seven-minute frosting and a forest of candles. Though she insisted on "no gifts," she loved any box or bag offered. She led the birthday song for herself, which embarrassed me when I was a child. Now, I think it was wonderful. I only wish that I could hear her sing again.

The lovely aroma of coffee drifted into my bedroom. I dressed quickly and headed to the kitchen, thinking Stephanie or Robert must have become ambitious. Instead, Lawrence sat at the table pecking away at his tablet. The kitchen table was full of books and papers.

"Morning, Jill," he said, cheerfully. He looked handsome even that early in the morning. "Hope you don't mind that I helped myself to your coffeemaker. I brought my own coffee beans and grinder, strange as seems. I'm kinda fussy about coffee. Hope you like it."

"I'm sure I will," I said. I wondered about a guy who travels with coffee beans and a grinder. Such behavior was new to me. Perhaps he'd also packed pots and pans. A new dishwasher would have been nice since mine was on its last leg.

"Guess it's odd for a person to pack coffee beans," Lawrence said.

"Most people I know wouldn't leave home without a few bags of coffee beans," I said. "You didn't happen to pack a side of bacon, did you?" I reached into the fridge for cream.

"You're not going to put anything in it, are you?"

"I was giving it some thought," I said. "Is there a problem?"

"Taste it first."

"I have to at least put sugar in it," I said. "Sugar's important, like gas to a car."

"Do me a favor and try it unspoiled. It's a special blend of Sumatra and French roast." He was so earnest that I couldn't tell if he was joking or just seriously hung up on coffee.

"Take a sip and let me know what you think."

I took a long slow slurp. It was mellow and delicious. "Where'd you get this?"

"A guy who teaches Russian history turned me on to it. It's roasted in Chicago. Costs a small fortune." Lawrence leaned back in the chair and took another long pull of coffee.

Hmm, I thought, attractive, single, writes books, packs coffee beans, can hold a conversation, seems normal. Lawrence intrigued me, but I was suspicious. He was sure to have a complicated past like most middle-aged people. "So, how's the New Deal coming along?" I asked.

"Well, if Roosevelt could get banking reform passed in the thirties, we should be able to do it today."

"Too bad the bankers make the rules about banking," I said.

Lawrence gathered his books and papers. "I'm sure you don't have time to talk about banking reform. By the way, the room is very comfortable. Can't remember when I've slept so soundly."

"It's the eiderdown pillows," I said. "They come from France and cost a king's ransom. People who sleep on those pillows report pleasant dreams. I bring them out for special guests." In my enthusiasm over the pillows, I'd gone a step too far and felt truly deceitful.

"I'm honored," said Lawrence, placing his hand over his heart. "So, I guess you have a big day planned."

"Yep. It'll be fun. But I'm going to the cemetery first to plant flowers. Want to ride along?"

Lawrence seemed familiar with the graveside custom. "A stroll around the Noblesville cemetery would be interesting," he said, "but I should keep working."

"See you later then," I replied. "Hope you'll join us for breakfast and the parade . . . and dinner on Pink and Rita's pontoon. We just drift around the rez drinking Pink's concoctions. It's low-key unless he overindulges. He can be quite entertaining."

"How did a burly guy like that come to be called Pink?"

"His name is Charles Wallace Restin the Third. In high school he wore a lucky pink t-shirt under his sports uniforms. The other boys called him Stinky Pinky, but after a while it became just plain Pink. He's not bothered by it. He owns the biggest Ford dealership in central Indiana, and he still doesn't care what people call him as long as they buy his cars and trucks."

"I can't quite place his accent. Did he grow up around here?"

"He's from Kentucky originally and so is Rita. His family moved to Noblesville when he was little. He ramps up the accent sometimes depending on his audience. Rita, on the other hand, is a true Kentuckian. We've been friends since high school. They're characters, but I love them. And, just for the record, it's not the Noblesville cemetery; it's the Bray Cemetery. It's on the other side of Mort's farm. Many a Bray rest in peace there. See you later." I grabbed the egg basket and headed outside.

The farm seemed particularly beautiful that morning. Dew lay on the grass and mist circled the trees. Mort's cattle and my sheep were already browsing and looked idyllic. My calico cat bounded out of the garden and rubbed playfully against my legs. Her yellow eyes were clear and bright and wise. She appeared sweeter and sleeker than ever.

Though the air was still, an odd little wind was blowing through me. My feet were on the ground as I walked to the hen house, yet I felt buoyant. I also felt strangely self-conscious as though Lawrence was watching me. His deep voice echoed in my mind. I wondered what he was all about. Nip it in the bud I told myself. I'm not screwing up my life again. Hadn't Jimmy the Monster cured me of men forever? Wake up and smell the coffee, I thought, and not Sumatra and French roast.

The hens were sulking and avoiding eye contact. As I stole their eggs, they looked away in disgust and refused to peck my hand. They flew from the nests in righteous indignation. I didn't bother talking to them; it wouldn't help. Mort would fill in the fox's tunnel, and I'd shut the door before dusk in the future. Time would mend their troubled hearts.

I deposited the lovely brown eggs in my fridge and then loaded my truck with the pink potted geraniums I'd been saving, a spade, and buckets of water. I don't love geraniums, but they withstand heat and are the flower of choice in the poor clayish soil around the headstones.

Lawrence suddenly appeared beside the truck. "Offer still good?" he asked. "A stroll would be good before it gets too hot."

We set off, and I didn't take the pickup out of second gear because of ruts and dust. We passed Mort's farm and his waist-high sweet corn, tomato patch, and cantaloupe and pumpkin vines.

"I'll bet you bought this truck from Pink," said Lawrence.

"It's a hand-me-down from Uncle Mort," I said.

Lawrence's blue jeans were creased as if dry-cleaned. His baby blue Polo shirt looked new and matched the color of his eyes. His fingernails were immaculate and appeared to be buffed. I tried to keep my eyes on the road, but it wasn't easy. We rolled along the shady lane leading to the cemetery.

The Bray Cemetery contains about a hundred graves in neat rows bordered by brambles and woods. Mort has been the groundskeeper all my life. At one point, a township committee tried to replace headstones older than one hundred years with commemorative plates. Mort was fine with the plates but fought to keep every crumbling headstone. As I'd expected, he won the debate.

I decided to go straight to work planting and not linger over the graves since that might be awkward for Lawrence. The soil around Buck, Mona, and Phil's headstones was packed hard. I jumped up and down on the spade but barely broke the surface. Lawrence took the spade from my hands and applied a little pressure with his foot. It sank as if going into sand. "I knew you had an ulterior motive for inviting me," he said.

"The county is always looking for grave diggers. You should apply."

"I believe they use backhoes now."

Lawrence wandered among the graves as I planted the geraniums. He stooped to read headstones and brush away debris. Oddly, it seemed natural to be there with him. I had the strange sensation that I had known him for a long time and that we were somehow kindred.

A car pulled into the cemetery parking lot. My stomach knotted up. It had to be a relative or friend because only these visit the Bray Cemetery. They would see me with a man they didn't know. They would be polite, but the mystery would have to be solved. I stayed on my knees to appear preoccupied. Female voices became recognizable. It was the worst-case scenario, the Mawbrey sisters.

Bea and Carolyn Mawbrey are elderly spinster sisters who own a small farm next to the Catzwell's place. Like me, they inherited their farm. Bea keeps bees and Carolyn is a retired school bus driver. Since they are relatives and neighbors, my mother invited them to her birthday parties but avoided them otherwise because they are "hard to take." I braced myself.

In seconds, Bea stood over me. "Why, Jillian, is that you?" she asked. Looking up, I saw that she was holding their huge, spoiled Persian cat, Mr. Fluffy. I greeted Bea and Carolyn and inquired after their health.

"We're well enough, but Mr. Fluffy has had quite enough of fireworks. The Catzwell children have nothing better to do than set off firecrackers all day and night. It's been going on for a solid week. Children don't need summer vacation in this day and age. They'd be better off in school. We thought Mr. Fluffy could use an outing, so we brought him along."

"You shouldn't bother with those geraniums," said Carolyn. "They'll be dead in a few days. It's too hot for them, and the soil is nothing but clay. You've wasted your money."

"Maybe so," I said, "but it makes me feel good to plant them here. It's my way of remembering Mother and Daddy and Phil."

"Yes, they were all fine people," said Bea. "I know you miss them."

"We've come to pay our respects and check on Momma and Papa and Uncle Thomas's graves," Carolyn said. "We heard from a little birdie that Mort isn't keeping up the grounds as well as he used to."

"He's getting on in years," said Bea. "Maybe it's time to let somebody younger have the job."

"The place looks beautiful to me," I said, defensively. "I think Mort is perfectly capable."

"Do you think you're planting those geraniums deep enough?" asked Carolyn. "Better snap off all the blooms so the energy goes to the roots. Those pink geraniums are nice to look at, but they aren't as hardy as the red ones. You'd be better off planting red ones."

"Who's that man walking toward us?" asked Bea. She shaded her eyes with her hand and squinted. "Do we know him?"

"I'm sure I don't know him," said Carolyn. "What do you think he's doing here? Do you think he works for the township? Maybe he's the new groundskeeper."

"If so, he'd be pushing a lawn mower, wouldn't he?" snapped Bea. "Besides, he's too well dressed. Maybe he's with the historical society. That bunch is always poking around cemeteries."

I got to my feet and attempted a smile as Lawrence approached. As I introduced him to Bea and Carolyn, he extended his hand for a shake. "Happy to meet you ladies," he said. Bea and Carolyn glared at him as though he had cooties.

"Milner, is it?" Bea questioned. "There was a Horace Milner on the town council years ago. Remember him, Jill? He was a Democrat who tried to spend the town's money on all sorts of foolish things, giveaways to anybody who put out a hand. Let the potholes go so everybody's car fell apart but supported any social program that came down the pike. He didn't last long. One term and we voted him out. Any relation to you?"

"I wouldn't think of being related to such a spendthrift," said Lawrence. His humor was entirely lost on Bea and Carolyn.

"Right," said Bea.

"Right," agreed Carolyn.

"So, where are you from, Mr. Milner?" asked Bea.

"Bloomington."

"What do you do there?"

"I write books about dead people and grade papers mostly."

"So, you're a teacher. At IU, I suppose."

"That's right."

"You must think me nosy to ask all that. Glad we cut to the chase. It's getting hot out here and time is short. Have you been seeing Jill for long?"

"For several months now," said Lawrence. "I do hope you ladies approve."

"It's not up to us what she does," said Carolyn, "but she's had a hard enough time, and we don't want to see her, well, mistreated by anyone."

"Lawrence and I are not seeing each other," I interrupted. "As I said, he's Robert's uncle and a guest this week." The exchange amused Lawrence.

"Don't you think those geraniums are too close together, Jillian?" Carolyn asked. "And how are you going to water them? Mort's never sunk a well out here, so you'll have to tote water from your place you know." Her absurd intensity about the geraniums would have been comical if it hadn't been so annoying.

As I stifled an uncharitable remark, Mr. Fluffy raised all twenty pounds of himself into the posture of a jungle cat and dug his claws into Bea's shoulder. The tighter she gripped him the more he struggled against her. Tiny Bea was no match for the wild-eyed beast that Mr. Fluffy had become. Using Bea's shoulder as a springboard, he leaped through the air, hit the ground on the run, and dashed up a maple tree. He had detected something we'd missed. The Catzwell's ever-straying beagle was darting between headstones and testing everything for scent.

"That wretched dog is a menace!" Bea shrieked. "This does it. I've told Catzwell ten times to keep that dog penned up. This time I'm calling the shelter. How will we ever get Fluff down?"

Mr. Fluffy was perched on a branch about twenty feet up. No matter how much sweet talk Bea and Carolyn applied, the cat sat motionless and stared into space. "Oh, my goodness," whined Carolyn. "What if a raccoon goes after him or what if he loses his balance? We'll have to call the fire department."

"Cats don't lose their balance," said Bea, sternly. "You should know that, and if we call the fire department they'll be annoyed. They're getting their trucks ready for the parade. They can't bother with a cat in a tree. I'll drive over to Catzwell's place and get that shiftless boy of theirs to climb up there. It's their fault anyway."

"I'll give it a try," said Lawrence. "I haven't climbed a tree since I was ten. Could be fun."

"You're kidding, right?" I asked. "He's way up there." Before I could caution Lawrence further, he was making his way up the branches with a nimbleness I wouldn't have expected from a middle-aged man. Bea, Carolyn, and I backed away from the trunk of the tree out of self-preservation. We watched in awe as Lawrence navigated the branches, measuring and testing each step up.

Bea asked a crucial question, "If he grabs Fluff, how will he get back down with one hand?" I ignored her question. My anxiety rose with Lawrence's every move. Visions of the local hospital trauma center raced through my mind along with mourners at a Bloomington funeral home. I had uncharitable thoughts about the two old ladies foolish enough to bring an unfettered cat to the cemetery. My father once referred to them as "daft," and I remembered why.

After a few more stressful minutes, Lawrence made it to Mr. Fluffy's branch. I cringed as he steadied his feet on a thin branch and plotted his move toward the cat. Cautiously, he reached for the skin on the back of Mr. Fluffy's neck and lifted the huge fur ball onto his shoulder with only a minor struggle.

We watched breathlessly as Lawrence eased down the tree, searching for footing. Mr. Fluffy blocked his view of the tree and the earth below. A branch under his foot cracked suddenly, and he lunged for a branch above with his free hand. He seized the branch and held it until he could find better footing. My heart was pounding, and I regretted inviting him to the cemetery.

"Steady, Mr. Milner," said Bea. "You're doing fine. Just a few more feet now and you'll be on the ground." Her comment was far-fetched since Lawrence was still a good ten feet off the ground. After another tortured few minutes of scraping himself along the tree trunk, his feet finally hit the ground. With Mr. Fluffy clinging to him, he looked like he was wearing a giant fur corsage.

"I told you it was best not to de-claw Fluff," Bea told Carolyn. "You wanted him de-clawed, but I wouldn't have it. Now you know why." She wrenched the cat away from Lawrence and tucked him under her arm. "What a nasty dog to scare you so. We must get you home where it's safe."

"That's right," said Carolyn. She stroked the cat's head and tried to finagle a cuddle despite Bea's death grip on him.

"It's getting late, and we still have chores to do before the parade," said Bea. "We can't stand here all day. We'll visit the graves when it cools off. Nice meeting you, Mr. Milner. Jill, cold water will get the blood out of Mr. Milner's shirt." She nodded at Carolyn to make for the car, and they scurried off. Stunned, I watched them drive away in clouds of dust. Lawrence was left bleeding and sweating. His once neatly pressed jeans were wrinkled and stained with bark residue.

"What awful creatures!" I blurted. "They don't deserve what you did for them, Lawrence." I kept myself from brushing twigs off his shirt and pulling bark out of his hair. Blood seeped through his shirt and scratches were swelling on his arms.

Lawrence stood at the base of the tree and looked up into the branches. "Can't believe I can still climb a tree like that," he muttered. "It must have been fate that I came out here, Jill. You needed help with digging, and the creatures needed a cat wrangler. It was meant to be."

"You could have been killed," I said. "You must have been twenty feet off the ground. Do you always do crazy things like that?" I immediately regretted such a forward question.

"Not as a rule. I didn't want you to miss the parade. Besides, it felt pretty good to climb up there. I feel a little more . . . I don't know . . . alive, I suppose."

I didn't know what to say, so I began watering the geraniums. Lawrence tamped down the mushy soil. We climbed into the truck and headed back to the inn. He rested his head on the back of the seat, folded his arms, and closed his eyes. I suspected the gravity of his heroics had sunk in. Since his eyes were closed, I felt safe examining his handsome face. His tanned complexion was flawless, with not even a razor nick. His cheekbones were high and his eyes set wide apart. His nose was the perfect size for his face—not too big or small. His forehead was not too high, and his sandy hair was still quite thick and perfectly trimmed to his hairline. His powerful forearms were covered in soft-looking blonde hair. I began speculating on the shade of his chest hair when his eyes opened slightly. I shifted my gaze.

"You're right," he said. "I suppose I could have been killed, but the cemetery would be a handy place to die." He let out a throaty chuckle and closed his eyes again. I wondered if he was in shock. As we drove on, the feeling that I had known Lawrence Milner all my life returned. I was drawn to him, and it felt exciting yet awful. I took comfort in the fact that he was only staying for the week, and I'd soon put him out of my mind.

CHAPTER 8

Not in My Playbook

Eddie's Café was packed. Townsfolk and visitors in red, white, and blue shorts, tank tops, flip-flops, and sunglasses filled the place. As the best-managed café on the Noblesville town square, Eddie's does a land-office business serving the courthouse crowd, shopkeepers, and farmers on weekdays, and families after Sunday worship. With only an hour to go before the town's biggest annual event, the place was up for grabs.

The cafe's wait staff maneuvered skillfully between fifteen tables covered with blue and white checked oilcloths. Short stacks with melting butter, eggs, sausage, crêpes, and hot coffee sailed around the place with amazing efficiency. Everybody knows everybody at Eddie's, so besides the tasty American cuisine, that's why most of us eat there.

Eddie Constantine is a sharp-eyed, no-nonsense businessman, who lives for his café. Stephanie and Lauren had both waitressed for Eddie. They learned quickly that he has low tolerance for tardiness, laziness, and sneakiness. Gossip in moderation is part and parcel of the job and usually tolerated. As a single mom raising willful daughters, I thanked Eddie many times for hiring my girls at his boot camp café. His approval of Stephanie and Lauren in their teen years gave me an enormous sense of relief. Curiously, it affirmed that they would be competent human beings able to survive in the world.

Eddie stood guard over the cash register, greeting every customer who entered the café, many by name. We exchanged hugs, and I introduced him to Lawrence, who by now was restored to sartorial perfection after the tree-climbing incident. Lawrence and I convinced the wait staff to jam a couple of tables together for our expected crew.

Stephanie and Robert arrived relatively on time. They looked groggy, but I refrained from mentioning the fact and so did Lawrence. We ordered coffee and scanned the extensive menu. Eddie's cooks are known for their fluffy pancakes and delicate crêpes, which made me think that I should add more variety of fillings to my crêpes at the inn.

Eddie also serves the best coffee in town. Lawrence waved his hand over the cup to bring the aroma to his nose. He sipped and nodded grudging approval. He then produced a pair of reading glasses from a trim tortoiseshell case and looked like a professorial Robert Redford. "What's good here?" he asked.

"Everything," Stephanie and I said in unison.

"I feel like ham and eggs with a raspberry crêpe on the side," Lawrence said. "Sound like a good pairing to you, Jill?" I was flattered that he sought my approval.

"Sounds perfect," I responded.

"So, where are the brats?" asked Robert. "Weren't they supposed to meet us here?" It was clear that Robert was in a sour mood. "Did anyone hear them come in last night? They get away with murder."

"They haven't killed anyone that I know of, Robert," I said, "and yes, I heard them come in about two o'clock. This wasn't exactly true, but I didn't like Robert's high-handed tone. "I didn't wake them, but I'm sure they'll be here soon."

"Don't pay any attention to Robert, Mom," said Stephanie. "He's mad at me because he thinks I was flirting with some of the other guys last night. It's ridiculous, of course, but Robert makes a big deal out of it when I so much as speak to another man."

"You weren't just speaking," Robert snarled. "You were batting your eyelashes and slipping into that little girl voice you use around men."

"That's ridiculous and you know it," Stephanie replied.

"It isn't ridiculous," said Robert. "It happens every time we get together with that bunch. I don't know why I agreed to go. When your high school pals get together, they act like they're sixteen. And none of them can even hold their liquor."

"Well, you were doing a pretty good job of acting like a teenager yourself," said Stephanie. "You were the first one to strip down to your boxers and swim out to the raft. Everyone followed you!"

"I swam out to the raft so I didn't have to watch you flirt with every guy there. I could have acted like a Neanderthal and dragged you home."

"Oh, really? I'd like to see you try it."

Lawrence was visibly annoyed by the squabbling. Stephanie and Robert were drawing the attention of other diners. All eyes seemed upon us.

"Keep it down," I whispered. "The owner of the newspaper is sitting right over there. He may ask for a story. And the mayor and her husband are over there. Don't embarrass me. This isn't like you two at all. It's Independence Day, and we should all declare independence from quarreling." It was such a ridiculous thing to say that the three of them stared at me quizzically.

Stephanie, forcing tears, turned to Lawrence and asked, "Uncle Lawrence, would you threaten to drag the woman you love?"

Lawrence placed his reading glasses in their case methodically, lifted his plate and flatware, and signaled a waitress. "We didn't come here to listen to this," he said. "Would you care to join me at another table, Jill?" Whether or not he was bluffing didn't matter. Stephanie and Robert settled down and our tasty breakfast was eaten in peace.

As I flagged our waitress for a second cup of coffee, a noisy bunch burst into the café. Thankfully, all eyes shifted to them. Some of the men wore huge hats with tall plumes in the style of the Musketeers and billowing white shirts. The women wore off-the-shoulder blouses, trussed bodices, and long skirts.

"Must have escaped from a parade float," I said, "but I thought the parade theme this year was "taking pride in Noblesville."

"Looks like they're taking pride in the Mayflower," Robert said, between bites.

The café was suddenly full of the pilgrims. The leader waved his sword and faked a gimpy leg. He shifted comically between the tables, swished his big hat, and bid diners "good morrow." He turned to a group of teenage boys with their mouths full of food. "Are you good men and true?" he asked. The boys rolled their eyes and continued eating.

One of the pilgrims wore a sandwich board advertisement for *Much Ado About Nothing*. "That explains it," said Robert, dryly, "but I don't see the brats."

Last to make a sweeping entrance was a party of three—Lauren in the persona of Hero, Chickie as Beatrice, and a tall, handsome young man, who could only be the demigod.

"Give us a bit of room, won't you good people!" the gimpy leader shouted. He signaled the wait staff to move away. "Where is Master Seacoal?"

Another actor answered from the opposite end of the café, "Here I stand good Master Dogberry."

Dogberry yelled in return, "You are thought here to be the most senseless and fit man for the constable of the watch; therefore, bear you the lantern." He contorted his body in a silly manner and grabbed a votive candle from a table. "This is your charge: you shall comprehend all vagrom men; you are to bid any man stand, in the prince's name."

"How if he will not stand?" Seacoal asked.

Dogberry wiped his mouth with his sleeve and responded, "Why, then, take no note of him, but let him go, and presently call the rest of the watch together and thank God you are rid of a knave. And now we must all away!" Though the language was confounding, the diners loved the spectacle. Eddie, on the other hand, had a line of customers waiting for seats and was getting annoyed. Most of the actors headed theatrically toward the door, bowing and bumping into tables as they left.

Lauren and Chickie pushed Craig to our table. "Friends, allow me to introduce Signior Benedick," Chickie announced, theatrically. "He has come from the wars to take shelter in our town and keep company with Count Claudio and good Don Pedro."

Lawrence rose and extended his hand to Craig, who in turn brought his huge feathered hat to his chest and bowed gracefully. Lawrence sat down again, quite amused. Robert reacted as though people dressed in seventeenth-century garb was standard at Eddie's.

I whispered to Lauren, "Hero, will you and Beatrice and Signior Benedick be joining us at the parade and on the pontoon later?"

Lauren leaned in. "Mr. Silvio invited the cast to a pool party at his house, and we're all going over there tonight. Do you mind, Mom?"

What could I say to a rising college sophomore who was eager to make a life for herself? I could only say, "Have a good time and be careful. You're right, by the way, he's dreamy." The trio hurried toward the door, clasped hands, and bowed before the diners. I hoped the demigod wouldn't break a heart and ruin a friendship.

We paid the check and our respects to Eddie and his crew then spilled onto the sidewalk, still leveraging breakfast bits from our teeth. It was eighty-five degrees already and the air was sticky. Noblesville's downtown merchants had moved their seasonal and hard-to-sell goods outdoors. Winter fashions, used books, jewelry, housewares, sporting goods, decorative pillows, scented candles, hand-made birdhouses, furniture, pottery, and other treasures were marked down and ripe for picking.

Stephanie and Robert headed for Mitchell's Used Books. "We'll meet you at the courthouse steps in a few," I called after them. "The horses come toward the end of the parade. Rita and Pink will be looking for us."

I expected Lawrence to leave my side and sift through merchandise on his own, but he stayed with me. We picked through clothing and hats and held things up for size. Lawrence tried on a misshapen straw hat and asked, "What do you think?"

"Perfect," I said, "but I think Jed Clampett wants it back." He actually looked charming in the hat.

Lawrence cocked his head in the direction of the Noblesville Antique Mart. "Wanna go in?" he asked. I was intrigued by a man who would initiate spending time in an antique shop.

The mart, lodged in one of our town's oldest buildings, is a consignment shop stuffed to its tin ceiling with remnants of the past. With only a few minutes to spare before the parade, we picked through clothes, linens, furniture, silver service, trunks, cut glass, books, old photos, kitchenware, and myriad other gems. It was clear that Lawrence was no stranger to antiquing and that he had an eye for the good stuff. He looked for manufacturers' marks and pulled drawers out of desks to examine craftsmanship. With the care of a trained archeologist, he examined a pen and ink drawing he'd pulled from a stack of artwork.

"It's a drawing of the Battle of Corydon," he said, excitedly. "I've never seen this one."

"Corydon, Indiana?" I asked. I had a flashback to the frustrated efforts of my seventh-grade social studies teacher.

Lawrence chuckled at my question but was graciously nonjudgmental. "That's right. It was one of the few battles of the Civil War fought in our state. I think I'd like to have this." He studied the figures in the drawing and tenderly wiped a little dust from the edges. The owner of the mart congratulated him on the purchase, and they discussed the artwork's possible provenance. Their discussion was interrupted by a loud boom signaling the start of the parade.

The Noblesville Fourth of July parade is a remaining bit of Americana that I love. All the cares of the world are suspended for one hour of bizarre behavior. People riding floats, farm tractors, trucks, and antique cars become celebrities momentarily as those on the sidelines yell for their attention. Families line the streets, with younger people standing and older people in lawn chairs. Girls and boys wave little versions of Old Glory in one hand and hold bags for catching candies in the other. I'm always let down when the parade ends.

As Lawrence and I weaved through the crowd, a certain vulnerability sapped my high spirits. Interspersed among the crowd were people I'd known all my life. There were the school teachers, mechanics, hairdressers, shopkeepers, relatives, neighbors, church friends, gardening friends, farmer's market friends, and so on. I was utterly exposed in the company of a tall, handsome stranger in happy possession of Civil War art and completely oblivious to my anxiety. It had all happened so fast. How could I explain that

Lawrence was Robert's uncle and that I had only known him for one day?

Had Lauren, Chickie, Stephanie, and Robert been with us that morning, friends and relatives would have thought Lawrence was a family acquaintance along for the day or a guest at the inn or a neatly pressed cowboy strayed from the trail—anything but "Jill's new boyfriend." As we greeted people along the way, eyes lit up with curiosity. I introduced Lawrence to a few people, hoping to heap a bushel of truth into the rumor mill. I needed my own sandwich board with the words, "THIS IS NOT MY BOYFRIEND, PEOPLE! I BARELY KNOW HIM."

We finally made it to the steps of the courthouse, quite near the judging platform. I was pleased with our location; my children could find us easily there. I noticed that the mayor, her husband, and the other judges were conferring with worried faces and looking at their watches. After desperately scanning the crowd, the mayor spotted me and yelled, "Jill, Jill, can you help us?" She motioned so frantically that I couldn't ignore her. I searched Lawrence's face to gauge his willingness.

"I'll do it if you will," he said. As we walked the steps of the judging platform, I thought of Marie Antoinette ascending to the guillotine. My head wouldn't roll, but I would become the object of gossip—a situation I like to avoid.

"Jill, two of our judges can't make it this morning," said the mayor. "Can you and your friend help us out? We'd be so grateful."

I knew all of the judges, of course. Besides Mayor Loretta Treadwell and her husband, Bernard, there was Bill Reeves, Hamilton County's public defender; Tim Johnson, owner of Johnson's Lawn and Garden Supply; Susan Marty from the Noblesville Visitor and Convention Center; Myrtle Justice, the mayor's cousin and owner of Midtown Art Studio; and Amna Jani, manager of the Noblesville Farmer's Market.

I quickly introduced Lawrence to the other judges, making sure they understood that he is Robert's uncle. We were welcomed warmly and the mayor hustled us to chairs in the front row, where we had a grand view of the parade and everyone had a grand view of us. This was not the location from where I'd wanted to view the parade. I admit, however, that sitting among the nearly prominent was a strangely heady feeling. Mayor Treadwell handed us the score sheets and clipboards and hastily explained the judging procedures.

Meanwhile, Myrtle Justice spied Lawrence's pen and ink drawing. Lawrence, completely at ease with our new situation, described the Battle of Corydon. It was clear that he connected easily with people; the judges seemed like his old friends. His good looks, soft voice, and affable manner were magnetic. I thought Myrtle might whip out a hanky as Lawrence explained the sad battle. Lawrence leaned toward me and nudged my shoulder. "Am I doing alright?" he asked. "I'm not making you too embarrassed, am I?" The musky scent of his aftershave and the sonic waves of his voice struck me in a zone of my body I'd all but forgotten.

"You're perfect, Lawrence," I replied. Fearing that I might be blushing, I didn't make eye contact with him. I didn't know why he had asked the question, but I was charmed, flattered, annoyed, and resistant.

By now, Main Street was packed with eager spectators waving flags, drinking assorted beverages and squinting under the July sun. There was no sign of Stephanie and Robert. My cell phone rang; it was Stephanie. She and Robert weren't coming. They were still quarreling about the silly business the night before and were going back to the inn. I was not happy with them but was resigned. My girls were living their own lives, and I must find a way to let go. My days of orchestrating family moments were washed up. An unexpected sense of relief accompanied my disappointment.

The parade began as usual with a color guard and somber veterans walking to a stately cadence followed by the high school marching band. These were followed by the grand marshal in a vintage car, screaming firetrucks, clowns with water guns, 4-H floats, fife and drum corps, pony carts, Little League teams, dance troupes, jugglers, hefty Shriners in tiny cars, and Miss Fourth of July riding in a sleek 1960s Thunderbird. It was all great fun, and I didn't want it to end. I had long since stopped thinking I was too sophisticated for corny parades. The spectacle and the lively conversations among the judges made it very difficult to focus on scoring the entries.

Craning his neck, Lawrence said, "I wonder when we'll see your friends." I spied the top of Pink's Stetson bobbing up and down to the rhythm of Big Dude's gait. I shifted my view constantly from the entries in front of the reviewing platform to Pink and Rita as they approached.

Pink riding Big Dude and Rita on Rhondo finally appeared before us. The foursome was a marvel and looked sharply out of place in a small-town parade. Pink and Rita were dressed in white fringed buckskin from head to toe, even fringed gloves. Pink with his Stetson and Rita with her pristine cowgirl hat nestled on top of her always-perfectly-touched-up auburn shaggy hairdo were the reincarnation of Roy Rogers and Dale Evans.

Golden streamers hung from the horses' saddles and fluttered with their movements. Their tawny coats glistened in the sun as sweat seeped from under the saddle blankets. Their manes and tails, the color of corn silk, swished elegantly as Pink and Rita pranced them from one side of the street to the other, whipping up excitement and pleasing the crowd.

Pink and Rita had mastered the art of appearing cool and completely in control of their show horses. I felt proud of them and of our long friendship. They were at my side when my first husband,

Phil, was killed and when my second husband, Jimmy the Monster, was at his worst. With all their quirks, they are as nestled in my heart as any friends can be. They maneuvered the horses squarely into position in front of the reviewing stand and reined them into bows. Pink lifted his Stetson and shouted, "Howdy Mayor! Glad to see ya!" Mayor Treadwell rose and blew him a kiss, which amused the crowd and drew applause.

Rita's eyes met mine. "Honey, what are you doin' up there?" she yelled. "And who's that good lookin' guy beside you?"

I blew a phony kiss to Rita but wanted to hide under my chair. Did she have to draw attention to Lawrence in front of the whole town? Of course she did because she's Rita Restin, and the Restins never do anything subtly. They must go big at all times, big dealership, big house, big horses, big money, big show. Love them I do, but there are times when I can wring their necks.

"Hey, Honey Lamb, you'll give us a good score, won'tcha?" roared Pink. He waved his hat in the air and swirled Big Dude in circles to hold the crowd's attention.

A familiar voice from the back row of the reviewing platform caught my attention, "Oh, my lord, Restin's got the biggest mouth I've ever heard." The voice was Tim Johnson's, owner of Johnson's Lawn and Garden Supply. "Putting up with him at Rotary is bad enough, but watching him show off like this is just obnoxious."

The other judges also heard Tim's comment, but we all chose to ignore him. I suppose we were hoping he would shut up. Apparently, he wasn't aware that there is a time and place for everything and that a parade reviewing stand is a bad place to air grievances. His remarks aggravated me greatly.

Tim's voice grew louder, "Jill, how can you stand Pink Restin? I've always wondered how a down-to-earth person like you can stomach that guy." A few of the other judges tried to quiet Tim.

Lawrence had become aware of the situation. He shifted his weight in his chair, sat up straight, and turned an ear in the direction of Tim's voice. "Is that guy talking to you, Jill?" he asked.

"I guess so," I said and shrugged. "He's just a loudmouth. I'm not getting anything started with him. I'm having too much fun."

Tim tried a stage whisper this time, "Go ahead and ignore me, Jill."

Turning my head slightly in Tim's direction, I asked, "What are you drinking back there, Tim? Why not share what's in your brown bag with all of us?" My remark made some of the other judges laugh, but I felt foolish for rising to Tim's bait.

"I thought you were going to ignore him," Lawrence said.

Tim continued, "Jill, maybe you and your fella would like to come back here and have a snort with me."

As last straws go, Tim had dropped his on the camel. Lawrence rose to his feet in tandem with Mayor Treadwell. He tipped his head slightly in the mayor's direction, indicating that she could relax and he would handle the matter. The mayor returned to her chair, looking embarrassed. My heart sank to my toes, and I wanted to run away. This situation was absolutely not in my playbook for the day's activities.

"Lawrence, please. Forget it," I pleaded.

Lawrence eased past the other judges, who sat motionless in anticipation of a good old fistfight there and then. Most would have loved to see Tim Johnson get his lights knocked out. It was surreal. I had expected to enjoy our little parade with my family. Now, deserted by them, I would soon be in a brawl in the town square. I envisioned blood on another of Lawrence's neatly pressed shirts simply because he was with me. I was no longer Marie Antoinette; now I was Calamity Jane. I didn't know whether to continue marking my scorecard or throw myself between Lawrence and the town loudmouth. As if the sun wasn't providing enough heat, I was perspiring from sheer fright.

Out of the corner of my eye, I could see Tim rise defensively to meet Lawrence eye to eye, though he was considerably shorter. The situation on the reviewing platform had become more entertaining for the judges than pony carts and jugglers. Their eyes were on Lawrence and Tim. Lawrence's tall, powerful frame made Tim look slight in comparison, but Tim is a hothead with a history of carousing that has lingered from his high school and college days. Would they put their money on Jill's new boyfriend or the obnoxious lawn and garden salesman? The wheels in the judges' minds were churning, and I could see delight in the eyes of some of the men. I held my breath.

Though Lawrence and Tim stood face to face, nothing violent was happening. Lawrence spoke softly to Tim. Tim's countenance changed from defiance to resignation. He shot a nasty look at some of the other judges and sat down. Lawrence walked back to his chair without a trace of triumph on his face. Somewhat disappointed, the judges resumed the task at hand. The mysterious stranger had won the day. But how?

The parade couldn't have ended soon enough for me. We handed our haphazardly-marked score sheets to the mayor and made hasty goodbyes. As we headed into the crowd, I asked Lawrence the obvious question, "What on earth did you say to Tim?"

"I told him I knew the secret he'd been hiding, and I'd tell everybody in town if he didn't shut up."

"How would you know Tim Johnson's secrets?" I inquired.

"Everybody has secrets . . . everybody," said Lawrence.

I couldn't wait to get back to the inn where it was cool, quiet, and private. As Lawrence and I drove home, I wondered about his secrets. I asked myself if I wanted to know.

CHAPTER 9

Lost Boys and Fireworks

I was relieved to return to the inn, my sanctuary and little kingdom. Lawrence made straight for his guest room, and, I supposed, the shower. The Jeep was in the driveway, so I assumed Stephanie and Robert were around somewhere, but there was no sign of them.

I was famished, but I didn't know whether I would be flying solo for lunch or to expect a crowd. I'd forgotten to check with Lauren and Chickie about lunch, and Stephanie and Robert hadn't surfaced. During the previous week, I'd scanned my cookbooks for summer recipes. In an old issue of *Food and Wine Annual Cookbook,* I found a perfect summer recipe called a knuckle sandwich. The sandwich is composed of succulent ingredients tucked between big slices of fried green tomato. I had plenty of green Big Boy tomatoes in my garden and all necessary ingredients.

Knuckle sandwiches call for fresh kernel corn, but Mort's patch of Super Sweet sweetcorn wasn't ripe. I settled for some of his corn that I'd frozen the previous summer. It was still amazingly sweet and tender. I also needed a couple of pounds of roughly chopped lobster for which I substituted crabmeat because this is Indiana, not Maine. I also needed minced garlic, mayo, chopped basil, chopped chives, red onion, lemon zest, pepper, flour, smoked paprika, eggs, milk, and oil. I zipped to the garden with my basket and scissors and snipped bundles of chives and basil, which fragranced my kitchen and delivered a punch of aroma therapy.

I'd planted ten Big Boy variety and ten Early Girl variety tomato plants in May, from which I was planning to fill my pantry with jars of luscious tomatoes. I would use them in recipes for the inn's guests and as Christmas gifts for friends and loved ones like Mort and my dear friend Mary Porter. For years, I'd gifted Rita and Pink with canned fruits and vegetables, but as I never saw the slightest trace of them in Rita's kitchen, I assumed she regifted them or tossed them out.

As I assembled ingredients, it dawned on me that I must remember to ask Teri to weed and water the vegetable garden on her next visit. I assumed she'd know the difference between tomato plants and quack grass, but I would take nothing for granted.

I was engrossed in lunch prep when the kitchen door sprang open and in tumbled three bedraggled thespians still in costume. Lauren and Chickie's pancake makeup had gone lumpy and their heavy mascara had shifted from their eyes to their cheeks. Their hair had gone quite flat. To my surprise, Craig Deluca was with them, also looking worse for the wear. The temperature in the kitchen rose instantly from their sweaty bodies.

The trio flopped onto chairs at the kitchen table. Lauren flung her arms and head onto the table in abject exhaustion and heaved breath in and out like a runner at the end of a marathon. Chickie's face was flushed, and she swiped at her chestnut page boy in a desperate attempt to pull the sweaty hair away from her face. Craig sat in a trance-like state for a few moments and then cupped his hand to his forehead as though fending off a migraine.

"Water, please, Mom. We must have water," Lauren pleaded, theatrically. "I didn't know it was possible to be so hot and stay alive. I came close to fainting so many times." Normally, I would have suggested she get the water herself, but seeing the trio nearly incapacitated, I rushed a pitcher of water to the table. They seemed to drink more than Rhondo and Big Dude.

"I can't believe Silvio made us tramp all over town like that," Chickie said. She grabbed a napkin and dabbed at eye makeup on her nose and cheeks. "He's inhumane and I'm going to tell him so. We could have died. Then what would he do for a cast? It would serve him right!"

"All I can see are faces when I close my eyes," Craig moaned. "All those blank faces in the crowd staring at us like we were freaks. Don't people around here know anything about art and theatre?"

"Hello to you, too," I said. "I thought you all looked terrific in your pilgrim costumes, though a little out of place for the occasion. It was clever advertising."

"No, no, our costumes are Cavalier period, not pilgrim," Chickie said. "Silvio is obsessed with the Cavalier period. He says that our costumes are mid-sixteen-hundreds, not early sixteen-hundreds, and don't we know anything about British history."

"Yeah, and aren't we all glad you're paying such close attention to what he says," Craig said. "Ask me if I care. All I know is that this costume is too damn hot to wear in twenty-first-century Indiana in July, and Silvio can stuff it. Sorry if I offended you, Mrs. Merrick."

"No offense taken, Craig," I said. "Why don't you all get out of your Cavalier period costumes and shower. You guys know where to find extra towels. Craig is welcome to use my bathroom. I hope you'll have lunch with us, Craig."

Waving his plumed hat, Craig channeled Signior Benedick and made a sweeping bow. "I would be honored to sup at your table," he said. Lauren and Chickie pulled him in the direction of the guest rooms. Over his shoulder, he said, "Your place is cool by the way, Mrs. Merrick."

I was a little confused about Craig. After meeting him for the second time, I decided he was a mere mortal after all. Clearly, he had a flair for the dramatic, but he also had a good sense of humor and a quick wit. Still, I wondered about the emotions flying around between the three of them. Was Craig becoming a romance for one of the girls? I knew that all would be revealed in a short time since the girls were open books.

As the thespians' voices faded into the recesses of the inn, Stephanie and Robert surfaced looking relaxed and holding hands. Apparently, they had worked out their squabble in the bedroom as newlyweds often do. I thought back to the days when Phil and I solved small differences of opinion in the same way.

"We're sorry for abandoning you and Uncle Lawrence," said Stephanie. "We just needed to work out some things. I hope you understand."

"Sometimes I can be a real jackass," said Robert. He embraced Stephanie and kissed her on the forehead.

So, what was I supposed to say about being abandoned again? Was I going to barrage them with another guilt trip and play the disappointed mother? They were too old for that, and I didn't feel like it. "It's okay," I said. "The mayor drafted Lawrence and me to be judges. We ended up sitting on the reviewing stand. It was, well, interesting." I decided to save the story of the near brawl. It might actually be funny at a later time.

We were all hungry, so I recruited help with lunch. I fried green tomato slices and handed them to Lauren and Lawrence; they sandwiched in the crab concoction. Stephanie and Robert set the table, sneaking little hugs and kisses. Chickie and Craig argued about adding sugar to the iced tea. Every chair at my kitchen table was taken, and my heart was just as full. Though I barely knew Lawrence and Craig, I felt a certain tenderness for them. They were at my table with my children, eating food harvested from my garden. The fried green tomato and crab concoction transformed them into kindred souls. With each bite, they became members of my inner circle. Whether or not I would get to know them better was unknown, but their baptism by knuckle sandwich was irreversible. The noisy banter was music to my ears. I wanted the image of this little party to lodge in my brain like a photograph on a hard drive, never to be deleted.

As always in life, perfect moments are fleeting. As the last of the knuckle sandwiches was lifted from the plate, an explosion jolted us into a new reality.

"Good god!" yelled Robert. He glanced out the kitchen window and sprang to the door. We all followed him onto the porch. Two scruffy-looking figures were milling around in the driveway. A sizzling flare was stuck in the ground beside them. They were lighting fireworks with amazing efficiency. The explosions were jarring. The two figures pushed and punched each other playfully between explosions.

"What in the world?" I asked. "Who are they, and what are they doing here?"

"Those idiots!" Chickie blurted. She exchanged knowing glances with Lauren and Craig, which linked them to the culprits.

"Do you know them?" I demanded. "Who are they? Stop them before they freak out the chickens and get Uncle Mort stirred up. What nerve!"

Another cherry bomb assaulted our ears, and the sulfur of a stink bomb reached our noses and throats. The trespassing perpetrators congratulated each other in shouts and hopped around with glee as a bottle rocked screamed and hissed through the air. We watched in disbelief. Lawrence, smirking slightly, cast his eyes in my direction, and swept his arm toward the porch door. I suppose there were limits to his interventions.

"Well, if you're all going to stand there, I'm not," I said, "but some of you have explaining to do." I hurried down the porch steps, sprinted past the herb garden and headed for the pyrotechnicians before they could light another fuse. Lauren, Chickie, and Craig raced ahead and reached the culprits before me.

"Dogberry, are you insane?" Chickie yelled. "You can't just come to someone's house and shoot off your crummy fireworks!"

"Dogberry?" I asked. "I thought I recognized you." The boys looked even shaggier in modern dress than they had in Cavalier period costumes at Eddie's Cafe. Dogberry's hair was long and flyaway, and the other boy's head was shaved except for a floppy little tuft on top that lurched in opposition to the rest of his body. Both boys were sallow and lean and wore wire-rimmed glasses. Dogberry's glasses were held together at the bridge by green tape. Remnants of pancake makeup remained on their necks and hairlines. Neither boy acknowledged us. They set up a bottle rocket as if we weren't present.

"Heavens, they've gone deaf," I said.

"No, that's how they are," said Lauren, earnestly.

"Stand back, everybody," yelled Dogberry. "This one is gonna shake the house!"

We all scrambled backward as the shrieking missile whirled skyward. Lauren, Chickie, and Craig took on expressions of wonder as the sound ricocheted from the barn to the chicken coop to the house. It was evident that the battle was in my hands since they were being seduced by the other side.

"Stop! Stop!" I yelled, cupping my hands to my ears.

"Cool, don'tcha think?" shouted Dogberry.

"I mean it now. That's enough!" I insisted.

"And now for the grand finale, we're gonna light four cherry bombs at once, so you better stand back," Dogberry warned.

"That's what you think," I said. I ran for the garden hose and turned it on at full power. A surge of hot water gushed from the sun-baked hose. I aimed the stream at the boys and the fireworks.

"No! No!" cried Dogberry. I turned the hose on his pile of unexploded armaments. "You've killed us. We're melting." Pretty soon both of the boys were on the ground, wriggling into the fetal position.

"Dogberry, get up." Chickie insisted. "You're not the Wicked Witch of the West and neither are you, Verges. Get up!"

I continued spraying the boys and their munitions even as they lay in pitiful heaps. I was tempted to fetch shampoo while they were wet. The boys crawled to their box of fireworks and pawed through it to salvage what they could.

"Do you know how hard we worked to steal these?" Dogberry whined. He retrieved a few damp sparklers and some soggy red, white, and blue boxes.

"I don't care," I said. "You can't go around shooting those things off wherever you please." I avoided the subject of stolen merchandise.

"Well, Beatrice here invited us," said the boy referred to as Verges.

"That's a lie, you little weasel!" said Chickie. "Lauren and I told you we were staying here this week. That's all. We didn't invite you here to shoot off your stupid fireworks. Tell the truth!"

After a moment's reflection, Dogberry said, "Okay, you said you were goin' home for lunch, so Verges and I thought we should serenade you with a few bang bangs. Thought you'd like it. We didn't mean any harm." He looked totally dejected.

I felt pity for the two waif-like creatures. "There's no sense baking in the sun," I said. "Are you two hungry?" Since the crab salad was gone, I wasn't sure what I could offer.

"Got any rattlesnake? That's our meat of choice," said Verges.

"Fresh out," I said.

"Rotten sardines?" asked Dogberry.

"Nope," I said.

"Stop it, Dogberry," said Chickie. "You're lucky to get an invitation."

"Truth is, we'll eat just about anything," said Verges. Finally came a statement I could believe. I invited Dogberry and Verges to pick green tomatoes for their knuckle sandwiches. Luckily, I had some leftover chicken breasts in the refrigerator, which I substituted for crabmeat. The recipe would be scaled back since I was entirely out of corn and chives, but I was sure they wouldn't care.

The boys' clothes were still wet, so they were served reluctantly on the porch by Lauren and Chickie. To my delight, Stephanie, Robert, and Lawrence remained on the porch as spectators instead of wandering off to engage in their own pursuits. Perhaps they stayed out of curiosity or because they had no place more entertaining to go. Lauren and Chickie called the boys Dogberry and Verges, as though they didn't have real names.

"'Tis good," said Dogberry. He stuffed his mouth, and a bit of green tomato hung precariously from his chin.

"Better 'n rattlesnake," said Verges. He wiped his mouth on his shirt sleeve. I handed him a napkin. Lauren, Chickie, and Craig exchanged eye rolls and sighs that were lost entirely on the ravenous Dogberry and Verges.

"Before we got here, we blew up a couple of garbage cans behind the liquor store uptown," said Dogberry. "We blew 'em sky high. Ol' man Pinter came out, but he couldn't see us 'cause we ducked behind a truck. You wouldn't believe what a bang bang that made. 'Twas a thing of beauty if ever there was. Think somebody called the cops on us, though, 'cause there were lots of cops around by the time we left town."

It occurred to me once again to congratulate Mr. Silvio for his masterful typecasting. He probably hadn't bothered with tryouts for these two. They were already slightly off-the-wall.

"Yeah, and you said the cops would be too busy helping little ol' ladies cross the street after the parade. Well, guess you was wrong," Verges said.

"Don't you two have anything better to do than vandalize the town?" asked Craig.

After mulling over the answer and taking a gulp of iced tea, Dogberry replied, "Nah, not really." Lawrence chuckled and then looked away. I supposed he was trying to remain detached.

"I'm curious about you two," I said. "Is *Much Ado About Nothing* your first play?"

"I've been in lots of plays," said Dogberry. "This is only Verges' second one. I started acting when I was in fifth grade. Everybody tells me I'm a chameleon. I can act like any kind of person. I can act stupid and wild or stuck up like them." He glanced at Lauren, Chickie, and Craig.

"Dogberry isn't much of a stretch for you," said Chickie.

"We're not stuck up. We just act like civilized human beings," said Lauren.

"We can't all act like morons," Craig added.

"And I've always been so nice to you," Dogberry responded.

"Always?" I asked. "How long have you known each other?"

"Oh, we go way back," said Dogberry. "I met Hero and ol' Bea here in drama club last year."

The puzzle pieces were fitting together. "What are your names?" I asked, excitedly. "I mean, your real names."

"He's Tom Laughlin. I'm Ted Bennett."

"Oh, my gosh! I just met . . ." I paused. A little shock traveled down my spine, and I refrained from telling him that I had just met Teri Bennett, his stepmother. I didn't know how he would receive the news. I didn't want to open an old wound. Ted seemed troubled enough.

"You met someone?" asked Ted.

"I met someone who, uh, looks a lot like you. He carried my groceries at Wilson's market. Do you know anyone who works there?" I asked.

"Yeah, I know people who work at the market. My dad keeps trying to get me a job there. I went there for an interview but didn't get called back. I guess too many people know me around here."

"You should try the Halloween store," said Chickie. "They'd hire you and Verges in a minute, but you'd have to show up for work and not steal anything."

"We applied there," said Ted. "When I called them last time, they said they had a lot of applicants for the fall. I thought, sure you do. Who wouldn't want to sell cheap wigs and fake tattoos to freaky little kids and bored housewives?"

My heart melted for Teddy Bennett and his friend. They seemed like lost boys. I thought of some of the lost boys I'd known in school. Some eventually landed on their feet. Maybe Teddy and Tom would be so lucky. They were certainly rich in imagination and street smarts, like two busy rats. Now, because of Teri, we were going to be linked. I didn't know how it would all unfold, but I knew it would happen.

CHAPTER 10

Terror on the Rockin' Rita

A cooling breeze off Morse Lake Reservoir brought relief from the clinging heat as Lawrence and I stepped into the pontoon boat. Twilight was closing down the day, and Pink and Rita were busy preparing for our cruise. The water was glassy and shimmering.

Large and small homes, long piers, and wooded lots line the banks of the reservoir. Pink and Rita's place is one of the grandest, a yellow brick manse filled with oversized furniture and huge modern art pieces. The garage doesn't contain a single automotive tool or garden rake since Pink and Rita drive vehicles from the dealership and employ a lawn service. That evening, the house was lit up like a hotel, and lights were beginning to shimmer on the water. Piers up and down the shore were festooned with speedboats, fishing boats, jet skis, pontoons, and sailboats—all rocking on the swells. Pyrotechies along the shore were setting up their annual fireworks displays.

Pink's newest toy, the *Rockin' Rita*, was decked out with plush off-white cushioned benches contoured elegantly on three sides.

There was enough space for ten or twelve adults, but that night it was just the four of us. The thespians were at Mr. Silvio's pool party, and Stephanie and Robert had begged off again, this time visiting Robert's parents. As usual, they had made last-minute plans and were heading for their Jeep when they shared their plans with me. I was upset that the manners I'd worked so hard to instill in my daughters had eroded to such an extent. I wondered if their regard for my feelings had vanished forever.

So, Lawrence was my sole companion at what I'd expected to be a family outing. He'd been in his guest room all afternoon, presumably rehashing old facts about the New Deal. He seemed excited about an evening on the water. In his crisp white Polo shirt, impeccable beige micro-fiber shorts, Sperry Top-Siders, and Indianapolis Colts cap, he looked perfectly in place with the boating set. I wondered why he owned a pair of boating shoes, but I thought it impolite to ask.

As we settled in, I was relieved that Lawrence and I were nothing more to each other than chance acquaintances related marginally through marriage. I could curse or spit off the side of the pontoon or drink too much alcohol, and he would have nothing to say about it. I didn't have to fuss about my hair and makeup. I could be at ease and detached from anything Lawrence did or said. I took no responsibility for him, and he took none for me. We were veritable strangers thrown together—again. It felt wonderful to be unattached to Lawrence or to any man. I leaned back on the seat, gazed at the rosy clouds draping the setting sun, and gave little thought to the damp breeze turning my hair flat. I was giddy with detachment.

Rita still has a good figure and rarely misses the chance to show it off in a bathing suit. Despite all warnings, she still exposes her skin to the sun and maintains a tan all summer. That evening, she wore a sheer white blouse with a stand-up collar to cover her bathing suit top and khaki shorts that had undoubtedly come from Nordstrom or Saks. Her hair, in its usual unmovable short shag, was weatherproof. Though it was dusk, her sparkly cat-eye sunglasses still sat upon her lovely girlish face.

Pink sat at the controls, as always. Since our high school days, he has been the one at the wheel, no matter what the circumstance or the vehicle. He's been the driver and all others his passengers. That's how he takes care of people. Though others may see Pink as a bombastic showman, he's a softy to me. That evening, with his yellow Wisconsin Dells t-shirt stretched over his paunchy tummy, sunglasses dangling from a DayGlo orange lanyard, lucky skipper's hat, and thick hands at the controls, Pink was feeling good.

"We have a surprise for you two!" Rita announced. Hopping out of the pontoon and back onto the pier, she waved to two figures carrying objects through the dusky light across the lawn, down the pier, and onto the pontoon. As they came closer, I could see they were wearing chef's jackets. Rita had gone to the trouble of having our little cruise catered.

"Isn't it wonderful, darlin's! Just look here at all these goodies," she said. She unwrapped a mound of shrimp and caviar on ice, fruit salad, cheeses, and crackers.

"Whatcha think, honey?" said Pink. "Like our little treat?"

I popped a plumb shrimp into my mouth. "Are you kidding? This is amazing," I said. "Love it."

"And we're mighty glad you could join us, Mr. Milner," said Rita.

"Please call me Lawrence, and may I say how glad I am to be here." He stretched out his arms casually on the back of a seat cushion and melted into a relaxed position. Rita settled up with the caterer and Pink maneuvered the pontoon gently away from the pier into deeper water on high alert to avoid colliding with other boats.

"Did I tell you how I happened to get this baby, Jilly?" Pink asked. "You know Charlie Hicks over at the Chevy dealership in Noblesville, don'tcha? Well, he's related to a guy over in Lake Shafer who just bought it from a dealer in Wisconsin. Well, the guy ended up having to bail his son outa jail, and he needed to sell her fast. It's all about knowin' people and bein' in the right place at the right time. That's what life is all about—connections. Don't you think so, Lawrence?"

"Sure," Lawrence responded. "But connections come easier for some people than for others."

Rita shot a quizzical look in my direction as though I could shed light on Lawrence's remark. I shrugged and looked away, still basking in detachment. Our conversation churned along almost as fast as the pontoon's propellers. It felt smooth, easy, and fun, nothing like Pink's forced conversations had been with Jimmy the Monster.

Pink and Lawrence chattered away; Rita and I interjected as we pleased. They talked about Pink and Rita's parade performance, fly fishing in the Appalachians, the recent Indy 500, Indiana's wine industry, and IU and Purdue basketball. Somehow, the history of the Ford Motor Company came up, which Pink turned into a truck sales pitch. Lawrence skillfully declined the "monster deal." Lawrence's mastery of conversation matched Pink's mastery of storytelling and bullshit. It was great fun.

Lawrence seemed particularly fond of the caviar, mounding perfect little bites onto crackers without using a plate or napkin or spilling a single little egg. It was as if he ate caviar every day and enjoyed it on the same level as a bologna sandwich. His nonchalance was infectious, so I found myself mirroring his

Gatsby-like casualness. It was a charade on my part, but Lawrence seemed to wear nonchalance and sophistication as perfectly as he wore his clothes.

The sound of water lapping the pontoon, the darkening sky, and the hum of the motor were mesmerizing. In his younger years, Pink would have opened up the engine to impress his passengers even in a pontoon boat, but he was content that night to cruise at a gentler pace. He speculated on the type of fish that jumped above the water and the amount of money his neighbors spent on fireworks.

Because of my happy detachment, periodic lapses in conversation were of no concern to me. I didn't attempt to force random topics upon us. I was free to sit back and drift into my own thoughts and be caressed by the washed evening air.

Rita was on a different path. "Jilly, I have something to show you," she said. Apprehensively, I followed her to a seat near the cargo box where she'd stashed extra jackets and her enormous purse. She glanced furtively in the direction of Pink and Lawrence, opened her purse, and pulled out her makeup bag. She whispered so earnestly that I giggled. "Honeylamb, what are you doin'? Have you lost your mind? Did you forget to put on makeup? The owl look doesn't work for everybody." She pulled out a small mirror and a pile of cosmetics. "They're not lookin' this way. Now's your chance to put on some blush and lipstick. If you need more time, I can distract 'em. Hurry up. It's not completely dark yet, and he can still see your face."

"I'm not putting on any of that stuff," I said.

"Are you crazy?" she gasped. "I've been watching him lookin' at you. He's definitely interested, Jilly, but you aren't even tryin'. Do you need a hormone shot? The man is a dream. I'm worried 'bout'cha. With a little rain dance, your drought could be over."

"Put that stuff away before they see you. I'm not in a drought, and I'm not doing a rain dance," I whispered. "I'm not interested in

Lawrence. Just because we've been thrown together doesn't mean I should pursue him."

"You mean to tell me that you wanna spend the rest of your life alone? That you don't want somebody to take care of you and cuddle up with you at night? The girls have lives of their own now. This could be your chance to pick a good apple off the tree. You've got a red delicious one sittin' right over there, and you're not even gettin' your basket ready. What are you thinkin'?"

"Stop," I insisted. "You're being ridiculous. Yes, I do want to spend the rest of my life on my own. Can't you see that I'm finally happy?"

"That's all fine now, but what's gonna happen when Mort dies and you've got that whole place to look after? Who's gonna pull your old truck out of the mud, feed your chickens, round up your stray sheep, and fix your pipes when they're leakin'?"

Rita's sudden practicality annoyed me. I didn't want to think about my truck in the mud at the moment, nor did I want to put on lipstick so I could find a man who would fix my pipes in my old age. I had never heard Rita talk like that. We had always talked about men in terms of Mr. Perfect or Mr. Dreamboat. Now, we were talking about Mr. Fix-It. I didn't want to talk about men at all.

"What's goin' on over there, you two?" yelled Pink. "Better let Lawrence and me in on the secret. I tell ya, Lawrence, those two are always up to somethin'. Gotta watch 'em every second." As Rita and I made our way back to Pink and Lawrence, I felt like a schoolgirl caught in a prank. I was unhappy with Rita for starting up about lipstick and for assuming too much. Her prodding had taken the fun out of the moment. I felt sulky.

The sun was nearly gone and the lake shimmered in every direction. Fireworks streaked through the sky and fell in colorful cascades. The stars were also becoming visible in the darkening summer sky. Pink dimmed the lights so we could enjoy the sights.

"What the hell?" Pink muttered. He sat up rigidly and squinted into the distance ahead. Lawrence did the same. "Is there a light comin' straight for us, or are my eyes goin' bad? Maybe it's the water patrol. Damn good thing I didn't bring booze on board tonight."

"Whoever it is, they'd better slow down," said Lawrence. The craft coming at us didn't slow down. Its headlights nearly blinded us as it sped straight for the pontoon, motor roaring. Lawrence, Rita, and I jumped to our feet.

"Jesus!" yelled Pink. He lurched for a cargo box filled with life vests. "Put these on fast!" We wriggled into the vests as fast as we could. It was dark and everything was happening so fast that we couldn't fasten the clips. "I'll kill that son of a bitch when I get my hands on him."

"Who is it, Pink? Do you know?" I asked.

"I don't know, but when I find out, I'm gonna kill him!" The speedboat was still roaring toward us, but the glare of lights and the spray made visibility difficult.

"Do you all know how to swim?" Lawrence yelled.

All I could think was my God we're all going to die here in these dark waters. I hate dark water, slimy creatures, and seaweed. I also thought about Lauren and Stephanie and how they couldn't plan their way out of a paper bag much less put on a nice funeral for me. Worse than that, for months I'd dawdled over my will. It was still unfinished, so the girls would spend the rest of their lives fighting over the farm and ancestral furniture. No, no, this couldn't be the end, not like this!

"Jill, Jill, do you know how to swim?" Lawrence repeated. He leaned his face close to mine and grasped my arms. "I'm a good swimmer. If we go into the water, I'll find you. Don't panic. We'll be okay."

"I love you guys," I yelled to Pink and Rita. It was all I could think to say.

The moment was surreal as the speedboat came at us. Then, just yards from the pontoon, it darted to one side. The boat made a wide circle around us with its engine still revving, making the pontoon roll so that we fell onto the cushions. There wasn't a chance of identifying the boat or the driver in the darkness.

"Hell, I know we're gonna be okay because I'm gonna shoot that SOB if he comes back," Pink yelled. He was brandishing something that could only be a revolver. Pointing the gun in the air, he blasted a couple of warning shots into the sky. A few moments later, we could see the speedboat's lights coming at us again, and its engine roared.

"Oh, my lord," said Rita. She held my hand and sat close beside me. "If this is a bad dream, I wish somebody would wake me up! Honey, if I die and you make it, you can have all my clothes and my new treadmill." I hugged her tight, not knowing whether to laugh or cry.

Pink lunged toward the front of the pontoon with his revolver in hand. "Damnation! Damnation!" he roared.

Lawrence jumped from his seat and tried to stop Pink from shooting again. "Look, Restin, let's not get crazy. It's probably kids trying to impress each other. Don't do anything you'll regret," he said. Rita and I looked at each other in horror. This wasn't the best time to tell Lawrence about Pink's legendary temper.

"Get outta my way, Lawrence. I'm not gonna sit here and let some jackass get away with this," Pink yelled in Lawrence's face.

Lawrence stared Pink in the eyes and held him by his shoulders. "I know how you feel, but you can't go shooting somebody. That's crazy." Pink jerked away from Lawrence's grasp. He shook his head in a quick burst trying to recalibrate his thoughts then lowered the gun.

Again, the speedboat circled the pontoon and left us rocking in its waves. As we braced ourselves, I could see enough of Pink's face to know that his skin was red with fury. The speedboat darted off into the darkness again. Pink jumped back into the captain's chair and turned up the motor. "Let's get to Wolfman's. It's closer than home." He placed the gun in the cargo box and closed the lid with a bang. Though we may have preferred to call it a night, none of us argued with him about going to Wolfman's.

We headed for Wolfman's Shoreline Tavern as rapidly as a pontoon can go, hoping we'd seen the last of the hit-and-run speedboat. We rode in awkward silence, which made the ride seem interminable. Even Rita was silent. Our brush with death combined with Pink and Lawrence's confrontation left us stunned and wondering what had just happened. Pink would need time to cool off if the evening was to be salvaged on any level. Through the darkness, I tried to make out the expression on Lawrence's face. He gave me a sweet little wave as if to say, "Everything's okay now, so you can relax." I did relax, slightly.

Wolfman's pier was well-lit and buzzing with activity. Some teenagers were milling around in a frenzy setting off firecrackers. Men and women lingered on the pier, and they chattered and laughed. I imagined that I might also see scruffy Teddy Bennett and Tom Laughlin lurking in the shadows but remembered that they were safely out of the way at Mr. Silvio's pool party.

Wolfman's is always crowded on holidays. I would have preferred a quieter setting to process our harrowing experience and have a nightcap, but Pink was determined to salvage our evening at the tavern. Our entrance drew the attention of several people sitting at tables and at the bar. Pink's mood lightened slightly as we exchanged greetings with half a dozen people and made our way to a table. He didn't mention the speedboat to anyone. He and Lawrence ordered beers. Rita ordered her favorite martini, and I asked for a Virgin Bloody Mary, in keeping with the events of the past hour. The mood was subdued as we settled in.

"That wasn't the ride I had in mind for us, Lawrence. I'm sorry," said Pink, shaking his head pathetically. "Nothin' like that's ever happened before."

"No need to apologize," said Lawrence. "But if somebody is unhappy about one of your truck deals, they chose a coward's way of letting you know about it."

"I never give anybody a bad deal," Pink said. "I always take care of people."

"You sure do, Honey. That's the truth," said Rita. "I thought we were all gonna die there for a couple o' seconds. I've never been so scared in my life. I'll have to call my beautician tomorrow for a touch-up 'cause some of my hair turned white when that boat came at us. Every time I close my eyes, I see those lights comin' right for us."

Pink took Rita's hand. "Now, now, Honey, calm yourself," he said. "Lawrence was probably right. Just kids playin' a joke. We'll never see 'em again. Don't worry. I'll let the cops know about it and everybody else on the lake. The truth will come out sooner or later. Always does. I don't want to spoil everybody's good time tonight."

Though we'd been munching on the cruise, Pink caught the attention of a server and ordered some appetizers. Before we knew it, she was plopping jalapeno poppers and seared tuna bites on our table. It was an odd combination, which I chalked up to Pink's upset. I picked at the food out of politeness and sensed that Lawrence was doing the same. Rita chased some tuna bites around her plate with a fork. Pink ordered another round of drinks, which nobody else wanted. The evening had been spoiled, and we all knew it. We tried small talk, and Pink attempted a couple of raunchy jokes that one of his salesmen had told, but the conversation was forced and self-conscious.

I felt protective of Pink and Rita and angry that someone would play such a rotten and dangerous trick on them—on all of us. The event robbed Pink of his equilibrium, and he would need time to recover.

Lawrence suddenly tapped my foot with his. Startled, I gave him a sidelong glance. With a subtle roll of his eyes and slight jerk of his head, he drew my attention to something he didn't want Pink and Rita to see. I scanned the place discretely. My eyes rested on Tim Johnson seated a few tables away. It dawned on me that Tim also lives on Morse Lake Reservoir. He appeared to be gulping beer and gobbling food in a big hurry. It was odd that on this festive night when families gather for food and fireworks, he would be eating at Wolfman's alone. He rose from his chair while still chewing, took a final pull on his beer, and threw a bill on the table. Wobbling slightly, he made his way to the kitchen of the restaurant, presumably to exit by the back door.

I glanced at Lawrence again, and we maintained poker faces. Had it been Tim who rushed us with his boat? Would Tim have the nerve to do such a dangerous thing? Was it possible that he could dislike Pink that much, or was he retaliating against Lawrence and me for the parade episode? How could he have known that Lawrence and I were with Pink and Rita? It all seemed crazy.

Lawrence and I excused ourselves on the pretense of needing to use the restrooms. Rita brightened and smiled to see us pairing off if only to use the facilities. When we reached the hallway to the men's and ladies' rooms, Lawrence whispered, "Do you think it was that guy?"

"I don't know," I said, "but he left awfully fast. The place isn't that big; he must have seen us."

"I saw him when we came in, and I'm sure he saw me," said Lawrence. "I think we'd better keep this to ourselves. Restin's had a couple of beers and he's got quick a temper. If we say anything about that guy, there's no telling how he'll take it. What do you think?" Lawrence leaned his face down until it was just inches from mine. His cologne was intoxicating, his breath sweet from beer and his deep voice mesmerizing. His blue eyes drilled into my eyes. My heart pounded and my knees buckled. Here was Howie Leonard again, my old high school crush. The sensation was delicious and all my senses were firing, yet I feared the feeling deeply.

"I think you're right. We don't have any proof," I said, finally. "I've known Pink a long time, and I've never seen him so thrown off. I'm not sure what to do." I pressed my fingers against my temples. The whole affair had brought on a headache, and I wanted to go home.

"Let's go on with the evening and keep this under our hats," Lawrence said. "We'll hope he's not out there waiting to try it again. I'm uneasy that Restin's got that gun, but I suppose he knows what he's doing. We'd better get back to the table."

"You go back," I said. I gestured toward the ladies' room. "I really do have to go." Lawrence chuckled.

We finished our drinks and headed back to the pier and onto the pontoon. I feared we were in for another long silent ride since Pink was still bruised and Rita had gone uncharacteristically quiet. Pink brought up the pontoon lights, and we cruised along. The stars put on a lovely show. Though we were on edge, the lulling water, night breeze, and galaxy above had a calming effect. Rita sat close beside me. We leaned back on the soft upholstery and gazed at the sky. Lawrence settled near Pink and the two did their best to resume small talk about fly fishing in some mountain area.

Rita, in a wistful mood, said, "Do you remember the night you, me, Phil, and Pink talked about skinny dippin' out here? Such a crazy night, but we had so much fun. Whatever happened to all that fun?"

"Whose idea was that, anyway?" I asked.

"Why, don't you remember, Honey? Pink bet Phil that he wouldn't get naked and jump in the water. It all started like that."

"I don't remember. Did any of us actually get naked?"

"Nah, but it was fun anyway."

"Now what?" Pink shouted. He sat up straight again and squinted at something in the dark waters ahead. "What the hell is this now?"

Just ahead were the lights of a craft that appeared to be drifting. The engine was silent, and the craft rocked quietly in the evening swells. Pink cut the pontoon's engine to a purr and we glided toward the mysterious vessel.

"Careful, Honey, this could be a trap. Let's keep goin'," said Rita.

Pink reached into the cargo box. It didn't take a genius to know he had gone for his gun again. Lawrence got to his feet and stood behind Pink. The evening had already been more than any of us bargained for, and now Pink was heading straight for more trouble.

"I think Rita's got the right idea," Lawrence said, calmly. "Let's move on. What's the point of taking chances?"

"Could be somebody in trouble," said Pink.

"Let 'em call 911, Honey. We're not the police," Rita said, sharply.

But Pink's mind was made up. The fear and humiliation he'd experienced at the hands of the phantom speedboat driver must be avenged. He needed to be the hero again—the master of his universe. The cost was irrelevant at that moment. The night turned terrifying again as he guided the pontoon alongside the silent craft.

I sunk my teeth into the sweatshirt I was holding, half expecting to be shot or blown up any moment.

Lawrence braced himself on the railing above the upholstered seat to get a better view of the craft. Through glaring lights, we could see that it was a speedboat bearing the name *Tim's Titan.* I couldn't make out the expression on Lawrence's face as he turned toward me, but I was sure he was anxious.

"Go away and leave me alone," croaked a male voice from the speedboat. "I don't need your help. I don't need anybody's help."

"Tim Johnson, is that you in that boat!" yelled Pink. "I know it's you. I know your boat. What's your problem? Are you okay?"

"Leave me alone I said. Are you deaf?" Tim's words were slurred and his voice shaky.

"He sounds drunk as a skunk," Rita whispered. She then shouted, "You sound drunk as a skunk, Tim Johnson."

"Go away and mind your own business," Tim yelled.

"What's wrong with your boat, Tim?" Pink called out in return.

"Nothing's wrong with my boat," came the answer.

"Will it start?" Pink asked.

"Not without gas. Got any?"

"Ha! Silly fool is out of gas," Rita scoffed.

"We don't have any gas now, but we can tow you to my place. I've got some there," Pink yelled.

"I don't want your help, Restin. Go away."

"Okay," said Pink. "You can sit there and let somebody crash into your boat and kill themselves. We'll leave you alone." We all went silent for a few moments, hearing only the lapping of water against the sides of both vessels.

"Alright, Restin, you can tow me, but you don't have to tell the whole world about it, you know. Got any rope?"

"The nerve of that skunk," said Rita. "He's going to let us tow him when he ran out of gas. It's just like him. Honey, let's leave him out here for the fish to eat. Too bad there aren't any sharks."

"Nah, we'll tow him," said Pink. "He won't remember saying any of this stuff tomorrow. Yeah, Tim, I have a rope, and I'll help you."

Lawrence cupped his hands around his face and chuckled in disbelief at the situation. The next twenty minutes were the definitive buzz kill, as the pontoon slowly towed the lame *Tim's Titan* toward Pink and Rita's pier. The mosquitoes were having their way with us since we were moving so slowly. Luckily, Rita had repellent on board, so we slathered up and put on windbreakers to fend off the hellhounds. I finally placed a towel over my head in mortal self-defense.

So, there I was with my hair smashed under a dampish towel, sweltering in an oversized windbreaker, and greasy from bug repellent. My exhaustion was exceeded by my disgust with Tim Johnson as well as with my daughters, who had scuttled what could have been a lovely holiday.

Again, I felt relief that Lawrence and I were only acquaintances and that he would be gone from my life in a few days. My flat hair, greasy body, and diminished grace were of no consequence to him or me. The thought was strangely reviving.

We finally reached Pink and Rita's pier with the disabled *Tim's Titan* in tow. I wanted to call it a night and break for my pickup immediately, but Lawrence wanted to see the business with Tim finished. Rita and I tidied the pontoon while Pink and Lawrence splashed enough gas into the *Titan* to get Tim home or at least to someplace where he could annoy someone else. Slapping at mosquitoes and tripping in the darkness, we managed to send the surly Tim Johnson on his way.

Rita and Pink tried their best to lure Lawrence and me into the house for a second nightcap, but we were both ready to leave. I hugged Pink tenderly and thanked him for being the protector as always. He took my hand in his two huge paws and kissed my fingers gently. "We've been through it all together, Honey," he said. "You know we'd do anything for you." I hugged Rita, and she kissed me on the cheek despite the bug repellent.

"Mr. Milner, you must think we're crazy people," said Rita. "Well, if you do, you're right, 'cause we are."

"I think you're terrific people," said Lawrence, softly. "I enjoyed the evening. Well, most of it. Thanks for the adventure."

It was a perfect night to ride home with the windows down. From the cloudless sky, the groupings of stars that I took to be the Big Dipper glowed as gloriously as the fireworks bursting here and there across the landscape. Fireflies hovered above the corn and soybeans and looked like a million glowing fairies. The air was damp and sweet as we passed fields of drying hay.

"Do you think it was Johnson?" Lawrence asked.

"I do," I said. "Do you?"

"I don't know, but he wouldn't look at me. Yeah, I think it was him. Will you tell Restin?"

"I'll tell him when the time is right," I said. "I thought it best to keep quiet tonight. With his temper, it could have led to big trouble. If it was Tim, he's lucky we didn't tell on him. Pink would have given him a lot more than gas."

It was very late when we reached Noblesville's town square and then Allisonville Road toward home. Lawrence sat back and stretched out his long legs as best he could. His cologne hung in the air, further perfuming the night. "Do you mind if I ask you something?" he said.

"Shoot."

"Is your life always this eventful? I mean, are cats in trees, loud-mouth bullies, and terrorizing speedboats daily occurrences for you?"

My eyes met Lawrence's in the dim light; I turned away quickly. A raw connection passed between us almost like an electric shock. I was glad the darkness hid my flushed cheeks. This guy had to go and the sooner the better. "No," I said. "My life is usually pretty dull, and I'm fine with that. In fact, I'm happy with dull."

"Not sure I believe that, but if you say so . . . ," said Lawrence. He settled his head on the back of the seat, closed his eyes, and folded his arms across his chest. We rode in silence for the last mile. When we finally reached the inn, all I could think about was getting into my four-poster where I'd be safe and alone. But, Lawrence's face and voice swirled in my thoughts as I drifted into sleep.

CHAPTER 11

A Better Man?

I awoke so early on Tuesday morning that I could have intoned reveille for the guinea fowl. I'd had a bad night's sleep. The image of the speedboat rushing toward us, Pink's unraveling, my disappointment with my daughters, and my free-floating attraction to Lawrence whirled through my thoughts. I couldn't brush the thoughts away gently as my therapist suggested during my split with Jimmy. There was nothing to do but get up and face the day.

I was accustomed to rotating a few favorite pairs of shorts and sleeveless tops as a summer wardrobe. Though I like looking tidy and put together, it had been a while since I gave great care to my outward appearance. I hadn't had a manicure in months, and though my weight wasn't a big problem, I was not in fighting trim. As I stepped out of the shower and looked in the mirror, I felt deflated. The crow's feet around my eyes weren't the only places the crow had landed. My hair was graying at the temples like the Bride of Frankenstein, and I had long since stopped waving "Hi Helen" in sleeveless tops.

This way lies madness, I thought. I had been perfectly happy with myself before Lawrence arrived, but now I felt self-conscious and chunky. I wondered how quickly I could work in a cut-and-dye job. That would be hopeless since I'd abandoned my stylist months ago because of her extortionate prices. Maybe I would have time to get an appointment at the local cosmetology school and stumble across a budding Vidal Sassoon. Yeah, right.

I didn't like being self-conscious. My neat little life had been invaded by a mystery man. I was perfectly fine with having a quick fling with the butcher in my mind and occasionally seducing my accountant in my dreams. That was all make-believe, and I could turn the thoughts on and off as I chose. I didn't have to talk to them. They never tried to tell me what to do, where to go, and how to spend money. If they had tried, they would simply go poof.

It was time to work out a dinner menu, so I slipped to the kitchen, grabbed a few favorite cookbooks, and squirreled them back to my bedroom. Nothing soothes me like leafing through recipe books with photos of pastries, casseroles, salads, sauces, wines, and exotic foreign dishes. There is something primal and satisfying in that. Food is the imaginary bridge I cross to unite with my mother, grandmothers, and other beloved relatives and friends both living and deceased. I settled on a recipe for tuna steaks with Provencal vegetables.

Unfortunately, my early July-garden could only provide the thyme sprig for the recipe, so a trip to the Noblesville Farmer's Market was necessary for the vegetables. The recipe called for zucchini, but this was only July, so squash would do. The tuna steaks, kalamata olives, and capers would take a little more energy, but sourcing is half the fun of cooking. The Fresh Market on 146th would have the freshest tuna steaks and any remaining ingredients.

A light breeze swept across the yard as I hustled with chores. While plundering the nests, I thought about my next paying guests, two couples from Holland, Michigan, who were due at the inn the following Wednesday. They would be easy to shop for since they hadn't checked boxes for lactose intolerance, gluten intolerance, vegetarianism, veganism, kosher, keto, diabetes, or dairy-free. The inn was fully booked until mid-September. My cleaning service was coming on Saturday afternoon for the monthly deep cleaning, and I remembered that Harlowe Barnes was to shear the sheep on Friday. Working with Harlowe would be no picnic, but the sheep were in need.

My mind continued to race as I plucked a few weeds in the garden. We'd had enough rain for the burgeoning vegetables. I couldn't wait to pick, eat, share, and preserve the bounty. I wasn't ready to make breakfast for everyone, so I tiptoed across the porch and into the kitchen. To my surprise, Lawrence was awake, sipping coffee, and at work on his book.

"Hi," he said, softly. "Ready for coffee?"

Again, he looked like he'd stepped out of *GQ* with his white tennis shoes, dark brown microfiber shorts, and crisp short-sleeved white shirt with an Oxford collar. His hair was perfectly in place and his face clean-shaven.

"Morning," I said. "Hope you slept well." I pulled a travel mug from the cabinet. "I'll take some coffee in this. I'm off to the farmer's market this morning. Kind of in a hurry."

"Want company?"

"Well . . . sure," I said, "but do you want another adventure with me?"

Before I knew it, Lawrence and I were back in my pickup. He drove this time. By now, he was wearing sunglasses and his Colts baseball cap. As I might have guessed, he handled the stick shift with ease, upshifting and downshifting without the jolting that I thought came standard. He didn't acknowledge the act of shifting gears or glance at the gear shift lever. He drove automatically with his eyes always on the road. We moved along as I directed, gliding to the market as if he had driven there a million times.

The Noblesville Farmer's Market attracts producers from across Indiana's midsection. I like walking from tent to tent, chatting with producers, and squeezing the goods. The stacks of colorful vegetables are a feast for the eyes. Pastries, jams, breads, cheeses, artisan vinegar, hams and sausages, bundles of flowers, herbs of all kinds, soaps, homespun woolens, and handmade jewelry fill the stalls. Many of the products are sold by Amish families.

As we hopped out of the pickup, Lawrence asked, "So, what are we looking for?" Though I expected him to try to grab my list from my hand, he did not. He moved closer to me, put on his reading glasses, and read the list aloud, "Fennel bulb, tomatoes, zucchini, and red onion. Do you think we can find zucchini now? It might be too early. Maybe you could substitute some kind of squash for the zucchini."

Who was this person and why did he know so much about zucchini? Was he an alien life form or on a mission to win my heart and disrupt my life?

"Do you use a lot of zucchinis in your cooking?" I asked.

"I make a mean stir fry with it. One of my neighbors unloads zucchinis on the neighborhood every summer. I have it coming out my ears. Several of my neighbors have gardens, in fact, and the wives are always bringing me vegetables. I guess they feel sorry for me."

"Oh, that's nice," I said. I couldn't help wondering if vegetables were the only thing his benefactresses wanted to share with him.

"I don't want to be underfoot," he said. "I'll be happy to hunt things down for you or I can just walk around on my own. Just tell me how I can help."

I hardly knew how to reply to such sensitivity. "Oh, just stay with me," I said. "You may spot things before I do. If so, just let me know. Okay?" My cheeks were flushed again.

The tomatoes were an easy find. My favorite local producers had bushels, though they had come from South Carolina and not from his farm. He cut open a large red and green heritage variety for us to taste. The warm, juicy goodness spurted out of my mouth. Lawrence produced a handkerchief and offered to wipe my chin. I wiped it myself.

"Will these do or should we keep looking?" he asked.

"These are perfect," I said. We were in luck; the same producer also had piles of red onions and straight-neck squash. "Now for the fennel bulb."

"I know about fennel," said Lawrence. "Granny Milner lived in a house on our farm when I was a kid. She had a big garden, and I helped her with it. She was a great cook. I remember her making leek and fennel soup. Vegetables would be spread out all over her kitchen. She made giant pots of everything. I helped her pull the leeks and cut the fennel bulbs. I wasn't a big fan of the soup, but I liked helping her. She was a very kind person, eccentric but kind.

"Eccentric how?" I asked.

"She was small in her ways, afraid to travel, barely left the farm, and she was superstitious. She wouldn't allow a black cat on the place. She had a fascination with owls. She'd listen for them at night and interpret their sounds. She also read tea leaves. My mother disapproved, so Granny read leaves for me in secret. Mostly things like how many points I'd score in a basketball game. I ate it up. Today, people would call her odd or crazy. There was a time when people could be different without being insulted."

"You must have really cared for her, Lawrence."

"Of course. She'll always be with me," he said, patting his chest. "May I tell you something?"

"I suppose so."

"I enjoy your company." He pressed his face so close to mine that the bill of his baseball cap almost touched my forehead. "You're easy to be with. I usually only talk this much during lectures, but with you I seem to run off at the mouth."

I smiled faintly and changed the subject. "Tell you what, let's split up and hunt for the fennel. Whoever finds it first can call the other one." I wagged my cell phone. When Lawrence walked away, it occurred to me that I didn't have his phone number in my call list. No matter, I could call Robert for it. My reason for wanting the number would be airtight.

In seconds, Lawrence was pointing to a stall like a bird dog. I made my way to him amid the growing crowd. On the table lay a pile of fennel. A deal was struck, and we pressed on for red peppers. Having bagged our lovely finds, we headed for the truck. The sun was already bearing down, and I looked forward to being under roof. As we passed the last few tents, I heard the unmistakable voice of Bea Mawbrey calling my name. I'd forgotten that Bea and Carolyn occasionally sell their honey at the farmer's market. Sure enough, Bea had spotted us from behind a table laden with jars of her sticky golden delicacy.

"You don't think she wants me to get Mr. Fluffy off her tent, do you?" Lawrence muttered. "My wounds are still fresh. Let's call the fire department this time."

"If we see Fluff, we'll run like the wind," I replied.

"Ah, Mr. Milner, I thought we might see you again," said Bea, as if performing. "Strong sense of that." She gazed in my direction and then back to Lawrence.

"You're a celebrity in town after facing down Tim Johnson," said Carolyn. "Nobody likes him."

"So, you're selling honey," said Lawrence. "Is it pasteurized?"

"Of course not!" Bea said, indignantly. "You can see that it's cloudy can't you and that I've left some of the comb in the jars. More antioxidants and antimicrobials that way. This honey will make you hale and hardy until you're a hundred years old. I eat it every day and just look at me." This was not an ideal piece of salesmanship since Bea is pale, brittle, and somewhat humpbacked.

"We use the honey for all sorts of remedies," said Carolyn, "and we even put a little in warm water to rejuvenate Fluff's fur from time to time. Makes it shiny and soft."

"And sticky?" I inquired.

"Never mind that," croaked Bea. "Mr. Milner needs to know how this honey is good for him. I'll tell you, besides allowing you to throw out your nasty white sugar, this honey will improve your digestion, lower your cholesterol, improve your circulation, thicken your hair, moisturize your skin, help you sleep like a baby, and heal your wounds. I'm sorry I didn't suggest it after our episode with Fluff yesterday, but that was a very trying moment for us. By the way, he calmed down and took the affair like a champ in case you were worried about him."

Lawrence maintained a straight face. "Well, I'm glad to hear it," he said. "I was concerned about him and about both of you after that ordeal."

"Oh, we came through fine, Mr. Milner," said Carolyn, "but Catzwell got a piece of Bea's mind after we left you."

"Yep! Marched right over there and straightened Catzwell out," Bea announced. "Won't see that beagle on the loose again. I should say not. At any rate, would you like to taste some honey on a cracker?" She opened a jar, spooned a little onto an unappealing saltine, and thrust it at Lawrence.

Lawrence bobbed his head up and down and smacked his lips. "Yes, very nice. Now how about you, Jill? Won't you have a taste?"

"Oh, Jillian's eaten our honey her whole life, Mr. Milner," Bea said. She replaced the lid quickly. "She knows all about it. Now, this honey is from our hives near the alfalfa field. Isn't it good?

Now, try some from this jar; this is from hives near our apple trees." She removed the lid of another jar and maneuvered a drop onto a cracker.

"Equally delicious," said Lawrence. "Tastes like apples."

"Well, what did you expect? Of course it does. And this jar is from the hives near the sour cherry trees," she said. She opened a fourth jar and repeated the process.

Lawrence accomplished enough saliva to swallow nearly dry crackers. "Well, I'm very impressed," he said. "You ladies have some amazing honey. Quite delicious. Thanks for the samples. Well, Jill and I are on a mission today, so we'll be leaving you now." He removed his baseball cap and bowed slightly to the Mawbreys as we backed away.

Bea raised an index finger. "That'll be twenty dollars, Mr. Milner. The jars are five dollars apiece."

"But, Bea, we didn't ask you to open those jars," I objected. "You opened them on your own."

Lawrence quickly fished a bill out of his wallet and handed it to Bea. She took it with gleeful satisfaction and bagged the honey. "Good doing business with you ladies," Lawrence said while struggling to juggle bags of honey and vegetables. "Give my regards to Mr. Fluffy, and try to keep him out of trees."

"Be sure to report back to us on the honey, Mr. Milner," Bea shouted in a phony performance for passers-by. "We'll want to hear how much you like it. You know where you can get more."

Once inside the truck, Lawrence laughed so hard that I laughed, too. "Those old crows," I said. "Bea is a scoundrel."

"Never mind," said Lawrence. "The laugh is worth the money. Besides, I'll be a better man and live to a hundred with thick hair and low cholesterol now."

A better man. The concept ricocheted in my brain as Lawrence cranked the engine. I wondered what kind of improvements could make him a better man. He didn't seem to need improvement. I didn't dwell on it for fear I was developing an affection for him. The prospect of falling into that chasm continued to unnerve me. Instead, I turned my attention to the market on 146th with hopes of getting my hands on some choice tuna steaks for dinner.

CHAPTER 12

Much Ado About Much Ado

The gang gathered at the kitchen table for an early dinner. Even Uncle Mort gave in to my invitation; albeit, I was apprehensive about serving tuna steaks with Provencal vegetables to a meat and potatoes man. I knew he wouldn't sit still long for the silly banter that was sure to follow. I also knew he would excuse himself early, saying that some cow, sheep, chicken, or rat needed his immediate attention. That was all fine. I simply wanted him to be with us and know he was loved.

Lauren and Chickie found it in their hearts to set the table without too much prodding while Stephanie and Robert ransacked my wine chiller for the perfect pairing with fish.

Lawrence, who had been in his guest room most of the afternoon, was now wearing perfectly pressed blue jeans and an Oliver Winery t-shirt. After introductions, Lawrence and Mort fell into easy conversation. Lawrence asked Mort about the history of his farm and his family tree, and they were off to races like old chums.

After searing the tuna steaks and sautéing a mountain of vegetables, I pressed the gang into further service and dinner was carried to the table. Grace was said, plates were passed, forks clinked. Robert poured the wine and we dug in. Mort was completely entertained by his exchanges with Lawrence, who pelted him with more questions about his farming operation and deceased relatives. I couldn't remember the last time I'd seen Mort so engaged and talkative.

"Good choice of wine," said Lawrence. "Rosé is right with fish."

"Yes, good selection, Robert. A lucky choice," said Chickie, with a snicker.

"What do you mean a lucky choice? I can imagine the wine you'd choose, probably the cheapest bottle of rot gut you could find," returned Robert. "You wouldn't know a bottle of good wine if it hit you on the head."

"If it hit her on the head, she'd be knocked out and wouldn't be able to taste it," said Lauren. Her comment drew eye rolls and sighs.

"The tuna is great, Mom. Just perfect," said Stephanie. I returned a self-satisfied smile.

To short-circuit further debate over the wine, I said, "Tell us about the play. How's it going, and when is the dress rehearsal?"

"Thursday night," said Chickie. She waved a fork in Lauren's direction. "Two days away and half the people don't know their lines yet. Crazy Dogberry and I are the only ones who have it down."

"Don't look at me like that," said Lauren. "I know my lines . . . well, most of them."

"Hero doesn't have a lot of lines, does she?" asked Robert. "Doesn't she just wander around looking pathetic? Beatrice and Leonato speak for her, don't they?"

"You got it," said Chickie. "I'm the one with all the lines, and I know them perfectly." She examined a vegetable dangling from her fork. "This has a very different sort of taste, Jill. I can't quite describe it. What is this?"

"Jill? What's this Jill stuff? She's still Mrs. Merrick to you," Robert scolded.

"It's fennel," I replied.

Chickie ignored Robert's protest and continued, "Even Deluca can't remember his lines. I mean, there's Benedick, finally declaring his love for Beatrice, and Deluca has to look at his script. Two days to go and he's still looking at his script! I told him that if he didn't have his lines down by tonight, I'd say them for him, and I mean it. I could deliver his lines better than he does, anyway. All this time, I thought he was some gift to the theatre."

"Maybe you should," said Robert. "Maybe you should say everybody's lines. I can see the headline: "Charlotte Stampler of Ball State University Fame Turns Shakespeare's *Much Ado About Nothing* into a One-Woman Show Entitled *Much Ado About Me.*"

"You're so hilarious, Robert," Chickie replied.

I inserted myself again, "Speaking of Mr. Deluca, has the demigod fallen from grace? Has he asked one of you out yet?"

The room went quiet. Lauren, Chickie, Robert, and Stephanie exchanged glances.

"What?" I inquired. "What's wrong? I hope nothing's happened to him. Is he seeing someone else? Well . . . what?"

"Yes," said Robert. "The girls discovered that Craig is dating someone else."

"Oh, that's too bad," I said, feeling a genuine pang of sympathy. "Is it someone you know?"

"Yes, it's someone we know," said Lauren, "but I don't know why Robert needs to know."

"He's dating Friar Francis," said Chickie, glumly. "Our demigod is dating Friar Francis."

After pausing, I said, "You mean he's dating the actor who plays Friar Francis?"

"That's the one," said Robert. "Friar Francis is Craig's sugar daddy."

I could see that Lawrence was amused by this revelation. "I'm ready for another glass of wine," he said. "I picked up this bottle today." Out of nowhere, he produced a bottle of Oliver Wine and hoisted it high. "Anyone else?" Mort, who seemed oblivious to the conversation, said he would take more water.

"Lauren and Chickie only get one glass," I said.

"Craig and Friar Francis were trying to keep it on the down low," said Chickie, "but Dogberry found out and blabbed to everybody in the cast. He told Lauren and me that he was saving us from ourselves."

"A full-time job for sure," said Robert. "Lauren, stop hogging the vegetables and pass them this way, please."

"How do you know so much about all of this, Robert?" I asked.

"Dogberry and Verges were here last night," said Stephanie, helping herself to more tuna. "It's obvious that Dogberry has a crush on Lauren. He also seems to know everything about everybody in town."

"The kid's actually pretty smart," said Robert. "He could work for the CIA if he doesn't wind up in jail first. You wouldn't believe the things he knows about people around here. For example, did you know that your mayor and her husband are being investigated for tax evasion?"

"That's old news, son," Mort interjected. "They've kept it out of the papers, but everybody knows about it."

"Yeah, but did you also know that a town councilman may have assisted them," Robert continued. "Apparently, he's also under investigation."

"Did Dogberry tell you that, too?" I asked. "How would a kid know that and why would he care?"

"Like I said . . . central intelligence," said Robert. "He's probably got a spy network."

"Dogberry and Verges were here last night?" I asked. "How did that happen?" I ignored Robert's gossipy rant, though I was curious about the councilman tidbit.

"They brought us home from rehearsal," said Chickie. "My car is in the shop, and we were desperate. We didn't invite them to stay, but they're like that gross fly paper my dad hangs in the garage. Once it's stuck to you, you can't pull it off. It just coils around you. I'm afraid we're stuck babysitting them until the show's over and we leave town. Dogberry's really brainy, but his home life is screwed up or something. I don't know what's wrong with him, really."

"Why don't we call him by his real name, which is Ted," I suggested.

"Most people call him Teddy," said Lauren. "He says his stepmother is working for you, Mom. Was that the lady we saw here on Sunday?"

"Yes," I said, sighing. "It's a weird coincidence. I met Teri in the grocery store on Saturday, and before I knew what happened, I hired her. She doesn't know one plant from another, but she's very sweet. I get the impression that life hasn't been going so well for her. I didn't think Teddy had anything to do with her now."

"Teddy likes Teri. The divorce really upset him," said Lauren. "He said he wants his dad and Teri to get back together. He says Teri was good for his dad." We all stared at Lauren in amazement. There was suddenly a chance that my younger daughter was concealing the heart of a caring human being. It also appeared that she knew more about Teddy Bennett than she'd let on. I wanted to interrogate her further, but that would have placed her in jeopardy in present company. I'd bide my time and catch her alone.

The perfect moment presented itself after dinner. Mort excused himself and headed down the lane, Stephanie and Robert grudgingly washed dishes, and Lawrence took dessert on the porch. Lauren and Chickie were ready to rush off to rehearsal, but they realized they didn't have wheels. Naturally, they asked to borrow my pickup.

Lauren would have to drive since Chickie was clueless about the stick shift. When the girls were fifteen, Chickie had asked if I would teach her to drive a stick while teaching Lauren. When I suggested that she ask her father to teach her, the subject dropped. Lauren nearly ground the gears to smithereens when she was learning, and she hadn't improved much over time. Consequently, I insisted upon giving her a quick refresher—just the two of us. She protested, "We'll be late for rehearsal, and I've driven this thing a million times."

"Do you want the truck or not?" I asked. "We'll go down the lane toward Mort's and be back in a flash." We lurched along as Lauren managed first gear and then second. I could see Chickie in the sideview mirror looking bewildered and pacing. Undoubtedly, she was anxious to get to rehearsal where she could say everybody's lines.

"Lauren, I was proud of how you stood up for Teddy Bennett," I said. "Do you know him well?"

"Oh, Mom," she replied. "I don't like Teddy like that. I mean, I don't like him like you're thinking."

"I'm not thinking anything," I said, "but you seem to know about his family situation. I'm wondering how you know about the divorce."

"Do you remember that I went to Noblesville High School? Everybody knows everything about everybody. Teddy was in my theatre class, and he was in *Charlie Brown* and that Broadway musical review."

"Well, you never mentioned him before," I said.

"Teddy was only a sophomore last year. He's so weird, and his friends are weird. I didn't pay much attention to him, but I did kind of feel sorry for him." She struggled with second gear, and we hit a large rut. "This truck is so lame. I wish you would buy a normal car."

"I like my truck, and I need it. I'm always hauling things around. You know that."

"Some cars have big trunks. You could probably fit everything in the trunk."

"Chickens, sheep, hay?" I said. "Is Teddy really as crazy as he seems?"

"Mom, what's this thing you have about Teddy Bennett? Why do you keep asking about him?"

"I don't have a thing, but I've hired his former stepmother to work for me, and I'd like to know a little more about her."

"Maybe you should try interviewing people before you hire them," said Lauren. "Make them take a personality test to see if they're all there?"

"Oh, sure, like I would have asked Mrs. Tubman to take a personality test to see if she was stable enough to pull weeds. Hiring Teri just happened . . . spontaneously. You would have understood if you'd been there."

"If I tell you something, Mom, would you promise to never bring it up again? Please?"

"That depends on what it is. I can't make a blanket promise, and you know it."

"Okay, then I won't tell you."

She had me. "I promise," I said, bracing myself.

"One night as I was leaving *Charlie Brown* rehearsal at school to get into this crate, Teddy was sitting on the hood of a car. He was crying. I could tell because he was wiping his eyes on his sleeve. I wanted to keep walking, but this thing was parked next to his car. I had to say something. We started talking. It was cold, so I asked him to ride to the gas station with me. I don't know why I did it, but I couldn't leave him sitting there alone."

"Sounds familiar," I said.

"Teddy told me that his dad had a drinking problem, but he'd married this nice lady, and he stopped drinking so much. But the fights were getting worse, and he didn't want to go home. He said he was afraid his dad might start drinking more again. He thought about running away, but he had no place to go. He didn't want to live on the street or something."

"So, what did you say?"

"Well, I told him about you and Jimmy and how I wanted to run away when he lived with us. I think it helped him a little. Then we talked about other stuff like how Mr. Silvio's comb-over lifts up in the wind and how his face gets white when he's mad. We've talked a few more times. I saw him at a party when I came home at Christmas. Things weren't much better then.

"Let's turn around so Chickie won't blow a gasket," I said. Lauren drove the truck to Mort's driveway, yanked the gearshift lever into reverse, released the clutch too fast, and killed the engine. She restarted somewhat frantically.

"This truck is a disaster! Doesn't it embarrass you?"

"No," I replied. "It requires tender loving care. You have to drive it with a soft touch. Does Chickie know about Teddy's family problems?"

"No, I've never told her anything about Teddy. She'd make fun of me. You know how she judges everybody."

"Well, maybe there's some way you can help him."

"Oh, Mom," Lauren said, impatiently.

"I mean, just be kind to him."

"Chickie's right; if I was nice to Teddy, he would stick to me like fly paper. He'd just get hurt."

"Hmm, I get your drift," I said, "but maybe something will come to you. Sounds like the poor kid could use a friend." The truck sputtered, and we lurched toward home. Chickie was impatiently kicking at gravel in my driveway.

"Mom, I have to ask you something," Lauren blurted. "Do you like Lawrence? I mean, do you think he's handsome?"

She'd stuck me with a two-edged sword. If I said "no" to her last question, she would know I was lying. If I said "yes," she would make assumptions and build it into a thing. I didn't want a "thing" to get started about Lawrence and me. I resolutely said, "Yes, Lawrence is handsome, but no, I have no interest in him in any way that you might be thinking. Okay?"

Knowing Lauren, she would read something into my abruptness. But there hadn't been time to practice a better response. If she brought up the subject again, I would be cooler. I took my time getting out of the truck on purpose. Chickie took my spot in a huff.

CHAPTER 13

A Single Touch

As Lauren and Chickie lurched down the lane in my pickup, I said a prayer that they would come home safely. It was dusk, and just above the vegetable and flower gardens hundreds of little fireflies twinkled away. I could hear the rumble of thunder and see flashes of lightning in the distance. Rain could be coming our way, or it could miss us entirely and enrich the crops and gardens of distant counties. I knew Mort would be pacing between the weather channel on TV and his screen door in anticipation.

I decided to check on the electric waterers in the chicken and sheep pens. Malfunctions are cruel in such hot weather. All was well with the hens. I closed the coop door quietly as if it were hinged on a sleeping baby's room then walked through the outer pen and slipped through the gate and secured the latch.

The thunder grew louder as I walked to the barn. My little flock of ewes and lambs had retreated to the barn for the night. Most of the ewes lay on their bellies coaxing coolness from the cement floor. Their bodies rocked with each breath, and when their lambs approached for milk, the ewes were annoyed. I was ready to take my chances with disagreeable Harlowe Barnes, the shearer. Mort was right, of course, Harlowe's personality had nothing to do with his ability to shear sheep. The goal was to make the ewes more comfortable and healthier; this he could do.

I strode through the mid-section of the barn and out the big east door and lifted the lid on the electric waterer. It was full; all was in order. The water looked so inviting that I plunged my hands in and rinsed off up to my elbows.

"I hope you're not planning to take a drink," came Lawrence's deep velvety voice from the open doorway of the barn. "The sheep might not like to share."

"Oh, sorry, I didn't see you there, Lawrence," I said.

"Didn't mean to startle you. I love a good thunderstorm. Thought I'd take a walk and see what you're up to. Hope you don't mind."

"No, no, just checking the waterer," I said. "Everything looks fine." Thunder clapped directly overhead and a cooling wind kicked up swirls of dust and rustled the trees.

"Bet you're glad Mort hasn't cut the alfalfa." That Lawrence knew about rain spoiling hay made him even more of a kindred spirit. Tepid raindrops hit my face and shoulders. I took refuge in the barn beside Lawrence. My heart began to race, and I felt self-conscious again.

The sky was laden with dark clouds as we stood together in the doorway and watched the rain wash the fields. The breeze swirled around us, and I felt wonderfully alive, exhilarated, and yet foolish for it. Lawrence moved closer to me, but I edged away. He shifted toward me again in what may have been an unintentional reflex, but I moved away again. An image of John Wayne and Maureen O'Hara embracing in rain-drenched clothes amid the ruins of an Irish abbey or cemetery—or whatever it was—leaped to mind. I despised the stupid thought. At that moment, I was even annoyed with poor, dead John Wayne.

"Well, I think I'll go in," I said, abruptly. "Glad it's raining."

"You're kidding," said Lawrence. "You're gonna miss this beautiful shower? Why not stay and enjoy it? You'll get soaked out there."

I raised my voice to be heard over the pelting rain on the metal roof, "I have things to do, and a little rain won't hurt me."

As I turned and started away, Lawrence caught my hand and pulled me back gently. His eyes were pleading. "Surely you can stay another few minutes. This shower is too good to miss."

It was a horrible yet delicious moment. I pulled away, almost unable to breathe. Evidently, I was wanted by this man, a man far more alluring than Stan the butcher or Larry the accountant in my imaginings. This wasn't a fantasy; it was flesh and blood and what flesh! I decided to accept the gesture as an act of friendship and not as an advance, but no matter what Lawrence intended, the reaction in my racing heart at that moment was anger. I hadn't invited his attention. I hadn't invited him at all.

"I'll stay for a couple of minutes," I said. I avoided Lawrence's gaze and folded my arms in a tight knot against my torso like a moat around a castle. Sensing my icy attitude, he placed his arms akimbo and moved to the center of the open doorway. He looked out into the pelting rain and stood in silence. When the rain eased, he helped me pull the track doors shut. We made awkward small talk and headed for the inn. That night, I undressed for bed in my closet with the light off just in case Lawrence could see through walls.

CHAPTER 14

Sincerely, Lawrence

I awoke at five o'clock a.m. on Wednesday feeling frozen in my bed. How could I relax and be myself now? Lawrence's one little gesture of taking my hand had spoiled everything. If only he hadn't done that, the week would have rolled happily on. I was enjoying his company and the thought of him. I didn't want anything real.

I propped my head on my pillows and pondered. Surely there were other women in Lawrence's life. He was probably taking a break from some relationship and decided to make me his project for the week. I'd thought of asking Steph for details about him. Did he have a girlfriend? How did he live? What were his habits? But asking Steph would be dangerous since she would devise a subtext for my questions. Besides, he would soon be gone. All I'd wanted was a nice week with my girls. Had I led Lawrence on? I did flirt with him slightly on the *Rockin' Rita*, but the man is so good-looking that a woman would have to be made of stone not to flirt a little.

My bedroom felt overly warm. I threw off the comforter and rooted around for a cool spot between the sheets. The pillows didn't feel right either, too big, too warm, oppressive. I threw them to the floor and tried lying flat, which was worse. I grabbed one of the pillows again and placed my head on the corner.

Why was I being such a coward? I had the power to shut down the game. I could tell Lawrence the truth: I'm simply not interested in a relationship. Yes, I'm very flattered, Lawrence, but not interested. That's what I'd say. But, was I making an assumption? Maybe he wasn't looking for a relationship. Maybe I had misread his touch. Maybe the gesture was one of friendship. Was it conceit that made me think otherwise? Did I think myself so irresistible?

I would straighten things out with him over coffee in a couple of hours. I would tell him exactly where I stood and that it was no dice. I was sure I could find the words to let him down gently. Exhausted, I fluffed up the pillow and sank my face into it. Sleep finally came again, if only by near asphyxiation.

It was eight forty-five when I awoke; the day seemed half over. Why hadn't the guinea fowl made a racket? Those little traitors. I'd planned to make waffles for Steph and Robert, but they were surely sipping Starbucks by now. Lauren and Chickie would sleep until noon. From my bedroom window, I could see that Mort had let the chicken out. Thank God for Mort. I would have to do something extra special for him.

I placed my face directly under the stream of hot water in the shower, and the sensation brought me to my senses. Yet, I was unsteady and a little dizzy. I braced myself against the shower wall, wishing for a grab bar. I rushed my hair and makeup routine, pulled on shorts and a blouse, and tried to dismiss the episode with Lawrence in the barn.

As I headed for the bedroom door, I noticed that my reading glasses were bracing a small envelope on the dresser. My name was typed in large font on the front. I opened it and found a tri-folded sheet of paper. The room became very warm again as I read the note.

Dear Jill,

Thank you for your gracious hospitality. When Robert and Stephanie mentioned spending the week at your inn, I hesitated because I didn't want to interrupt a family get together. They assured me that you would be warm and welcoming and they were right. To be honest, I have wanted to see you again ever since their wedding. You captured my attention that day and you've stayed in my thoughts. I enjoy your company very much and hope that we can become good friends and perhaps even more. Forgive me for saying these things in a letter. I'm not always good at expressing my feelings in person.

Sincerely,
Lawrence

I jammed the note into my sock drawer and sat down on my bed in a panic. I couldn't possibly open the bedroom door and walk to the kitchen. I felt terror, anger, fear, and pleasure all at once. It was true, a strikingly handsome and accomplished man was interested in me. He had noticed me at the wedding and thought I was something special. I suddenly experienced a shameful sense of power over him, power over the whole world. If he cared for me, then the whole world should kneel at my feet. No, I'm going crazy, I thought.

I wondered if Lawrence was deliberately trying to ruin me with his dreamy eyes, tantalizing voice, intoxicating cologne, hairy forearms, and good coffee. Somehow, this had to be my fault, but how?

Though I wanted to stay in my bedroom, I had to face the day and everyone who would whirl in and out of it. I had no reason to hide or feel self-conscious. The house was very quiet as I took the dreaded walk to the kitchen. The drainer beside the sink was piled with dishes, and the dishwasher was filled with dishes from last night's dinner. A note from Stephanie said she and Robert were getting breakfast out. She said that Lawrence was also leaving to do some research at a library in Indianapolis; he asked that we not wait for him at mealtime.

After reading Lawrence's note, I couldn't go on with my day as normal. Nothing was normal now. I unloaded the dishwasher in a dream-like state. After placing an empty bowl in the refrigerator, I sat at the kitchen table to think. What was I supposed to do? Was I going to track down Lawrence at one of the city's hundred libraries and set him straight? I couldn't call him because I didn't have his phone number.

I decided to visit my dear friend Mary Porter immediately and discuss everything with her. Mary would help me get my head on straight. I grabbed the egg basket and a pair of scissors. I couldn't drop in on her without some eggs or herbs or flowers. The race was on; I had to leave for Mary's house before the children appeared. I would call her on the way.

CHAPTER 15

How Hard Can It Be?

Mary Porter had been one of my mother's dearest friends, and now she is one of mine. She has lived in the same charming home on Walnut Street in Noblesville for eighty years. She grew up in the house with two younger sisters. The girls were raised by doting parents. Mary never married.

Mary was also my piano teacher from the time I was eight until I turned thirteen. Around my thirteenth birthday, she must have had a heart-to-heart with Mona concerning my future as a pianist. Though it probably pained her to say it, she had gone as far as she could with a mediocre piano student, who didn't like practicing. Mother took it well and excused me from piano lessons on a permanent basis.

When my mother died, it was Mary who consoled me. Her wit, wisdom, and no-nonsense approach to life have fed my soul and lifted my spirits countless times. She's taken care of me, and I've tried to respond in kind.

When I arrived at Mary's that morning, I lingered in the pickup for a few extra moments and gazed at her compact white frame house—the house I knew so well—with the orange tiger lilies and blue delphiniums against the wrought iron fence.

On one side of the house are the brick steps that once led to Mary's piano studio. I often sat on those steps doing homework while waiting for other students to finish their lessons. When I was in seventh grade, the horrible Michael Fleming took his lesson before mine. When finished, he would burst through the door and step on my homework before bounding down the steps. He grew up to be a stock broker and lives in California.

I was at Mary's house again to share my troubles. I knew she wouldn't mind and that she'd be glad to see me. I also knew that I wouldn't have her forever, though I wanted to keep her forever. She is the last of my mother's lifelong female soulmates. To think of life without Mary Porter was too bleak to dwell upon. Since I was already in panic mode, there was no sense in adding morbidity to my distress.

Mary met me at her front door wearing the powder blue duster I'd given her on her eightieth birthday. Her bright smile lightened my heart. Her short bluish-white pageboy fluttered slightly as she jolted backward on her walker to admit me into the entryway. She eyed the contents of my basket. "You look peaked," she said. "Eggs? Good. I was nearly out . . . and flowers. How nice. Tomatoes already?"

"These are from the farmer's market," I said. "Mine aren't ripe yet, but I can bring you some green ones if you want them."

She waved her hand. "I'm not that hard up."

I followed Mary's jolting steps into her kitchen, placed the basket on the counter, and eased onto a chair at her table. It's a privilege to be invited into her kitchen. As a child, my interaction with her was limited to the four walls of her piano studio. On very rare occasions, I would be admitted into the living room when accompanied by my mother but never into the kitchen. The kitchen was the inner sanctum, a place of mystery off limits to children. In fact, the house beyond the studio had been a source of great mystery during my childhood. As I grew up, went to college, and got married, I was admitted more and more until finally I was accepted into the elite clique of women allowed to gather in the kitchen.

Mary's kitchen is bright, cheerful, and cluttered with cookbooks, magazines, and mail. Though outdated, the appliances are immaculate and uncomplicated. The pale-yellow walls and wooden shelves are graced with antique blue and white plates and ceramic pieces, some of which I have purchased for her with great pleasure. Her kitchen was a safe harbor at that moment, and I wanted to stay indefinitely.

"Kettle's hot. Tea in a jiff," Mary said. She shuffled to the stove and began the ritual of placing loose-leaf tea in the pot and laying out cookies on a plate, this time Walkers Shortbread. "Get some milk out, Jilly, and put it in this creamer." I obeyed. "I know you're bursting with something, so let's hear it."

I gathered my thoughts. "Well," I began, "there's this man and he's interested in me, and I don't know exactly how to handle it. I don't want a relationship." The words seemed ridiculous.

Mary placed her china tea strainer over my cup and poured. "Good heavens!" she said, "How hard can it be to tell a man to get lost?"

"It's not that simple," I said. "He's Robert's uncle, and he's staying at the inn with us this week. You wouldn't believe how charming he is and how handsome. I mean, he looks like a movie star."

"You're not still taken in by good looks, are you? From what I've seen, it's the good-looking men that give women the most trouble." Mary poured herself a cup and settled into her chair.

"It's not just his looks," I said. "He's also intelligent, polite, and warmhearted. There's something about him, something magnetic.

Every time we're in the same room it's like nobody else is there. He's all I see. I hate being so drawn to him. I'm furious with myself, and I'm furious with Steph and Robert for inviting him. Frankly, he's ruining the week. I want to kick him out, pull down the shades, jump in bed, and hibernate until he gets out of my head."

Mary peered at me over the top of her glasses. "That's not the most mature thing I've heard you say. How do you know he's interested in you? Has he made a pass or something? How old is this Lothario, anyway?"

"I don't know. I suppose he's about my age."

"And he's single without any attachments. Really? Come now."

"I'm not sure about attachments. From all accounts he's single. He lives in Bloomington, which isn't that big. Steph and Robert would know if he had attachments, and nothing's been said about that."

"Nothing has been said? You mean you haven't asked them about him?"

"If I ask about him, they'll be suspicious. I don't want to show any interest in this guy at all. You know Steph; she'll jump to conclusions," I nibbled a shortbread and poured a dash of milk into my tea.

"So, back to my questions. What makes you think he's interested in you?"

I produced the note and handed it to Mary. "He left this note on my dresser. I found it this morning."

"There's a reason I ask you to pick up big print books for me at the library."

I gently pulled the note from Mary's hand and read it to her. When I finished, she took a sip of tea, sat back in her chair, twisted the little napkin on her lap, and fixed her eyes on the ceiling for what seemed like an eternity. "Hmm," she said. "Looks like you have a little situation, my dear, but I'd give this a lot of thought if I were you. This could be an invitation to trouble. I'd hate to see you have more trouble. What do you think your mother would say if she was sitting here?"

I sighed. "You know what she'd say. She'd warn me to be careful."

"How long has it been since your divorce from . . . um . . . what was his name?"

"Jimmy."

"Yes, him. How long?"

"Four years."

"He wasn't good for you and the girls. He was a tyrant as I recall."

"He was a jackass and a colossal mistake, but that doesn't mean ..." I stopped.

"No, it doesn't mean there might not be someone else for you, but it means taking your time and being selective, doesn't it? There's no rush. You don't need anyone to help you raise the girls now, and the inn's solvent, right?"

"The inn is solvent, and I've worked my tail off for that. It feels strange, but I'm finally at a place in life where I don't need the help of a man, except for Mort, of course. So, why mess it up? Why invite someone to complicate everything?"

Mary cocked her head. "Why indeed?" she asked. "But could you be jumping to conclusions? Was an engagement ring taped to the note? Did he ask your permission to have the banns of marriage posted in the church bulletin?"

"No, no," I said, chuckling.

"As I see it, the problem isn't your Lothario. You could give him the brush in an instant if you wanted. The problem is within you. As they say today, you're conflicted. You wonder if a relationship could make you happy, so you're tempted."

"But that's just it," I said. "I am perfectly happy as I am. I'm able to come and go as I please. I make decisions without interference or approval. If I want to take a little trip, I take it. If I want to spend some money, I spend it. If I want to eat crackers in bed, I eat crackers. If I want to dye my hair green, I can do it, and there's no one to tell me otherwise. As much as I loved Phil, he had an opinion about everything I did, and I was always accountable. Jimmy the Monster was forever breathing down my neck. Who needs it?"

"I think you're still angry."

"I suppose I'm getting carried away," I said. "I suppose in my heart of hearts I would love marital bliss, but I don't see it in the cards."

Mary took my hand. "Jillian, you'll make the right decision, and when you do, tap the gavel on it—done—and move on. If you really listen to your heart, you'll do the right thing. But go slow."

That was the crux of the problem. If I listened to my heart, I might have jumped at the chance to start a romance with Lawrence. But the voice of reason deep within said that I would be happier and that my family would be happier in the long run if I proceeded with my life as it was—solitary.

I left Mary that morning just as confused as when I'd arrived; yet, being in her home and in her presence calmed my soul and boosted my confidence. The thought of not having her counsel and friendship was unbearable.

CHAPTER 16

Market Therapy

My next stop that morning was Wilson's Farm Market just a few doors from Eddie's Café. The bakery and market, owned by Tom and Nona Wilson, is a frequent stop for me. Though small and old-fashioned, the store bursts with Amish breads, pastries, cinnamon twists, tea rings, ginger cookies, and other assorted marvels that my guests devour. The shop sells divine produce and only the best cuts of meat, fish, and poultry.

Tom Wilson himself was at the check-out counter. I selected lavender-infused lemon bars, crispy cinnamon twists, juicy peaches and locally grown asparagus to take home for the gang and share with Mort.

"Nice choice there on the peaches," Tom said, as he rang up my purchases. "The only trouble with those peaches is the juice drips onto my shirt every time. I hold a towel under my chin to eat 'em."

"I don't see that as a problem, Tom," I said. "Will you still have them next week? I'll come back for a bushel to freeze. I'm too busy this week."

"Should still have 'em, but don't wait too long 'cause they'll be gone mighty quick." Tom lowered his voice and thrust his torso over the counter. His face was suddenly so close to mine that I backed up. "Say, I was glad to see your fella put Tim Johnson in his place the other day," he said. "Tim's not a bad guy, but he gets outta hand sometimes. Your friend pulled him up short from what I hear."

Lawrence and Tim Johnson's standoff had become a topic of gossip, as I'd expected. Tongues were wagging and speculating about "Jill's new boyfriend." My heart sank.

"Just for the record, Tom, the gentleman who was with me is not a friend of mine. He's my son-in-law's uncle. He's staying at the inn this week. I barely know him. I thought he might enjoy the parade, so I invited him along. I hadn't planned to judge the parade. It was sort of a crazy deal." I couldn't believe that I was actually explaining myself to Tom Wilson. Must I also go to the butcher, baker, and candlestick maker to squelch rumors? It was no one's business but my own, and poor Lawrence was an unwitting actor in all of it.

"Well, whatever," said Tom. "We was all on your friend's side. A few folks was hopin' your fella might sock him in the jaw." It was hopeless. Lawrence was pronounced my boyfriend. I gathered the shopping bag of meticulously packed food, shoved the change in my pocket atop Lawrence's note, and bid Tom farewell. I soothed myself by thinking the gossip would be short-lived. People would soon forget Lawrence if they didn't see him. With any luck, I'd forget about him, too. I took a cleansing breath and headed for the truck.

As I secured the goodies on the seat, my cell phone rang. It was Rita calling for our daily gab. I hadn't decided if I would tell her about Lawrence's touch and his note. Knowing Rita as I do, she would make a huge fuss over it. Yet, keeping such information from one's best friend leads to trouble when they find out, and they always find out. There would be hell to pay later if I didn't spill it.

"Hi, Honey, watcha doin'?"

"Hi. Steph and Robert went out for coffee; Lauren and Chickie are probably still in bed, and Lawrence went off to a library. I took some eggs to Mary and stayed for tea. I'm at Wilson's now and getting ready to leave. Thought I'd bring some goodies home. Need anything?"

"Gracious, no. The stuff in that bakery'll kill ya. It's death by sticky."

"Yeah, but what a way to go."

"Jilly, I had a bad dream about you last night."

"Oh, dear. Really?"

"You're in trouble, aren'tcha?"

"No, I'm fine," I lied. "What makes you ask?"

"Well, in my dream we were little kids ridin' our bikes down Anthony Road where the big trees on both sides of the road make it like a tunnel. We were ridin' along and then you rode into a deep ditch. It was a dark, bottomless ditch—like a cliff or somethin'. You kept callin' my name, but I couldn't find ya. Oh, Honey, it was terrible! I looked and looked for you and called your name. And you were callin' my name, and I couldn't find ya. Jilly, Jilly, I said, but I couldn't see ya. I finally woke up and went downstairs for a glass of Bourbon to calm myself. Is it money, Jilly? Do you need some money? I know Pink'll help ya. Is that it?"

"No, I don't need money. I'm fine for money."

"Are the girls in trouble? I hate to say it, but I've never exactly trusted Chickie Stampler. Her daddy was in trouble with the IRS some years back. I think he was cheatin' on his taxes. Remember that? Almost went to jail. He had to get some big lawyer out of Indianapolis to keep him out. They say he's kinda sneaky, too. Is she gettin' Lauren in trouble?"

"No. Lauren isn't in trouble . . . that I know of, anyway."

"Is it Steph? Don't tell me she and Robert are splittin' already. They haven't been married long enough to hate each other. Why, they're newlyweds, for goodness' sake! Did he do somethin' to her? Is he cheatin' on her already? That skunk. I'll let him have it with both barrels, and then I'll sick Pink on him."

"No, stop, Rita. Nothing is wrong with the girls. Everyone is fine."

"No, it's not. If everybody is fine, why did I have that bad dream? I can still hear you callin' Rita, Rita. I don't have bad dreams for nothin' and you know it. You're not telling me the truth, and if you don't tell me the truth you're betrayin' our friendship. Now what's goin' on? I hope your good-lookin' guest hasn't made himself a nuisance. Has he done somethin'? Has he?" I didn't answer immediately.

"It's him, isn't it?" Rita continued. "Did he steal your silverware? Did he say somethin' rude? Did he ask you to iron his blue jeans?"

"Rita, if I tell you, will you promise to remain calm?"

"Oh, my God. You found out he's some kind of pervert, didn't ya? No wonder he isn't married. How did you find out? What'd he do?"

"Stop. Stop," I insisted. "Lawrence isn't a pervert, as far as I know. It's nothing like that. Can I tell you about it later? I'm burning up in this truck, and I can't drive the stick shift and talk on the phone at the same time."

"Are you kiddin'? You're gonna leave me hangin' like this? Are we best friends or not? Tell me right now."

"I'm burning up here."

"Well, get out of the truck and walk over to Eddie's for a Coke. You can tell me about it from there."

"I have to go home, so I'll just tell you that Lawrence left a note for me that's troubling."

"A note? What'd it say? Do ya have it? Read it to me."

"Can you come over to my place? I don't want to read it over the phone."

"This is cruel and inhumane. I have a hair appointment at eleven o'clock. My roots are showin', and the girls get mad if I cancel. Then, I have to run up to Kokomo for a ridin' lesson. I'll be back later and come straight to your place. Pinky can pick up somethin' for his dinner. I'm not happy 'bout this, Jilly. The next time I have a secret, I'm gonna make you wait for it."

"I'm sorry," I said, "but I'm still processing. I'm not ready to talk about it. Just be patient with me. I'm rattled right now and not sure what to do."

"Well, for God's sake, that's what friends are for. We can process together. Don't know how I'm gonna get through the day wonderin' about your note. See, my dream was right. I knew you were in trouble. Never fails. Call me if anything else happens. I mean it. My roots can't wait, but I can cancel the lesson. Okay? I love you, and I'll see you later."

"Love you, too."

"I'm still not happy with you, girl."

By now, perspiration was beading on my face. As I backed the truck out of the parking space, my phone rang again. Teri Bennett's name appeared on the screen. I pulled forward, jumped out of the airless truck, and dashed under Wilson's awning. I assumed Teri was calling to discuss her next assault on my garden.

"Hi, Jill. It's Teri Bennett. After an uncomfortably long pause, she began in her soft, faltering voice, "I . . . I know we don't know each other well, and I . . . I shouldn't ask you for help again, but I'm sort of in a pinch."

"What's up?" I wondered uncharitably how bad it would be. Her additional long pause frayed my nerves. The sun was glaring in my face, and I imagined my lemon bars melting into goo in the pickup.

"Well . . . well, I got up the nerve to call Jerry. I just wanted to see how he was doing."

"Uh-huh."

"And before I knew it, I invited him to my place for dinner on Saturday."

"That's great, Teri. I'm glad to hear it if that's what you want." Another pause.

"Yeah, it's great, and I'm excited about it, but there's a big problem.

"Uh-huh."

"Remember that I told you I'm a terrible cook?"

"I remember," I said, suppressing a chuckle. "You're probably not that bad."

"No, I'm really bad. I need help. I know you have your family with you this week, and I hate to ask, but . . . but if I cook something nice for Jerry, well . . . I think he would really like it."

"Do you mean you want me to cook something for you?" I asked. "I'd be happy to do it, but I don't think it will help in the long run."

"No, no, I don't want you to cook, but could you possibly . . . would you have time to . . . give me a lesson before Saturday night? If you can't, I'll understand, and maybe we can make it another time."

After another deep breath and despite near heat stroke, I mulled over my schedule for the next few days. Tomorrow night was the dress rehearsal for *Much Ado About Nothing*. The cast's immediate families were invited so the actors could get a sense of crowd reaction. Harlowe Barnes was coming to shear the sheep on Friday, and that would be exhausting. On Friday night, *Much*

Ado would open, and I might see the show again to support the girls. Stephanie, Robert, and Lawrence were leaving on Saturday morning, and my cleaning service would arrive that afternoon.

"Can you get off work a little early and come to my house this afternoon, Teri?"

"I think so."

"By the way, what does Jerry like to eat besides Chinese?" I asked. "Chinese cuisine isn't exactly my thing."

"Well, I know he doesn't like fish. Well, he might kind of like shrimp, but I don't. I had some bad shrimp once. Made me sick. I don't think I want to cook shrimp. He once told me he likes oysters."

"Oysters? We're pretty far from an ocean, so I'm not sure where I'd get my hands on anything but frozen oysters," I said. "We don't want frozen oysters. Oysters are an appetizer, anyway, and they're tricky to prepare. What else?"

"Well, I think he might like steak, but he likes it bloody. We went out to a fancy steak dinner for my birthday once. Jerry ordered his steak rare. When it came to the table, I almost puked. It ruined my birthday. I just kept thinking about that poor dead cow. I could never make steak the way he likes it. Uh-uh."

"There are always pork chops. You could serve them stuffed with mushrooms and served with grilled vegetables. Maybe with baked apples?"

"Oh, no, I can't make pork chops. Jerry told me that his first wife made great pork chops. We argued about it. He'd think I was trying to outdo her."

"Do you really think Jerry would remember a quarrel over pork chops?" I asked. "I mean, if you made him a delicious pork chop, he'd probably be so grateful that he wouldn't dare mention her."

"I don't think I want to risk it."

I was growing impatient with Teri. I wanted to tell her to buy Jerry a Big Mac and call it done. From what I could tell about Jerry so far, food out of a bag would suit him just fine.

"What about chicken? Does Jerry like that?"

"He loves chicken. I think everybody loves chicken." Mercy, why hadn't she told me that in the first place?

"Okay," I said. "Let's go with chicken. I have an easy recipe for chicken. You can't go wrong."

"That sounds good, Jill. I can go to the store when I get off. Ugh … what should I buy?" How could a middle-aged woman not know how to buy some chicken and a few vegetables to throw into a pan? It was too hot to ponder, and I had more pressing matters to worry about.

"I'm at Wilson's market now. I'll pick up what we need. I'll be cooking for my gang tonight, anyway, so it will be chicken for everybody. Can you get to my house by four o'clock?"

"I'll be there. I'll tell Bud and Billy that I'm sick or something. Billy can handle the phones. Oh, Jill, I'm so excited! Thank you; you're a lifesaver."

With that last comment, my frustration with Teri melted away, much like the lemon squares in my truck. I retrieved the shopping bag from the front seat, took it back into the cooling oasis of Wilson's market, and shopped for chicken. Perhaps I owed Teri my thanks. Preparing for her lesson would keep me from thinking about Lawrence and his note.

Anyway, nothing revives my spirits like shopping in a good market. The sights and smells connect me with the earth and refresh my soul. The market was familiar territory, and my equilibrium was returning.

CHAPTER 17

Fugitives

I wondered who I would find at the inn when I returned. Would Steph and Robert be there? Would Lauren and Chickie be stirring? Would Lawrence be there or would he still be deconstructing the New Deal at some library? A plan was kicking in. If he was still at the inn, I would play it cool. I would take him aside and let him down gently but firmly. No dice. Not interested. I'm flattered and you seem like a wonderful guy, but no thanks. I was sure I could find the right words when the time came. Other than being overheated, I was feeling restored.

Rita's comment about Chickie returned to my thoughts. I'd known Chickie for years but didn't know much about her family. I'd met her parents on a few occasions, but we were not friends. Could there be some darkness there? Yes, she was outspoken and a drama queen, but I had never found a reason to question the girls' friendship. Rita, too, has a flair for the dramatic. Was she trying to start some new drama?

As I whirled into the driveway, I was alarmed to see that another drama was playing out at the inn. Two Noblesville Police cars were parked in my driveway. Blind panic made me fear the worst. The

Jeep was also parked in the driveway, ruling out a traffic accident involving Steph and Robert. I clutched my grocery bags as though they might protect me from shock, climbed the porch steps, and hurried to the kitchen door.

Police Sergeant Lloyd Hoggard opened the door and admitted me. With Lloyd was a young policeman, whom I didn't know and wasn't anxious to meet. Lloyd tipped his hat and offered a reassuring wink, which lowered my blood pressure. Lauren, Chickie, Stephanie, and Robert stood stiffly in the kitchen.

"What's going on?" I asked, placing my crushed groceries on the counter.

"There was some vandalism in town on Monday," said Lloyd. "We're looking into it. The owner of a liquor store on Second Street said some boys destroyed some trash cans behind the store. He wants to be repaid or he'll press charges. We got a tip that the boys might be involved with the outdoor play in the park. Someone said your daughter is in the play and might know the boys."

Naturally, Chickie piped up first. "We told the officers that there are a bunch of boys in our play. The watchmen are all high school boys. We don't know them. We're just here for the week to help out Mr. Silvio."

"Didn't you go to high school with some of the boys?" asked the younger officer.

"We didn't pay attention to those boys," said Chickie. "They're mostly skaters and goths. Not exactly our type. You should ask Mr. Silvio about them. He's got their names."

"We've been to the high school this morning and to the park, but we haven't been able to locate Mr. Silvio. We'll try his house next," said Lloyd. "I'm sure we'll catch up with him. We would appreciate any help you can give us. The owner of the liquor store is pretty upset. You understand, I'm sure. Thank you all for your time."

"You're welcome," I said. "We'll certainly help if we can." I played along with Chickie and Lauren's silence with great apprehension. I wanted to hear their side first and listen to their rationale, but that didn't excuse my collusion. As Lloyd and the younger officer left the inn, I had an impulse to stop them. The girls knew Teddy Bennett and Tom Laughlin, and they should have said so. In retrospect, concealing the truth from police was foolish and could have been a dangerous move for an innkeeper in need of their cooperation and protection.

"Now you've done it!" said Robert. "You've lied to the police and made us all accomplices. "You know those boys. Why didn't you say so?"

"It's a long story, Robert. You wouldn't understand. We have our reasons," said Lauren.

"Your reasons better be good," I said. "And you'd better spill it right now or I'm calling Lloyd back here to straighten this out. You can't lie to the police. Don't you know that?" My tirade was interrupted by the sound of scuffling and muffled voices coming from my pantry. To my disbelief, Teddy Bennett and Tom Laughlin burst through the pantry door and into the kitchen. They looked just as scruffy and urchin-like as they had on Monday when I hosed them down. "What in the world?" I demanded.

"Ah, you guys are cool," Teddy said. "I can't believe you held up under the scrutiny of law enforcement." He ripped a sheet of paper toweling from the holder and handed it to Lauren. "Here's your certificate of bravery in the face of tyranny."

"Tyranny?" I objected. "You're the ones who committed the crime. The police are doing their job. Now, you've gotten us involved."

"Mom, please don't freak out," said Stephanie. "This wasn't murder. It was just a couple of garbage cans."

"So, you're going along with this? You condone this?" I asked Stephanie.

"Well, I'm not going along with it," said Robert. "These two menaces and their primary accomplices better get this straightened out."

"We just need to evade the long arm of the law for a couple of days," said Teddy. "We'll repent and make good on the cans after that."

"Yeah," Tom said. "We wouldn't want to deprive the town lushes of their highly prized receptacles. I know how much they'll appreciate shiny new cans."

"That's not the point," I said. "The cans weren't yours. Please tell me you get that."

"They get it," said Robert, coolly. "They like causing havoc."

"We'll go to the cops after the matinee on Sunday and pay for the cans," said Teddy. "Honest, we will."

"What about your parents?" I asked. "Where are they in all of this? Do they know you're hiding from the law?"

"Well, they're busy with meetings a lot," said Tom, "and can't be bothered with a couple burnt up trash cans."

"Maybe they should get out of their meetings and pay attention to what you're doing. Are they business people?" I asked.

"Not exactly," said Teddy.

"What meetings could be more important than you?" I continued. "What kind of meetings?"

"They take steps, a lot of steps," said Tom.

"Oh, you mean they're at the gym all the time?" I asked. The boys laughed uneasily, and Lauren gave me a censoring glance.

"Well, since they only take twelve steps, they don't really need to go to a gym," said Teddy. The boys chuckled again.

I quickly dismounted my high horse. "Oh," I said. "I didn't know. But you have to promise you'll get this straightened out on Sunday. If you don't, I will."

"The cops will be back, you know," said Robert. He grabbed a bag of potato chips from the counter and began munching. "They'll never make it to Sunday."

"I've never seen that younger officer," said Chickie. "I wonder if he's married."

CHAPTER 18

The Gathering Storm

After inviting Teddy Bennett and Tom Laughlin to vacate the inn at their earliest convenience, I announced that Teri would be arriving at four o'clock for a cooking lesson and that dinner would follow. Everyone was welcome for dinner. I wondered when Lawrence would reappear, but I didn't want to seem anxious about it, so I refrained from asking Steph and Robert about him.

I'd expected a certain amount of chaos that week, but I hadn't anticipated dealing with Lawrence Milner and two fugitives from the law. I let the children make lunch for themselves and fled to the garden for a few moments of tranquility.

A thunderhead was taking shape in the southern sky once again. The wind was rising, and the air had cooled considerably since my foray to the market. My straw hat and hoe were waiting for me in the garden shed like two old friends. I needed soil time. For the first time in my life, I was glad to see crabgrass and pigweed popping up. I attacked the little criminals with savage strokes to relieve some frustration.

While striking the earth, my thoughts turned dark. It was clear that Stephanie and Lauren were moving on with their lives, and I was no longer the pivot point. I feared growing old alone and becoming irrelevant. Had I done anything right with my life? Would I become an aged gardener to be found dead one day under a tomato plant? Rita's words haunted me. What happens when I lose Mort? Will I become a lonely old lady working my fingers to the bone in a falling-down inn?

At length, my pity party was so pathetic that I laughed at myself. Such is life, I thought. Was I expecting a bed of roses? Yes, I was expecting roses, and I already had them in abundance, literally and figuratively. All I had to do was open my eyes and count my blessings. They were all around me, so I'd better appreciate them and take life one day at a time.

My most pressing dilemma was what to do about Lawrence. Would it be so terrible to open the door to an intimate relationship? If I dipped a toe in the dating game, would I find myself in a quagmire? I'd been content prior to Saturday. Why should I change anything? I knew so little about Lawrence. A relationship with him would be risky at best. Still, the chemistry did feel great. Maybe we could simply be friends. Sure . . . friends. That never works.

"Keep that up and you'll wear yourself out," came a familiar voice. Mort's pickup truck was stopped at the edge of the garden. "I'm takin' some hay to the market tomorrow," he yelled. "Got anything you want to sell?"

"Nothing here but green tomatoes and some bush beans. I'll can the beans," I replied.

"Don't forgit Harlowe's comin' on Friday bright 'n' early."

"I remember," I replied, unenthusiastically.

"I'll let you shut up the chickens tonight. Don't forgit 'em," he said.

"I won't," I replied. "Don't you forget about the girls' play tomorrow night. It's the dress rehearsal, and they're counting on us to be there. Starts at eight o'clock."

"In the park, right? Better take bug spray. It's 'bout to rain, ya know. I'd say you got ten minutes to put up your hoe and shut up the chickens." He rolled up his window and cruised toward his place.

I wanted the rain to hold off so I could finish hoeing and determine my game plan concerning Lawrence. He seemed like a good man. Inviting him into my life could mean happiness, but it would certainly mean compromise. He could lend physical strength, ingenuity and know-how to my operation, but at what cost? He was sure to have ceaseless opinions and suggestions for improvements. Yet, weren't improvements a good thing? Was I so smart? Mary Porter asked if an engagement ring had come with Lawrence's note. It was a silly question, of course, but she made her point. The note opened the door for so many questions and so much angst.

A raindrop hit my forehead as the wind swept fine dust in my face and rustled through the garden. The sky was a dark, silvery blue. Hoe in hand, I fled to the hen house and hustled the hens inside. I then hurried to the barn and shut the big east door so the ewes and lambs would stay dry.

As I left the barn, the sky opened up and rain fell sideways. It was too late to make it all the way to the inn, so I darted around streaming puddles to the garden shed. From the shed's little window, I could watch Mother Nature showing off. A beautiful summer shower was cleansing and nourishing the earth. I was content to sit on mulch bags and watch the show. Stephanie rang my cell phone to check on me and to say that she and Robert were leaving to meet friends at the movies. A few minutes later, the sun peeked out, so I freed the captive hens and sheep and headed for the inn. The rain shower left me feeling optimistic.

CHAPTER 19

Fugitives Discovered

It was time to get organized for Teri's cooking lesson. From a well-worn *Cook's Country* cookbook, I found the "Chicken Baked in Foil" recipe. Even a novice cook like Teri could conquer this one. The only ingredients that I still needed to gather were fresh chives and thyme. Luckily, both were only a few steps from my kitchen door.

Footsteps on the porch led me to believe that Teri had arrived early. Instead, Rita rushed in still wearing riding jodhpurs. Her eyes held an expression of hurt. "Some friend you are," she said. "How could you make me wait for hours to tell me what's goin' on? And where's this note?"

"Shoosh," I said. "I don't want the girls to know about this." I escorted Rita to the porch and directed her to a chair.

She swiped her bottom and said, "Can't sit down. Horsehair."

"Never mind that. Sit down, and I'll tell you about it. This is exactly why I couldn't talk this morning. I knew you would get all worked up. I'm still not sure what to think about it."

"So, where is it, Honey? Let me read it," Rita insisted. I retrieved the note carefully from my pocket since it had gotten wet in the rain and was curled. Rita read it to herself. "Oh, Jilly, he's crazy about you. I knew the way he looked at you on our little cruise he has a thing for you. And you weren't even wearing makeup. He must like a gal 'au naturel.' Aren't you excited?"

"No, I'm not excited. If Lawrence thinks he can come here and sweep me off my feet, he's wrong. I'm not interested in a relationship now and may never be again. I made a mistake last time, and I'm not making another one. I know exactly how I'll handle this. I'll talk with him as soon as I can and let him down gently. No sense stringing him along."

"Honey, do I need to fetch smelling salts?" Rita proceeded. "You gotta get a grip. Don't blow this. I don't mean to burst your bubble, but do you really want to go on slavin' away for lodgers just makin' ends meet for the rest of your life? You deserve to be the one on vacation once in a while. Do you want to be washin' everybody's sheets and cookin' their breakfast when you're seventy-five? Like I said before, Mort is a sweetheart, but he's not gonna live forever. Lawrence really likes you."

"Oh, I don't know what to think," I said.

Rita studied the note again. "Besides, he doesn't ask you to marry him. He just says he hopes y'all can become good friends."

I grabbed the note from her. "Look, it says 'and maybe even more' right here."

"That's a big maybe, Honey. Lots has to happen first, like maybe dinner and a show. Nothin' may even come of it. Give the man a chance."

"He lives in Bloomington. He won't want to move here, and I can't move there. If we got involved, I'd never be able to trust him with a town full of college girls and faculty on the make. It's too complicated, and I'm absolutely not interested in a complicated relationship again. Do I have to remind you about Jimmy?"

Teri's car pulled into the driveway.

"Who's that?" Rita asked.

"It's Teri Bennett. I introduced her to you and Pink when you stopped the other night. She's helping me with the gardens. She's coming over for a cooking lesson to try to impress her ex-husband, although I'm not sure why. My impression of him is less than favorable, but she still loves him, I suppose."

"Poor things," said Rita. "What's she cookin' for him?"

"I've got an easy chicken recipe for her."

"Chicken? How's she gonna win back her man with chicken? Men like steak, roast beef, lobster. Can't she do better than chicken?"

"We've been through that. Trust me, chicken is best in this case."

I opened the screen door to welcome Teri; she looked ghostly pale. She headed straight for a rocking chair, perched on the edge and cupped her hands to her face. Rita gave me a "what the hell?" sort of look.

"Teri, are you alright? What is it?" I asked. I knelt beside her with dread in my heart.

"He's in trouble, and I don't know what to do."

"Who's in trouble," I asked. I had reasonable suspicion.

"Teddy," she blurted. "The police are looking for him. Somebody told Buddy Wren, and he couldn't wait to tell me and blab it to everybody at work. He said he wouldn't be surprised if Lloyd Hoggard is looking for me, so I told him I was sick and left. I'm scared for Teddy. Maybe he's done something terrible. Oh, my gosh!" Teri rocked back and forth unaided by the chair.

"Teri, Teri, Teddy didn't do anything terrible. He just blew up some garbage cans by the liquor store downtown." I handed her the tea towel draped over my shoulder to wipe her eyes.

"What? How do you know about it?" she asked.

"It turns out that my daughter, Lauren, knows Teddy. In fact, she's in a play with him this weekend. They've known each other for a few years. You were right; they were in drama club together. Teddy and his friend were here on Monday shooting off fireworks."

"What? I wish you would have told me this before."

"I just put it all together," I said. "When I met you on Saturday, I didn't know Teddy."

"His dad needs to know about this," said Teri, still dabbing her eyes. "Did they damage your place?"

"No, but he and his friend had an arsenal of firecrackers, which by the way I think they may have stolen," I said. "I turned the hose on them before they could do any damage. They were boasting about blowing up trash cans after the parade. They were here again today and so was Lloyd Hoggard. My girls hid them, I'm ashamed to say, and now they're also involved in the mess. I don't think Teddy and his friend are bad kids, but they could use some supervision."

"Was Tom Laughlin with Teddy?" Teri asked. "Teddy's the brains and Tom goes along with everything."

"I can't vouch for brains, but Teddy does seem to have a knack for trouble," I offered.

"Oh, I forgot my manners," said Teri. She looked at Rita. "I didn't even say hello to your friend before I started talking."

"I'm Rita Restin. We met the other night. Pleased to meet you—again."

"You were here with the horses, right?" asked Teri, still dabbing her eyes. "I saw you and your husband and the horses at the county fair. You were the best in the show."

"That's right, Honey; that was us," Rita responded, sympathetically.

"Jill, I have to beg off on the cooking lesson," said Teri. "Teddy's in trouble, and I've gotta find him."

"Wait a minute," said Rita. "This is none of my business, but why should you rescue the boy? If you and the boy's daddy are divorced, this is his problem, Honey. Why don't you let him hunt for the boy?"

"I agree with Rita," I said. "It's up to Jerry and Teddy's mother to work this out with the police. Maybe you'd better let them handle it. Isn't it time Jerry puts some energy into his son?"

"Great," said Teri, "that will give her another excuse to get Jerry in her clutches."

"Teri, is this about what's best for Teddy or for you?" I asked.

Teri cupped her hands to her face again and moaned. "You're right. I'm making this about me. I've got to find Teddy."

"No, Honey," said Rita. "You need to call his daddy and let him take care of the boy. Is the man a stallion or a gelding?"

"A what?" asked Teri.

"I think chicken serves him right," said Rita.

"Chicken?" Teri inquired.

"I think you should call Jerry right now," I said. "Tell him that Lloyd is looking for Teddy and suggest strongly that Jerry handle the situation pronto. He can pay for the cans and be done with it."

"You're right," said Teri. "I babied Jerry and picked up the pieces with Teddy all the time when we were married. He spent too much time at work and at the bar. He never made enough time for Teddy. I was afraid to speak up—afraid he would go back to her, I guess."

"That could have been your lucky break," Rita quipped.

I suddenly caught sight of two figures darting through the yard. I silenced Rita and Teri and motioned them to keep a low profile. Following my lead but confused, they shifted their attention to the side yard. Unaware that we were watching, Lauren and Chickie rushed from the corner of the house to a large oak tree and then to the back of the garage. They stooped at the waist like combatants sneaking up on the enemy. Whispering and giggling, they surged forward in bursts, jostling what appeared to be dishes, undoubtedly from my kitchen. We rose from our chairs to take a better look.

"What the heck?" whispered Rita. "Who are they hidin' from?"

"Is that your daughter?" Teri asked.

"Yes, and her friend," I said. "Wonder what they're up to now?"

Seconds later, the girls scurried from the garage to the small door at the front of the barn. They cracked the door open, squeezed through, and quickly shut it behind them.

"What do you think they've got stashed in there?" asked Rita. "Lauren hasn't gone in the barn since her pony died years ago."

"I have a pretty good idea," I said. "Let's go out there."

"I'll stay here," said Teri.

"I think you'll want to see this," I said.

Dodging puddles, we made our way to the barn. I pulled open the track door with determination, praying that my hunch was right and that we weren't on the verge of some horrible embarrassment.

In the center of the barn floor stood Lauren, Chickie, Teddy Bennett, and Tom Laughlin. The boys were stuffing their mouths with contraband from my kitchen. Straw clung to their hair and clothes. We all stood in shocked silence, Teri most of all. "Teddy!" she blurted. "What are you doing here? Are you alright? Everybody's looking for you."

"Oops. Guess we're busted," Teddy said. Bits of food flew from his mouth.

Tom snatched another sandwich from Lauren's tray. "Just when the set-up looked good," he said.

Teri, Rita, and I moved toward the fugitives and their accomplices, while the ewes and lambs went about their business around us. "What's going on?" I asked Lauren.

"They had nowhere else to go," she said, pitifully. "If they turn themselves in now, the play will be ruined. We don't have understudies."

"They'll pay for the cans," Chickie said. "We only have to keep them free until Sunday afternoon. We've worked our butts off, and we're not letting them mess it up now."

"I don't think Lloyd would put two kids in jail 'cause of some burnt up trash cans. Do you, Jilly?" asked Rita.

"Of course not," I said. "I'm sure this can all be settled quickly. You can't stay in a barn." I suddenly wished Lawrence would appear. I could have used his steadying presence and sense of humor. Yet, the fact that I was longing for Lawrence seemed all wrong. I couldn't keep myself from thinking of him and wondering where he was. I'd only known him a few days, but I thought of him in that moment of crisis.

"Teddy, your dad can help you," said Teri. "Let me call him."

"Go ahead. Call him," said Teddy. "He'll say he's with a client or getting ready for a conference call or some bogus excuse like that. I'm not your problem anymore, Teri. You can stop worrying about me."

"I can't stop worrying about you, Teddy. I love you," said Teri.

Teddy bowed his head and gazed at the floor. "I know," he said.

I was steamed at Jerry Bennett, a man I'd never met. Drinking problem or not, he had no business neglecting his son this way. I didn't want to get involved in their family problems, but I thought Jerry had been bogus long enough. He allowed his first wife to lead him by the nose, ignored Teddy, and didn't appreciate Teri's obvious good nature. His big thrill was eating Chinese takeaway and bloody steak. The thought of providing Teri with a cooking lesson to please him had lost its appeal. He could go on eating egg rolls and chop suey for all I cared.

Rita's eyes met mine. She searched my expression. "Well, Honey, where do we go from here?" she asked.

"Teri, please call Teddy's father and ask him to meet us here now," I said. "I'll call Lloyd and see if he can meet us, too. Wish I had his direct number."

"Pink has it," said Rita. "Lloyd and Pink go way back. Do you want Pink to come out here, too?"

"No thanks. We can handle this," I said, projecting as much confidence as I could muster.

"What about the play, Mom?" asked Lauren.

"Yeah, what happens if they get hauled off?" protested Chickie.

"They should have thought of that before blowing up those trash cans," I said.

"We're still here, you know," said Teddy, pulling straw from his matted hair. "We can hear you."

Tom began walking toward the open barn door. "This is a conspiracy," he said. "I'm leavin'. They won't take me alive!"

"Stop, stupid!" Teddy said. "This is our best chance. We might as well get it over with. The cops will hound us until that old man gets his money. They know we'll be at the play tomorrow night. Do you want the cops to shake us down in front of the whole town?"

"The whole town?" asked Lauren with a nervous expression. "I hope it won't be the whole town." Tom stopped in his tracks, appeared to weigh his options and rejoined our little circle.

"Look, the guy wants the money for the stupid cans. Just cough it up or get your parents to cough it up. Problem solved," said Chickie. "Why do you have to be such weasels about it?"

"Maybe that's how it works in your family," said Teddy.

"If your dad won't pay for the cans, I will, Teddy," said Teri. "Don't worry."

We placed the calls. Lloyd was on another case and would be tied up for some time, even with Pink's intervention. As predicted, Jerry had an "important" meeting to attend before he could meet with us. I wondered if his meeting was with Benny's Hunan House of China or a local tap.

Our oddly assorted troop walked back to the inn. I suggested that the thespians run lines for the play until Lloyd and Jerry arrived. To my surprise, they agreed and moved to the living room. As in many other trying times in my life, I turned to cooking as a balm to soothe my nerves and bring order to the chaos.

"This may not seem like a good time for your cooking lesson," I told Teri, "but how about it?" She agreed reluctantly.

Rita said, "I'll leave you two with the mess. I smell like a horse, and you know I hate cookin' anyway. If I want chicken, I'll order it cooked. Can't stand makin' all those dirty dishes. I'm goin' home to freshen up, but I'll be back. Don't want to miss anything. Jilly, walk me to my car." Rita and I barely made it onto the porch before she asked, "Where's the hunk, Honey? Why isn't he here? When's he comin' back?"

"I don't know," I said offhandedly. "I told you he was going to a library. That's all I know. I'm not keeping track of him."

"What if he didn't like your bad attitude and left for good?"

"Bad attitude? I don't have a bad attitude about Lawrence. I told you how I feel, and you don't listen. Case closed."

"Okay, okay. It's your loss. Just don't come cryin' to me when you realize your mistake."

"When have I ever come crying to you? Don't answer that, please," I said.

Rita gave me an angry look and jumped into her SUV. She shut the door with a bang and pulled away in a huff. Moments later, she backed up her big machine, climbed out, and gave me a bear hug. "I just love you, Honey, and want you to be happy," she said.

"I know," I said. "I love you, too."

With Lloyd Hoggard and Jerry Bennett due to arrive any time, Teri's cooking lesson would be abbreviated. I pulled the fat chicken breasts out of the refrigerator and began placing them on a cutting board to be seasoned. "These are going to be great," I said. "You can finish unwrapping, Teri. I'll pick some chives and thyme." I grabbed my scissors and a basket.

Teri backed away from the meat as though it was diseased. "Do I have to touch them?" she asked. "I don't like touching raw meat. It feels like a person's skin. Makes me weak in the knees."

"Oh," I said. "I didn't know that. You didn't say. When we talked this morning, you liked the chicken idea."

"I know, but I didn't think about having to touch it."

I was exasperated with a woman afraid to touch a piece of raw chicken. "It's a good thing you don't have to wring their necks and pluck their feathers," I said. "You'd starve."

I handed Teri my tongs in hopes she could use them to finish the job in my brief absence. When I returned with the herbs, she was using the tongs to pick up a breast that had fallen onto her shoe. I could only chuckle, and despite her embarrassment, Teri managed a dejected half-smile.

We set to work peeling potatoes and carrots, which Teri seemed to enjoy more than touching raw chicken, but soon her peeler slipped and cut her finger. We managed to keep the blood away from the food. After that, she was content to observe the lesson rather than participate. Clearly, her mind was not on cooking. She regaled me with more stories about Jerry and kept watching the clock. I had no idea how she would manage to cook for him on Saturday, but that was out of my hands. "I'm sorry," she said.

"I thought it was a good idea to call Jerry, but now I'm not sure. I haven't seen him in months, and I'm so nervous. Wish we hadn't called him."

"So, who is going to take responsibility for getting his son out of this jam if he doesn't do it?" I asked. Teri shrugged and looked away. When we finished cooking, we moved to the porch and perched on rocking chairs. I rocked back and forth and thought I'd rather be doing almost anything than waiting for her ex-husband and the town constable to arrive and hash out Teddy's fate.

CHAPTER 20

Faux Negotiators

Teri tried rocking to soothe her nerves, but she was soon pacing the porch floor and wringing her hands. The weather was very warm, the air was still, and cicadas sang shrilly in the trees. Storm clouds were gathering once again, and thunder rumbled in the distance. I hoped the darkening sky wasn't an omen. "I'm sorry we brought you into this," Teri said, softly, "but I'm glad you're with me, Jill."

"You didn't bring me into this," I said. "Lauren and Chickie got me into the situation. I regret that they didn't tell the truth when they had the chance. I'm sure things will work out, one way or another." Moments later, a little red sportscar swung into my driveway. Two men squeezed out and headed up the walk.

"Is that Jerry?" I whispered.

"Jerry was driving," Teri said, "but I don't know the other guy. Maybe it's his lawyer. Oh, I'm so nervous."

When Jerry reached the steps, I recognized his face from Noblesville High School parent nights. I had also seen him at Mike's Café with what may have been insurance clients. He was very neat in appearance with a fresh-from-the-barber precision haircut. One might take him for a former captain of the football team. He wore a pristine short-sleeved white shirt with a baby blue tie, impressively creased slacks, and expensive-looking shoes and belt. Where Teddy was concerned, the apple had fallen so far from the tree that it was in another county.

As I admitted Jerry onto the porch, he looked into my eyes for an instant but looked away quickly. His eyes were bloodshot and his demeanor uneasy. He flashed a salesman's smile, the phony smile Pink sometimes uses with customers—the shark smile. I'd already been pre-judging Jerry, so I resolved to wait and see.

From his appearance, it was highly doubtful that Jerry's companion was in the law profession. He wore a plain red t-shirt with a pocket that bulged from a pack of cigarettes. He was slight, bony, sallow, and stooped. His saggy blue jeans were held up by an aged belt, and his black lace-up sneakers looked vintage. He nodded slightly in my direction as he followed Jerry onto the porch. I invited Jerry and his companion to be seated on rocking chairs. Jerry avoided the chair beside Teri and motioned his companion to take that one.

"I'm sorry we have to meet you under these circumstances," Jerry said, shifting his gaze from me to Teri. She sat still and perched on the chair's edge. "Hey, Teri." Teri gave Jerry a nod but said nothing. Jerry turned to me. "This is Mr. Sidney Pinter. Mr. Pinter is an insurance client of mine. He contacted me and said the police think my son and another boy destroyed some garbage cans at his store on Monday."

I extended my hand to Mr. Pinter. "I'm Jill Merrick and this is Teri Bennett," I said. Mr. Pinter nodded in response but did not take my hand. He gave Teri a disinterested glance.

"Teri is my ex-wife," Jerry explained. Mr. Pinter showed no interest.

"May I offer you gentlemen a glass of lemonade or iced tea?" I asked. I couldn't suppress my innkeeper persona.

"We didn't come here to socialize," said Mr. Pinter, abruptly. His eyes appeared to be settled on some object beyond the porch. "I've got a store to run and need to get back to it." Perhaps life had not been a cakewalk for Mr. Pinter. I couldn't help wondering if his smile had atrophied along with the robust health he may have once enjoyed.

"That's a kind offer, Mrs. Merrick, but I'd like to talk with my son and the police. Mr. Pinter and I will leave you alone then," said Jerry. Such a conversation would not be easy. Jerry and Mr. Pinter were not exactly jovial, and both were anxious to complete the business and move on.

"Teddy and his friend, Tom, are in the house running lines for a play," I said. "I suppose you know that the boys are in a play this weekend. My daughter and her friend are in the play, too. It's *Much Ado About Nothing*. You know, Shakespeare. I'll ask them to join us."

"I know about the play," Jerry said, flatly. "Ted told me about it. He's supposed to be looking for a job this summer, but he's more interested in that play. Can't see how that's gonna get him any spending money."

As I opened the kitchen door, Lauren, Chickie, Teddy, and Tom rushed onto the porch. Chickie planted herself directly in front of Jerry and Mr. Pinter. She signaled Teddy and Tom to stand to the side and spoke as if on stage, "I'm Charlotte Stampler and this is Lauren Merrick. We're representing the accused, Theodore Bennett and Thomas Laughlin." She grabbed Jerry's hand and gave it a shake. "I trust you are Mr. Bennett, father of the accused." She attempted to shake Mr. Pinter's hand. "I assume, sir, that you are the owner of the liquor store on Second Street where the vandalism took place."

Mr. Pinter looked puzzled and pulled his hand away to avoid Chickie's touch. "Say, what is this?" he asked. "I didn't come here for some kind of show. I mean business. I want to be paid for those cans. What's going on, Bennett?"

"Mrs. Merrick?" said Jerry, quizzically. His eyes searched my face for an explanation.

"Mrs. Merrick knows nothing of this," Chickie said. She made a sweeping gesture toward Lauren and continued, "Ms. Merrick and I are colleagues of the accused, and we have, out of the goodness of our hearts, volunteered to handle the negotiations."

"Negotiation? What negotiation? Nobody ever said nothin' about a negotiation." Mr. Pinter protested.

"Well, Mr. Theodore Bennett and Mr. Thomas Laughlin here are ready to face up to their lapse in judgment, ask your forgiveness, and make reparation, sir," said Chickie.

"The name is Pinter, Sid Pinter. You mean these two admit blowing up my garbage cans?" He looked at the boys. "Why did you want to go and do that?"

Chickie continued, "They were like two lost sheep gone momentarily astray, sir, I mean Mr. Pinter. Ms. Merrick and I have known these young men for years, and we know they have never done anything like that before. Theodore is actually a good student and a promising actor and Thomas is . . . well . . . promising."

"Yes, promising," Lauren interjected.

"I want to hear it from them, if you don't mind, Missy," said Mr. Pinter. "What made you boys think you could destroy somebody else's property?"

Teddy and Tom shifted uncomfortably and cast their eyes downward in a show of abject shame. They transformed into very different boys than the cherry bombers I'd met on Monday. If they were play-acting, they were good at it.

"Speak up, Ted," said Jerry.

"Well, sir, we just got a little carried away, I guess," said Teddy.

"Theodore and Thomas are actually budding scientists. They were conducting experiments with chemically reactive materials," said Chickie.

"Ya mean they was havin' a field day blowin' up the town while the police was occupied with crowd control," said Mr. Pinter. "I wasn't born yesterday."

"Well, at any rate, Mr. Pinter . . . would you mind if I call you Sid?" Chickie inquire. "You know, one of my favorite professors is named Sidney. Such a strong and honest name. If I call you Sid, that will put us on equal footing while we talk."

"Equal footing? We ain't on equal footing," Mr. Pinter objected. "What's she talkin' about, Bennett?" Again, Jerry looked to me for help. I didn't know whether to try to bring sanity to the conversation or allow Chickie to hang herself along with Teddy and Tom as they all deserved. "Oh, call me whatever you want, Missy, as long as somebody comes across with some cash for those cans and I can get goin', or do we have to let the cops settle this?" As Mr. Pinter pushed the words through his bluish lips, a flash of lightning streaked across the darkening sky, and his threat was punctuated by a thunderclap. In another circumstance, the coincidence would be comical, but comedy was elusive just then.

Chickie proceeded undeterred, "There's more to our defense, Sid, but with the impending weather event, I'll come straight to the point . . . unless you want to meet another time and hear about Theodore and Thomas's quest for scientific discovery."

"No, thanks!" said Mr. Pinter, rising to his feet. "I'll collect seventy-five dollars here and now and get back to town. Who's payin'?" Jerry made no offer. He seemed to be waiting for Chickie to finish her pitch.

"We fully appreciate the timely manner in which you want to settle the matter, Sid, especially since we also have an impending engagement. In fact, Mr. Silvio, our play director, is waiting to meet us for a final costume fitting. So, with a storm coming, I hope you will allow us to quickly offer a solution." Mr. Pinter sighed and sat down, exasperated.

"Theodore and Thomas would like to ask you if they might work off their debt at your store. They may look scrawny, but they're wiry and strong. They can lift heavy objects, organize things, mop floors, and pick up trash in the parking lot."

"That's not possible," said Jerry, shaking his head.

"I've got this, Bennett," Mr. Pinter interrupted. "Let me get this straight. You think I should take on them two vandals as employees so they can lift crates of liquor around my store and sweep floors? So, you want the cops off their behinds and onto mine? They're underage. I can't hire them!"

"No, no, not at your liquor store, Sid," said Chickie, without hesitation. "We know better than that, but what about your lovely thrift shop on Tenth Street? Theodore and Thomas would like to work for you there at least until they've paid for bright and shiny new cans. When you get to know them and see how hard they work, you'll thank yourself. What do you say?"

"Thank myself? Doubt it," said Mr. Pinter. Yet, he rubbed his chin and paused to consider Chickie's proposal. He sat back in the chair, closed his eyes, and rocked back and forth. The rest of us were motionless as though waiting for a decision from the Supreme Court and old Mr. Pinter had the deciding vote. He finally opened his eyes. Again, he seemed to be staring at an object somewhere in the distance.

Teddy and Tom were somber, moving only to shift from one foot to the other. Jerry had a poker face, and Teri massaged her temples as if in pain.

"Might work. Might just work," Mr. Pinter pronounced. "Okay, I'll give 'em a try. They can start at Thrifty Mart on Monday at seven o'clock in the morning and work until noon. They can do that every day 'til they work it off. And since you're so fond of negotiations, they can negotiate their pay with the manager. She's the meanest old woman in town, my wife. Nobody gets away with nothin' on her watch, and she's been askin' for more help. Yep, I think this might work out just fine. But if it don't, you'll all hear from me again. Let's go, Bennett." Jerry looked pleased with the outcome.

The sky was on the verge of releasing another torrent. To my great relief, Mort's truck pulled into the barnyard. He'd returned from wherever he'd been and was shutting in the hens and the sheep to keep them safe from the storm. I would call him later with my excuses and my thanks.

As Jerry and Mr. Pinter discussed getting to Jerry's car in the rain, a police car swung into the driveway. An officer hurried up the walk, holding down his hat. I could tell from his build that it was not Lloyd Hoggard. It was the young officer who had accompanied Lloyd earlier that afternoon. The inn was beginning to feel like Grand Central Station, and I was growing impatient with the entire mess.

I held the porch door open for the officer, and he squeezed in dripping water from his shoes and wide-brimmed hat. He was tall with a sturdy build and handsome boyish face. It seemed like God had placed a boy's face on a man's body. Lauren and Chickie brightened up considerably with his arrival. He quickly removed his hat. "Afternoon, everyone. Martin Hines," he said. His demeanor was outwardly meek, but his eyes had the look of a hawk as he scanned our faces. "I was here earlier with Officer Hoggard. Maybe you remember."

"We remember you, officer," said Chickie. The tone of her voice changed from serious negotiator to blatant flirt.

"Thank you, Chickie; I'll take it from here," I said. "Welcome, Martin . . ."

"No, I'll take it from here," interrupted Mr. Pinter. "Marty, you're too late. We worked it out. I'm gonna own these two for a while until they earn enough to pay for the cans. They'll be workin' at my store on Tenth. It's all settled. I won't press charges as long as they show up and do the work."

Officer Hines looked sternly at Teddy and Tom. "Turnin' 'em over to Big Sue then, Sid?" he asked.

"Yep. She'll keep 'em in line."

Teddy and Tom's fate was sealed, at least until they worked off their debt to society. Lightning flashed among the billowy dark clouds and thunder pealed. Just before he and Mr. Pinter dashed for his car, Jerry smiled faintly at Teri and then turned to Teddy with a deadpan expression. "I'll see you at home, Ted," he said.

Officer Hines returned his hat to his head, tipped the brim in my direction, and said, "Well, if it's all worked out then, I'll let Officer Hoggard know so we won't bother you folks again. Glad you worked it out."

"Wait. Wait!" Chickie blurted. She scrambled for the kitchen door. "Don't leave! I'll be right back." Moments later, she appeared with tickets to *Much Ado About Nothing* and pressed them into Officer Hines' hand. "You and your wife or date might like to come to our play tomorrow night. It's our dress rehearsal for family and friends. We'd love it if you could come."

"Thanks. I'm not married, but my buddy might like to go with me if I don't have to work. Things can get crazy in town some nights." Chickie and Lauren watched Martin Hines intently as he darted through sheets of rain on the way to his car. Chickie had extracted from him the information she wanted. She and Lauren exchanged self-satisfied grins.

"Big Sue? Big Sue? So, this is what you negotiated for us? A stretch with Big Sue?" Teddy protested.

"That ain't hap'nin'," said Tom, shaking his head. "No dice. I ain't workin' with that old Amazon."

"You're a couple of ingrates; that's what you are!" insisted Chickie. "I had to do some quick thinking to get you off the hook. You should thank me."

"Thank you? My old man was sitting right there. He would have coughed up the money," said Teddy.

"Or I would have," Teri interjected.

"You said yourself that your father wants you to get a job. I got you a job, and all you can do is complain," said Chickie.

"We were trying to help you," Lauren said, "but I think we may have overplayed it a little."

"You didn't overplay it," Teddy said. "Our star negotiator did." He glared at Chickie.

"Yeah, when you're back in your dorm safe and sound next week, we'll be Big Sue's creatures," said Tom.

"Mr. Silvio's waiting for us," said Lauren. "Can we borrow the truck, Mom?"

The squabbling thespians gathered their belongings and headed for the truck in drizzling rain. Teddy and Tom rode in the bed of the pickup. I felt sorry for them. Teri and I packed up some baked chicken for her supper. I handed her a recipe card on which I had dutifully printed the *Chicken Baked in Foil* recipe. She thanked me again sweetly for the lesson, but I suspected that she and Jerry would be dining at Benny's Hunan House of China on Saturday night.

"I've known Big Sue all my life," said Teri. "She's a distant cousin and a battle ax. Maybe the boys will learn something from this if they can last a few days with her. Teddy's job may put Jerry in a good mood on Saturday night." I wasn't concerned about Jerry or his mood, but I was glad that the trash can calamity was resolved—at least for the moment

"When can I work in the garden again, Jill?"

"How about Monday evening? My family is leaving on the weekend, so I can spend more time showing you around."

Teri opened the kitchen door to leave, and Rita rushed in. "I've done it!" she announced. She threw her hands in the air. "Ooh, you're gonna thank me for this one. I've set you two up with a gal who's gonna get you both straight. You're gonna love her. Can't believe I was able to get you an appointment with her tomorrow."

"What are you talking about?" I asked.

"It's great to have connections," Rita continued. "I made a few phone calls, and she's gonna see you tomorrow!"

"You said that, but what are you talking about?" I repeated.

"I never told you this, Honey, and this has gotta stay in this room," said Rita, glancing at Teri. "A few years ago, Pinky and I were havin' some troubles. He wanted to buy that dealership in Kokomo and spend all that money, and I said over my dead body. It was too risky. Remember? Well, I didn't sleep with him for a month 'cause I was mad at him for buyin' the dealership anyway. We almost split up. Remember, Jilly?"

"Remember? You spent a week at my house and cried the whole time," I said. "I don't think I would forget that."

"Well, I told you we went to a marriage counselor, but I didn't tell you the whole story 'cause . . . well . . . you can be a wet blanket sometimes."

"You mean I can be too practical," I said.

"Anyway, we didn't see a regular counselor. We went to see a wise woman. She's like something out of this world. After two sessions, we were back in love and it all worked out."

"There weren't any flying monkeys or cauldrons involved, were there?" I inquired.

"Jilly! You're tryin' to be funny 'bout something precious to me," said Rita. "I nearly divorced my sweet husband that winter and you're makin' a joke. This is your chance to talk with the best money can buy. I had to pull strings to get you in so fast. She has a big clientele. I've already paid for your sessions; it's all set up. She can get you on the right track about Lawrence. She'll see Teri, too, about Jerry. She's like talkin' to a big sister who's got all the answers."

"I don't need a big sister or a wise woman or a fortuneteller to help me make decisions," I said.

Rita persisted, "I've seen how you look at him and how he looks at you. You haven't got much time to think about it, Sister; he's leavin' in a few days. You gotta give him a little sign of encouragement." I gave Rita a censoring glance since Teri knew nothing about my situation with Lawrence.

"I've heard about the wise woman," said Teri. "She's not a fortuneteller or anything. People swear by her. I want to see Jerry again, but I'm not sure it's the right thing. Maybe she can help."

"No thanks," I insisted. "I'm absolutely not interested in what some charlatan thinks I should do with my life. I'll be the one to decide that."

"Okay, tell me that everythin' is clear in your mind now. Tell me what you're gonna do 'bout Lawrence," Rita insisted. "Tell me right now."

I heaved a long sigh, sat down at the kitchen table, and stared out the window. Rita and Teri waited for my answer. "Well . . . maybe I could use a little help," I said. So that was that.

Despite the day's aggravations, the evening was pleasant. Steph, Robert, and I joined a hundred other Hoosiers at an outdoor concert by the Indianapolis Symphony Orchestra at Connor Prairie Homestead to celebrate the nation's birthday. It was the first time that Steph and I had really connected that week. We laughed and kidded each other over silly things. I was tempted to tell her about Lawrence's note but knew that she and Robert would jump to conclusions and things would get very complicated.

Steph and Robert were in particularly high spirits as the dreamy music and pastoral setting soothed our souls. I couldn't help wondering if a baby would soon be in their future. The very idea was exciting. I relaxed on my lawn chair and reflected on the day's events. What a day it had been. I'd found Lawrence's note first thing that morning. His words had looped in my head all day. There had been loving guidance from Mary Porter, near heat stroke at Wilson's market, the discovery of teenage fugitives in my barn, a hopeless cooking lesson with Teri, and a homespun trial on my porch. And now Rita was prodding me to talk with some wise woman. No wonder I enjoyed the tranquility.

The evening grew delightfully cool. Steph and I covered our legs with a blanket, and the music played on until after dark. I could have stayed much longer—especially since the area had been treated for mosquitoes.

Lawrence didn't return to the inn that night. He texted Robert and said his research had led him to a library at Notre Dame in South Bend. He wasn't sure how long he would be there, but he'd be in touch. He also sent an apology to me for his "unannounced absence." I felt disappointed that he would be away yet relieved.

CHAPTER 21

Wise Woman of Lapel

Thursday arrived way too soon. I'd envisioned a week of shopping, eating, and relaxing with my girls. Instead, I found myself riding shotgun in Rita's SUV on the way to see a wise woman. Rita, Teri, and I were on the road to Lapel, Indiana, and running late for our appointment. Buddy Wren had given Teri a hard time about leaving work, resulting in her delay. Rita was in a panic about being late. When we were a safe distance east of Noblesville, she engaged her police scanner and put her foot to the floor.

"Jilly, watch for cops on the north-south roads," said Rita. "Teri, watch behind us." She was driving twenty miles an hour over the speed limit.

"Feels like high school days," I said. "At least we're not smoking and drinking while we speed now. These ditches are pretty steep. Better slow down."

"Don't worry, Honey, I'll get us there on time," said Rita. "Lillian will see us." Her hands gripped the steering wheel while her sight was glued to the blacktop."

"I'm not worried," I said. "This whole adventure is your idea. So, that's her name, huh, Lillian?"

"Yeah, Lillian. Don't ask me her last name 'cause I can't pronounce it."

Teri, who sat in the back seat behind Rita, looked pale and dug her fingernails into the cushy leather like someone clutching at the seat of a tilt-a-whirl at the county fair. Her wide-eyed expression revealed nothing short of terror.

"Rita, slow down," I insisted. "Lillian can't help us with our future if we don't have one."

"Lillian lives near downtown Lapel somewhere," said Rita. She took a hand off the steering wheel and began digging in her purse.

"For heaven's sake," I said, "keep your eyes on the road! What are you looking for?"

"I can't remember exactly where she lives. I gotta put her address in my GPS."

"You can't do that while you're driving," I protested.

"Okay, there's a piece of paper in this mess with the address. You'll have to find it. Put it in my phone and get the voice. Gotta have the voice."

After a few minutes of stressful hunting and bickering over passwords and apps, I loaded Lillian's address into the GPS on Rita's cell phone. Finally, a soothing British voice was guiding us to our destination like a magical Bluetooth fairy. If the voice had belonged to a real person, I would have given her a bear hug. Although still exceeding the speed limit, Rita was calming down. Teri's face regained some color as we reached Lapel's city limits.

The small town of Lapel is not far from Noblesville, but it's not on a major highway and a bit remote. The brick buildings on Main Street stand in two short, neat rows like oaks lining a shady lane. The town could be featured on a poster representing very small Midwestern towns. In the center of town stands a huge grain elevator skirted by railroad tracks and bearing the look of bygone prosperity, yet still imposing and with a long and proud farming heritage.

The British Bluetooth fairy guided us to a small, tidy white house on a side street just off the main drag. My stomach was cartwheeling, partly from our wild ride and partly in nervous anticipation of meeting the renowned wise woman. The idea that I'd soon be getting advice on how to live my life from a perfect stranger made me feel sulky and irritable. Would spells and voodoo be involved? Why had I allowed Rita to talk me into another ridiculous adventure anyway? How would I keep Steph and Lauren from learning about this? How would I explain such a squandering of my time during their visit?

As Rita pulled up to the house, I attempted a game plan. "If I get in there and want to leave at any time, I'll give you a wink. Teri, the same goes for you. If you want to leave, just start coughing. That'll be your signal. Okay?"

"Okay, Jill," came Teri's shaky voice.

"Oh, brother! Lillian isn't an old witch or something," said Rita, grabbing her purse. "We didn't drive way out here to turn tail."

"Rita, I mean it," I said. "I'm walking out if I don't like anything about this. Can't believe you talked me into this in the first place."

Unwilling to brook further resistance, Rita sprang from the car. Teri, still looking pale from the ride, followed Rita's lead. I wanted to melt into the seat of the SUV and stay put. Rita was already ringing Lillian's doorbell, and Teri was beside her.

I ventured onto Lillian's sun-bleached front lawn with trepidation. The one-story house looked innocent enough. Lush Boston ferns flanked the front door shaded by a small porch overhang. Knock Out roses lined the short driveway leading to a garage at the end of the house. A shiny yellow and red bass boat named *Wake Up* sat on a trailer in the driveway. I hoped "wake up" wasn't code used by a satanic cult. On the other side of the driveway stood a white lattice-work fence bordering a vegetable garden. A host of ripening tomatoes in the neat little garden was oddly comforting. Could the ferns, tidy garden, and sporty little boat be a cover for something sinister?

As Rita rang Lillian's doorbell a second time, I caught up with her. A moment later, a woman whom I took to be Lillian thrust open her door as wide as its hinges allowed. She greeted us with a radiant smile. She was perhaps in her late sixties. She stood about five feet tall and was amply built. Strands of brown hair mingled naturally throughout her thick, gray pageboy. Her hair appeared completely natural with no hint of chemical coloring. She wore tight-fitting jeans, red lace-up tennis shoes, and a crisp yellow t-shirt imprinted with the words "Gone Fishin'."

But it was Lillian's eyes and warm hugs that banished my sulky mood. Her eyes were pinched by her broad smile and exuded the sparkle of holiday lights. It was impossible not to return Lillian's smile. Her complexion was peaches 'n' cream with scarcely a wrinkle. Her face was at once mesmerizing, familiar, endearing, and tranquil. I sensed immediately that I was in the presence of a joyful woman at peace with herself and the world.

"Welcome! Welcome!" said Lillian. She made a sweeping gesture with her arm as she stepped back to admit us into her living room. "Oh, my goodness, I'm so happy to see you, Rita, and you've brought your lovely friends. I'm glad you've come. What can I offer you girls? Have you had your coffee this morning? I have strawberry Danish from our little grocery here in Lapel. Let's eat while we're getting acquainted."

Lillian led us to her dining room, where the table was laid with Blue Willow plates and white linen napkins. I couldn't pair Satan with Blue Willow and white linen.

While we introduced ourselves and feasted on good coffee and fresh pastries, I snatched furtive glances at Lillian's decor. The walls of the dining room and living room were strewn with lovely artwork, mostly wildlife and water scenes hung in perfect symmetry. Her home was beautifully decorated. She had managed to match the floral print of two overstuffed club chairs with the checked pattern on her sofa. The drapes perfectly complemented the furniture, and the oriental rugs in her living room and dining room added charming richness and harmony. Clearly, she was some sort of wizard! I also noticed that the rooms were void of pictures identifying her as a wife, mother, or grandmother.

"I'm not married, Jill. It's just me here," Lillian said. She gave me a sweet smile. Was she a mind reader? If so, my session with her was probably doomed.

Rita was completely at ease with Lillian. I think she could have taken a snooze on Lillian's sofa. Teri, on the other hand, was on edge and cautious. I was camped somewhere in the middle. As we made small talk about our annoyance with fireworks continuing past the holiday and buying whole coffee beans as opposed to pre-ground beans, Teri finally managed a few bites of her Danish and a sip of black coffee. She may have been waiting to see if Rita and I survived the food.

Lillian chattered happily as though we were old friends and had all the time in the world to linger at the table. As we talked, she studied our faces and seemed to be searching our souls. Finally, after brushing a few stray crumbs from her lips with her napkin and placing it methodically on the table, she said, "Jill, would you like to talk with me for a while in my study?"

"Sure," I said, with an eagerness that surprised even me. Rita smiled triumphantly. Lillian led me to a sunny little room with baby blue walls, loaded bookshelves, and two huge over-stuffed leather chairs. With a smile and gracious sweep of her hand, she invited me to select the chair that suited me. The chair's embrace was as soft and comforting as Lillian's had been.

"Would you mind if we sit without talking for a few moments, Jill?" Lillian asked. "I must clear my mind and focus entirely on you." Her voice was so calm and tender that it seemed like I was speaking with my mother. She closed her eyes and sat perfectly still for a couple of minutes before saying, "Rita wanted to tell me about you when she called yesterday, but I stopped her. I'd rather hear about you from you. So, where have you taken your life so far and where are you heading?"

I'd never been asked to talk about my life like that, as though my life was a vehicle on a clearly marked road. Lillian had me on the ropes already. "Well," I said, "I've been married twice and have two grown daughters. I own a bed and breakfast and a farm, and I work all the time. My neighbor, who is like an uncle, is my right-hand man."

"I'm sure you love him."

"I owe him so much. I'll never be able to repay him."

"Do you think he expects payment?"

"No, I don't think so. I mean, absolutely not."

"And your girls? Are you close?"

"We've always been close, but they're strong-willed, and now they have their own lives. I'm trying to let go but not doing such a hot job of it."

"And your marriages? Did you love your husbands? How did the marriages end?"

"I loved my first husband very much. His name was Philip. We met at college. He was smart and endlessly cheerful. He was a brainy engineer. We were soulmates, you could say. He was a great dad. He was killed in a car accident when my girls were eight and twelve. After that, I moved us back to Noblesville to be near my parents. They helped me through some tough times."

"And you inherited the farm from them and turned it into a bed and breakfast? How marvelous!"

"That's right. It's not always marvelous. I mean, I love the place but there's a lot involved in running it. I'm also the chef. That's what I love most."

"Cooking?"

"Yeah, the satisfaction of creating beautiful food. There's nothing like it."

"What about your second marriage?"

"I was hoping I could get you off track."

"I know. Tell me about it though."

I sighed. "When we moved to Noblesville, I worked for the city clerk's office. Jimmy had a law practice in town, mostly personal injury cases. He was smooth; I fell for him. He wanted me, but as it turned out, he didn't want to be a father. He seemed to like the girls at first, but he didn't know anything about dealing with kids, and they didn't understand him. It caused a lot of tension. In the end, he became a world-class jerk, and I couldn't stand him. I gave him lots of chances, probably too many. My folks despised him, which didn't help matters. He was damaging to all of us, so I ended up divorcing him."

"How long ago?"

"Um, about four years, I guess."

Lillian sat back in her chair and closed her eyes again for what seemed ages. "For some reason, I'm getting a picture of a woven basket in my mind's eye, Jill. Does a basket have significance for you?"

"I'm not sure. Can you describe it?"

"It's large with a handle and something yellow draping off the side."

"There's a yellow ribbon on the basket I use in the garden. I collect herbs and flowers in it. Maybe that's it."

"Maybe. You're a gardener then."

"Yeah, that's another passion of mine."

"I'm not feeling the basket connected to gardening in your case. I think it's connected with your generous nature. You give a lot of yourself to others, family, friends, guests." Lillian closed her eyes again and breathed deeply. "Oddly enough, the basket is on its side. What do you think that could mean?"

"Maybe that I'm clumsy and prone to spilling things."

"Are you clumsy?"

"Not really."

"I'm reading it a different way. I'm wondering if you're closing yourself off and not receptive to an idea or to change or maybe to a person. Positioned that way, the basket could also mean that you're giving away a lot of yourself and you might be depleted. Does any of this make sense for where you are right now?"

"Well, what's the choice? I have to keep everything running."

"You can work with me, Jill, or resist me? It's your call."

"Sorry, guess I'm a little defensive," I said, "but isn't every woman depleted for one reason or another?"

"Probably. So, let's look at you from another angle. "I get the feeling that you've come to a crossroads and you're a little panicked about it. There's a push and pull going on inside you. Am I getting warm?"

"Are you sure Rita didn't fill you in about me?"

"Perfectly sure."

With a sigh, I said, "A man has suddenly appeared in my life out of nowhere, and I'm drawn to him. He's charming and commanding and smart, but I've been happy alone. I don't want to mess up my life and the girls' lives by getting involved with him. I don't want a romance, but he's completely magnetic. He's surrounded by this force field."

"You said your girls have their own lives now, so let's concentrate on you. Can you separate your needs from theirs?"

"I'm not sure. I can try."

"If I asked you to name an object or an idea or anything under the sun that symbolizes you, can you do that? Please try."

My mind was racing. After a minute that seemed like ten minutes, I said, "I suppose the basket is a good symbol for me. Heaven knows I carry baskets around the farm often enough, and I share produce in baskets all the time."

"In my mind's eye, I see the basket again but it's right side up now. Yes, the basket may symbolize you very well, Jill. You like nothing more than to share with others, whether it's from your garden, your kitchen, or from your heart. True?"

"That's true."

"But there's a complication."

"Really?"

"You may not be as generous with yourself as you are with others."

"What makes you say that?"

Lillian shook her head gently in the affirmative as a sign of reassurance and smiled sweetly. "Do you love yourself, Jill?"

I paused again. "I'm not sure what that even means. I didn't like myself when I was married to Jimmy, but my farm and my friends and family have helped me heal. Yeah, I like myself again. I have confidence in myself."

"Does that mean you trust yourself?"

"I think so. I make a hundred decisions every day without questioning myself, but right now with this current thing maybe I don't trust myself completely. This is a lot bigger than which cut of meat to buy."

"Is that why you're here . . . because you don't trust yourself to make a good choice in this matter when you trust yourself in so many other ways?"

"Ye gads," I blurted. "That feels lame, but I think you're right. I could blame Rita and say she dragged me here, but I'm really here because I don't trust myself to make the right choice concerning romance."

"Wait, now. I didn't say that. I just asked the questions. Here's another question: What did you learn from your marriages? How about Philip?"

"How many hours do we have?" I asked. Lillian chuckled.

"I put my full trust in Phil, and he never let me down. I was young when we met and hadn't dated much. I was never serious with anyone else. My father had been trustworthy, too. That's all I knew. I took Phil's love and his character for granted, I'm sure. His death taught me that the love of a good man should never be taken for granted and to appreciate the hell out of it every day."

"And Jimmy?"

I groaned. "Jimmy also taught me about love or whatever that was. He wanted to own me not love me. When things didn't go his way, he freaked out. He tried to isolate and control me. He was a classic control freak. He was desperate for my undivided attention and jealous of the girls. I was dense and kept thinking he'd calm down, settle in, and change. I was fooling myself. He always wanted what was best for himself not for me. Yeah, I learned a lot from Jimmy."

"So, now you're standing on the brink. You don't know if you should encourage a new relationship or let it pass."

"That sums it up."

"Are you lonely, Jill?"

Another sigh. "I've asked myself that several times in the past few days, but I never get a straight answer. Can't seem to complete the thought."

"It's not an easy question. Could it be that you keep yourself busy at all times so you don't have to think about it?"

"Maybe."

"Let me give you some time right now. Clear your mind and go deep into your core, your gut. That's where our truth camps out. Tap into your gut, Jill. There's so much wisdom there. Be completely honest with yourself."

I sat back in my chair, closed my eyes, and thought about the inn, my guests, the farm, the girls, Mort, Rita, Pink, and Mary Porter. I delighted in them, but was I missing what only an intimate partner can provide? Intimate partnership is very complicated. Did I want the complications? After the initial thrill and ego boost, would a relationship bring me joy in the long run? After a few minutes of contemplation, I said, "I've worked very hard to make it on my own. If I invite another man into my life, it will be because he's very special and because I want him there. But I don't need someone else to make me whole."

Lillian extended her hands heavenward. "Clarity!" she exclaimed. "That's the spirit! That's what we're looking for—clarity. You've allowed distractions to keep you from deciding what's best for you. We must be crystal clear about what fulfills us and go after it. It takes guts and focus to look life in the face and say what we want."

"I suppose it does," I said.

"I urge many of my clients to wake up and live intentionally by clarifying their lives. You're doing this, so you're in an enviable position. You already know that you're a whole person. You aren't caught in the illusion that you need someone else to complete you. You embraced the opportunity to grow strong on your own, and you can say yes or no in making decisions about your life. This is beautiful! Listen to your gut, Jill. Trust yourself. You've probably already decided how to play this. Now . . . listen to your decision."

"I will. I am," I said.

"Here's another thought . . . though you don't need another person to feel complete, might you want to share yourself with someone and add to their happiness?

"Hadn't thought of it that way," I said.

"Let me ask you something else. If you should decide to get involved with this gentleman, what do you want your relationship to be like?"

"That's putting the cart before the horse, isn't it?" I asked. "I don't even know that I want a relationship."

"I think it's the exact thing to ask yourself right now. It's easy to get off track when a romance is new. You know, stars can get in the way and hormones kick up. What are the essential elements for you?"

"Well, . . . if there would be somebody and if I encouraged a relationship, it would only be with a person who cares for me above himself . . . a guy who is as committed to my happiness as he is to his own. Wow, is that a crazy expectation?"

"Do you think it's crazy?"

"No, no, I think it's smart," I said. "Might be the smartest thing I've said in a while."

"I'm going to tell you something, and this will probably sound pretty woo-woo. As you've been sitting here, the ring on your right hand has drawn my attention. Does it have a connection to your father?"

"Yes. How did you know that?" I asked, amazed.

"I just get these feelings sometimes."

"I had the ring made from Daddy's favorite stick pin. He was a quiet, unassuming guy, but he had an eye for good jewelry. The ring keeps a little part of him with me."

"He's still with you, Jill. I'm sure of it, and so is your mother. Lillian closed her eyes again, sat back, and took a few deep breaths. Her name began with . . . an . . . M?"

"Mona," I said. "Mona was her name. How could you know that?"

"As I said, I have these perceptions."

"Thank you," I said, brushing away tears on my cheeks.

"You okay?" Lillian asked, tenderly.

"Yeah, I'm fine," I said. My mind was reeling. We sat in silence.

"Well . . . I'm running late for Teri. I'd better let you go," Lillian said, finally. She reached out and took both of my hands in hers. "It's been my privilege to talk with you. Be sure to go to your gut for answers, and don't make a move until you find clarity. Trust yourself and live intentionally. Should you ever need me again, I'm right here in little ol' Lapel." We exchanged a final warm hug. I wanted to bring her home with me.

I was in an altered state of mind. Rita led me to her SUV, and we drove to a cafe in downtown Lapel while Teri took her turn with Lillian. Rita ordered box lunches for the three of us, and I tried to gather myself. She had come through for me again. I would surely need to return the favor.

The ride home was quiet and within the speed limit. Rita barely spoke, and Teri stared out the window seemingly transfixed on the corn and soybean fields. I was sure she wasn't thinking about corn. I was tempted to ask her about her conversation with Lillian and to share bits of my own, but I decided to wait for a time when it would be just the two of us. I, too, had a lot to consider, but I was quite sure now of my decision regarding Lawrence.

As we drove into the lane at the inn, Rita asked, "Well, Honey, was it worth the drive?"

"Yeah, it was worth it. You're the best," I said. I hugged Rita. "I'll see you both tonight at the park. Curtain goes up at eight o'clock."

"Sounds good, Honey. Pink and I'll be there with bells on."

"I'll be there. See you then," said Teri.

I watched Rita and Teri's vehicles pull away and then surveyed the garden on my way to the inn. Even with the storm the day before, the tomatoes called for water. That little chore must be done right away, as well as preparing an early supper for Lauren and Chickie. I was sure they would have butterflies before dress rehearsal. I opened the porch door and found Stephanie, Robert, Lauren, and Chickie sitting on rockers and sipping sodas.

"Hi. Where have you been, Mom?" Stephanie asked.

"Rita wanted Teri and me to take a drive with her," I said. "It was very spur-of-the-moment." How could I possibly tell Steph and Lauren that I'd consulted a wise woman about whether or not to start up a thing with Robert's uncle? Telling the truth in this case was unthinkable. No one in her right mind would tell her children such things. They would never understand, and it would be impossible to describe the experience. "Ready for tonight?" I asked Lauren and Chickie.

"I'm ready, but my nerves aren't," said Lauren.

"Don't worry. If you forget your lines, Chickie Baby will say them for you," said Robert. "Don't you guys have a prompter?"

"Silvio says prompters are a crutch and make actors lazy," said Chickie. She gave a perfect impersonation of Mr. Silvio. "It's sink or swim. Anyway, I'm ready."

"Will you all be there?" Lauren asked.

"Of course," I said, "and Pink and Rita and Uncle Mort and Mary. They're all excited."

"Uncle Mort is excited?" Stephanie asked, dubiously.

"Well, he'll be there," I said.

"My parents are coming on Sunday," said Chickie. "My father wants to see the play without the kinks and opening night jitters."

"We'll be there, if only to watch Chickie Baby say her lines and Signior Benedick's, too," said Robert. "Can't wait to see this."

"Teddy Bennett said Teri will be there tonight," said Lauren. "His real mom is coming on Saturday."

"Really?" I asked. I was surprised that Lauren would admit to knowing these details about Teddy's family.

"Speaking of Mort, he was here looking for you this morning," said Robert. "He said everything is set for your sheep shearing tomorrow. The shearer will be here about nine o'clock."

"Okay," I replied. "So, what about dinner? Big meal, small meal, or something in between?"

"Something light for me," said Lauren, clutching her stomach. "Maybe crackers."

"I could eat a horse," said Chickie.

"The neighbors have one if you can catch it," said Robert.

I retrieved some frozen pizzas.

CHAPTER 22

Much Ado and Lawrence, Too

Ronaldo Silvio enjoys celebrity status in Noblesville. He is a second-generation Italian American with a big personality and passion to spare. Few can remember a drama and debate teacher at the high school before Ronaldo. He knows theatre well from directing high dramas to light musicals. His outdoor productions over the years have been legendary. He once borrowed a construction crane to hoist Peter Pan and company in the air, and he outfitted the entire high school band in period uniforms for *The Music Man*. A few of his former students have had Broadway success. Two generations of lawyers have praised him for demanding airtight evidence in debate class.

Mr. Silvio's patrons are generous, which translates into high-quality sets and costumes. With a reputation for flamboyance and volatility, one might expect high school students to avoid him. Instead, they flock to his classes and vie for his attention because he loves them and is interested in each of them.

Ronaldo himself settled our little group in the third row of the outdoor seating. He was dressed in tux and tails. His much-talked-about toupee, bushy mustache, and neatly trimmed Van Dyke contributed to his theatrical appearance and to the very atmosphere of the evening. He was all smiles.

Also contributing to the ambiance was a woodwind trio playing lively selections under the branches of an oak a few paces from the stage. According to the playbill, the music was "thoughtfully selected to engage the audience in an English frolic."

Teri Bennett arrived solo. Naturally, I invited her to join our little company. I was seated between Rita and Mary Porter. To Mary's right sat Teri, Stephanie, Robert, and Uncle Mort. Mort insisted upon an aisle seat. Pink sat next to Rita on the opposite end of our group. Though Pink, Rita, Mort, and Mary weren't technically family, I invited them. The inn had made a substantial donation to the production and was listed among patrons in the playbill, which pleased me. I assumed Mr. Silvio would approve of a few extra guests.

The weather was pleasant and the sun was setting in a clear sky. It was a perfect summer evening, and I was feeling lighthearted. The more challenging events of the past few days were replaced in my mind by the excitement of seeing Lauren and Chickie strut their stuff on stage. I was proud of them and eager for the opening line.

Lauren had been in plays since grade school. Since her first role as the star of Bethlehem in her school's Christmas pageant, she was hooked. After that, it was *Peter Pan, Annie, A Midsummer's Night Dream, Aesop's Fables, The Sound of Music,* and *You're a Good Man, Charlie Brown.* I thought of the many hours I'd spent shuttling her to play practice and running lines. Theatre made her a happier girl, which was all that mattered. Each time the footlights came on and the curtain rose, I was breathless. As Hero, she would take on her most challenging role so far. I marveled at how she was grasping Shakespeare under Mr. Silvio's direction. Yes, it was English but as tricky to get right as a foreign language. The role was perfect for her—a lead role but not the central role. She hoped she would be offered leads at Ball State in the years ahead, which would be very exciting.

Chickie, too, was seasoned on the boards. She had been in several plays at school and in community theatre. The girls had been friends since junior high but became glued to each other while rehearsing *You're a Good Man, Charlie Brown* as seniors. Chickie was always ready to take on the world, and tonight she would give us her best.

I was also anxious to watch the ever-entertaining Teddy Bennett and Tom Laughlin—but this time from a safe distance. It was a relief to know they wouldn't be arrested during intermission.

The stage set reflected the courtyard of an Italian villa and contained three arched doorways for the actors to enter and exit. A long balcony topped the arches and was festooned with white flowing fabric. The stage right archway was flanked by artificial shrubs ready to conceal the deceived Signior Benedick. The hundred chairs set up in the grass for the audience were filling up quickly. I recognized many of the faces streaming in and nodded a greeting to several people. The mood was festive and the anticipation palpable.

"I have to go," Mary whispered, discreetly.

"Aren't you feeling well?" I asked.

"I'm fine, but I need to use the ladies' room."

"There's no ladies' room here. Only port-a-johns," I whispered, grimly.

"That'll do," she responded. "Any port in a storm."

The thought of Mary using a nasty port-a-john was revolting. I wondered if she and her walker could navigate the uneven earth all the way to the john, much less squeeze inside the awful thing. My heart sank.

Mary shook her head apologetically. "You'll have to come with me," she said.

"Of course. Let's go," I replied.

"Where ya goin', Honey?" Rita asked.

"Mary has to use the ladies' room."

"Now? It's about to start. Does she have to go that bad?" I glared at Rita as the stage footlights came on. The play was indeed about to begin. I felt guilty for putting Mary through such a trial. She'd come to the play reluctantly, and I should have been more sensitive. Her sacrifice dawned on me. We moved at a snail's pace down the center aisle. All eyes were upon us, or so it seemed. The port-a-john was a good distance from the seating area. I feared that she might fall or that she wouldn't make it in time.

Suddenly, almost out of thin air, Lawrence appeared and took Mary's arm. She pulled away from him at first, but upon examining his handsome face and solicitous expression, she accepted his help. I braced her other arm, and an usher raced to our aid and patiently helped Mary steady her walker as we puttered along. Lawrence reassured Mary with his soothing baritone and coached us as we inched across the rutty lawn toward the john. He did his best to joke and put us all at ease. After a few tense minutes, we reached the port-a-john. I helped Mary inside as discreetly as possible. The usher politely excused himself from the scene.

Standing guard at the port-a-john with Lawrence was awkward to say the least. Besides the obvious embarrassment for Mary, other topics loomed large. Lawrence had written a note revealing his feelings for me. He had positioned the note prominently on my dresser and then taken off with barely a word. These facts hung in the air around us like a pea soup fog, but this wasn't the right moment to talk intimately. Our relationship had changed because of the note. I wasn't sure how to talk with him now, but talk we must and soon. Consequently, small talk was uncomfortable.

"I'll help you get your friend back to her chair if that's okay," said Lawrence.

"I won't turn down the offer," I said. "Looks like I owe you again."

"I know you're surprised to see me."

"Well, yes. How's the research going?" I asked, coolly.

"Notre Dame was helpful."

"Glad to hear that."

"Robert left a ticket for me with the ushers. Sounded like fun. Haven't seen Shakespeare in years. Hope you don't mind that I came."

"It's open to the public. Well, it's supposed to be for family tonight, but you qualify," I said.

"Didn't want to miss it," Lawrence said, sheepishly.

Our stiff conversation was interrupted by Mary pounding on the door of the john. Once outside again and settled on her walker, her mood lightened. We began the walk back to the seating area. "That was a close one," she said. "You young people will understand someday. Mother Nature is a tyrant."

"Mary, I'd like you to meet Robert's uncle, Lawrence Milner. Lawrence is staying with us at the inn this week," I said. "Lawrence, this is Mary Porter, my lifelong friend and another of my guardian angels."

Mary chuckled. "Don't listen to her, Mr. Milner. I'm no angel, but the friend part is true." I was afraid Mary would let slip our chat over tea, but she's too cunning for that. She added only, "Very nice to meet you, Mr. Milner. Can't thank you enough for coming to my rescue." Lawrence smiled. "I'm going to be lost when we get back, Jillian. Tell me the plot quickly, Dear."

"Oh, okay, I'll try," I whispered. As the three of us made our way slowly to the seating area, I did my best to set up the plot, "So, a young soldier named Claudio falls in love with a sweet girl named Hero. She's the daughter of the town's mayor. Hero's cousin and best friend, Beatrice, has decided that she's off men entirely and will never marry."

"Which means she'll get married soon," Mary interjected. Lawrence laughed.

"Of course," I said. "So, Beatrice claims she despises Signior Benedick, another soldier, and friend of Claudio's.

"Which means she likes him," Mary interjected again.

"Right," I said. "Beatrice and Benedick bicker a lot. Their friends trick them into thinking they love each other, so then they do. Go figure. The good Prince Don Pedro is hated by his bad brother Don John for some reason. Don John and his pals trick Claudio into thinking Hero has been unfaithful. Claudio makes a terrible scene at their wedding and humiliates Hero. She faints and plays dead."

"Poor girl. So, there's a lot of tricking going on," said Mary.

"Naturally. At first, Hero's father believes she's unfaithful," I continued.

"Typical. Men always stick together," said Mary. Lawrence raised an eyebrow.

"Then, the town's goofy policemen do a stakeout and find out Hero's innocent. Hero's father punishes Claudio by pretending to make him marry another niece, and Claudio is fine with that."

"Makes no sense," said Mary.

"It's Shakespeare; what can I say?"

"So, the stupid boy doesn't marry the sweet girl?" asked Mary.

"Wrong. He does marry her. She was pretending to be the other niece at the wedding."

"The girl is a fool for marrying such a stupid boy," said Mary.

"Agreed," I said.

"What do you think, Mr. Milner?" Mary whispered.

"I'm impressed that Jill knows the play so well," said Lawrence.

"I watched it online," I said.

"I suppose Lauren is playing the sweet girl and Charlotte is playing the quarrelsome girl," said Mary.

"How did you guess?" I responded. Mary rolled her eyes.

We had missed several minutes of the action, but I consoled myself by thinking I could catch another performance on the weekend. The Sunday matinee might be best since, as Chickie's father observed, mistakes and jitters would be worked out by then.

We couldn't get back to the third row without making a scene. All the other seats were taken. The same helpful usher produced three extra chairs, so Mary, Lawrence, and I formed a new back row. It was difficult to see the actors and hear the dialogue. The location was especially hopeless for Mary. I feared she would get very little out of the performance. Yet, she looked perfectly happy.

As we settled into our new seats, I tried to decide if that night had been the fourth or the fifth time Lawrence had come to my aid in as many days. I wondered how I'd managed life without him. I did my best to focus on the play, but from that remote vantage point there were too many distractions and too many heads in my way. Mary's comfort concerned me, but the bigger distraction was seated next to me wearing perfectly pressed microfiber shorts and a yellow Polo shirt. Even the rise and fall of Lawrence's chest as he breathed was a distraction. I wondered how and when I'd be able to talk with him about his note. Would it be tonight after the play or tomorrow? And what would I say? How could I possibly concentrate on the play seated next to him? Here was another situation gone awry this week.

Also distracting was the sight of Jerry Bennett in the audience several rows ahead. I could only see the side of his face, but I was sure it was Jerry. I resolved to confirm this during intermission. I wondered if Teri knew he was there.

The play had been in progress for twenty minutes before we were seated in our little back-row annex. I finally shifted my attention to the stage until Lawrence whispered, "I feel bad for your friend. I'm sure she can't see much from back here. I'll get Robert to trade seats with her."

"Robert's in the third row," I whispered. "We'll make a scene."

"He won't mind," Lawrence said. He stood suddenly and was poised to walk ahead fifteen rows to fetch Robert.

"No, no," I said, grabbing Lawrence's arm and motioning him to sit down. "It's nice of you, but, please, no. Mary will hate the fuss."

"It's just friends and family tonight, right? Wouldn't they want her to actually see what's going on?"

"Too embarrassing," I said. Some heads turned in disapproval of our whispering.

"I'm not embarrassed," said Lawrence. He turned toward me and stared deeply into my eyes. My heart raced.

"What's going on now?" Mary asked.

"I think Beatrice is complaining to everybody about Benedick again," I said.

"I mean, what's Lawrence saying?"

"Oh, he's worried that you can't see the stage. He wants you to trade places with Robert."

"Now? In front of all these people? On this contraption?" Mary shook her walker. "Forget it."

"That's what I said."

After a moment, Mary said, "He's thoughtful, isn't he?"

"Let's just watch the play," I said. Mary smiled knowingly.

Lauren and Chickie looked beautiful in their off-the-shoulder white flowing blouses and long skirts. Their hair was pinned away from their faces, blending neatly with hairpieces at the back of their heads. They were young and vibrant, and I loved watching them glide across the stage. They had learned to relax and move naturally. Chickie's stage voice was especially clear and strong. Though the lines she spoke were from an earlier age and nearly impossible to fully grasp, her gestures, timing, and facial expressions helped tell the story. She often used the same snappy sarcasm with Robert. The audience laughed and even clapped several times.

Craig Deluca, as Signior Benedick, gave as good as he got during the spite fights with Beatrice. Chickie's complaint that Craig didn't know his lines was not bearing out. He had mastery of every line it seemed. His tall muscular form, handsome bearded face, and Cavalier costuming made him the audience darling. Women's faces lit up with his every entrance. There was a reason that he was making a splash in the Indianapolis theatre scene. I wondered how Mr. Silvio had snagged Craig's talent for the summer. I also wondered how Friar Francis fit into the equation.

Lauren, too, was doing admirably as Hero. Though Hero has comparatively few lines, it's her job to look alluring and innocent. Lauren nailed it. In past productions, she'd struggled to speak naturally. As Hero, it hardly seemed that she was acting. She floated gracefully through her scenes, giggling convincingly with Beatrice and showing the unrestrained zest of a blossoming young woman. She was maturing before my eyes. Maybe my years as a struggling single parent and then as Jimmy's unhappy wife hadn't wounded Lauren to the extent I'd imagined. Maybe she would be okay after all.

Mary nudged me suddenly and asked, "Why are they wearing masks?"

"They're at a masquerade ball. Prince Don Pedro proposed marriage to Hero on behalf of Claudio," I whispered.

"You mean he can't ask her himself?"

"I'm not sure why Don Pedro does that, but he fixes them up in the end. Now, Don John is plotting with the other bad guys to make Claudio think Hero is cheating on him."

The play moved along briskly. Don Pedro devised his scheme to get Benedick and Beatrice together. Don John and his thugs plotted to wreck Claudio and Hero's wedding. Hero and her maid schemed to make Beatrice think Benedick loved her.

I was startled by a tap on my shoulder. Robert stood behind me. "Uncle Lawrence wants me to help you and Mary get back down front," he said. Robert's attempt at whispering failed, so more members of the audience glared at us.

"How did you know that?" I asked.

"Text," he said.

Lawrence stood up in a genteel gesture to let Mary and me pass in front of him.

"What does he want?" Mary asked.

"They think we should move back to our seats down front."

"I thought we settled that," Mary said with an edge to her voice.

"We can't move now. We're waiting for intermission," I told Robert. "Go back."

"I can't walk back there now," Robert objected.

"Then pull up a chair," I said, sharply. Hoping to quell our disturbance, the usher rushed to find a chair for Robert as well. Now we were all stuck in the back row. I scowled at Lawrence.

"Just trying to help," he said. He smiled mischievously with no hint of remorse. I wasn't sure if he was flirting or testing my patience.

"What's happening now?" Mary whispered.

"Lawrence thinks he's being funny . . . or something," I said. "I mean on stage."

I caught the action for a few moments and replied, "Don John wants Claudio and the Prince to meet him under Hero's window later so they can catch her in the act."

"Oh, good," said Mary.

The actors exited the stage and were quickly replaced by the woodwind trio playing a romping Renaissance tune. We made it to intermission with Mary still in good spirits. The crowd was heading for the refreshment table. Mary, Lawrence, Robert, and I proceeded slowly to our seats in the third row. Darkness had fallen and the area was dimly lit by strings of tiny lights draped between poles and by the rising moon. We walked at a snail's pace, guarding Mary closely. Robert snagged a chair and placed it at the end of our row for Lawrence, who seemed perfectly happy to sit in the aisle beside Mort.

"Where have you been, Honey?" asked Rita. "I thought you went home."

"They made a new back row just for us. I'll tell you about it later."

"So, the hunk turned up, I see. Thought we might see him tonight." She nudged my arm playfully.

"Don't look at him," I insisted. "He'll think we're talking about him."

"We are talking about him, Honey."

Teri had been to the refreshment table and was now squeezing back into her seat. She leaned forward in her chair and looked in my direction with a horrified expression. With Mary between us, it was hard to talk.

I mouthed the words, "What's wrong?"

"Jerry's ex is here," Teri whispered. "I just saw her. Teddy said she was coming on Saturday night, but she's here!"

"Is she alone?" I asked.

"I don't know. She was getting a drink. I didn't see anybody with her." Teri looked stricken. I thought of our first meeting at the grocery store on Saturday and how distraught she was over her split with Jerry. This was not a love like Claudio and Hero's or Beatrice and Benedick's. Teri truly loved Jerry. She was floundering without him. She wasn't whole.

"Jerry's here. I saw him," I said, before considering my words.

"Was she with him?" asked Teri.

"I don't know. I only got a glimpse of him."

"Oh," Teri said with downcast eyes. "Do you think you could walk past him and see if she's with him? I have to know." Such an assignment held little appeal, and I wondered why I'd bothered to come to the play at all. I didn't mind spying on Jerry but didn't want to maneuver around Mary's walker, step on toes, and face Lawrence again so soon. He might think I wanted to get near him. I was seated dead center in the row, so walking in the other direction meant stepping over Rita's monstrous purse and Pink's long legs.

"Pinky says they're servin' wine," Rita said, excitedly. "Let's go."

The woodwind trio ended their tune, and Don John, Claudio, and Don Pedro made an entrance. It was too late for the free wine. I signaled as much to Teri. Through the dim light, I could see her expression was bleak. The off-stage intrigue had to wait.

The intrigue on stage, however, was heating up with Don John baiting Claudio and Don Pedro to witness Hero supposedly making love with Borachio. Claudio played the betrayed, heart-sick lover to the hilt. If I hadn't known the rest of the story, I would have felt sorry for him.

At last, stomping onto the stage came the ragtag town watchmen. Teddy as Dogberry, the leader, owned the stage at once. Tom as Verges, second-in-command, played the perfect fall guy.

Shakespeare created the characters for comic relief, and Teddy and Tom delivered. Dogberry's ridiculous malaprops and mistreatment of Verges had the audience in stitches. Teddy delivered the lines more like a seasoned professional than a high school kid. Even if one didn't understand all the wordplay, the slapstick silliness was hilarious. Maybe Chickie hadn't missed the mark when she lauded the boys to Sid Pinter, and maybe Robert's remark about Teddy summed it best, "The kid's actually pretty smart." I couldn't believe these were the same sniveling pyromaniacs I'd sprayed with my garden hose earlier in the week. Come Monday, Big Sue might outsize them, but she'd never outsmart them.

The play moved along to its happy, if implausible, conclusion. In the final scene, Hero and Beatrice were poised to marry their sweethearts. The ensemble hopped and whirled to the tune of an English country dance. Lauren and Chickie looked radiant. Their expressions were a mixture of joy and relief, perfect for Hero and Beatrice.

The curtain call brought loud applause. Dogberry, Verges, and the men of the watch bounded on stage, clasped hands, and bowed low. The audience was thrilled. I felt an odd sort of pride at having the inside track on Teddy and Tom, the biggest scene stealers. Next to bow were other lesser characters, Friar Francis, Don John and his bad boys, Don Pedro, and Leonato. Then, Hero and Claudio took their bows. Claudio kissed Hero's hand and lifted it high in triumph. Stephanie and Robert clapped for Lauren enthusiastically, which made me happy. Maybe my girls were coming to appreciate each other's successes. What can be better than this for a mother?

Finally, Beatrice and Benedick took triumphant bows. I was thrilled for Chickie and proud of her, yet I knew there would be no living with her now. She would sail to new heights of self-esteem and pester me again for permission to address me by my first name.

I'd have to think of an airtight argument. I wondered what would become of the girls' relationship with Craig Deluca. Would their acquaintance blossom into a lasting friendship or fade after the show? The crowd loved Craig. Was he headed for New York or Los Angeles? Both seemed possible.

Then something shocking happened. Teddy Bennett collapsed in the middle of the curtain call. His crumpled body lay center stage. Laughter rose from the audience at first since the fall seemed like part of the show. The laughter turned to gasps. Since there was no curtain to close, the events of the next few minutes were on full display. The actors surrounded Teddy quickly and tried to help. The actor playing Claudio had already begun administering CPR when Mr. Silvio reached Teddy.

"Stand back, everybody. Give him room," Mr. Silvio shouted firmly to the actors. "Call 911, somebody, please."

Jerry Bennett sprinted onto the stage. "I've already done that," he shouted. The actors, including Lauren and Chickie, stood by in shock. Most everyone in the audience sat quietly, fearing the worst. This was something new for the Shakespeare Summer in the Park Series. This was more drama than anyone wanted. Whispers rippled through the crowd and fear mounted.

Teri leaned forward in her seat again. "Jill, what should I do? I want to go to him."

"Go then," I said. "Teddy might need you."

"What about her?"

"Worry about her later," I said. "Teddy's the important thing now."

Lawrence's eyes were on Teri and me. He signaled Stephanie, Robert, and Mort to allow Teri out of our row quickly. He escorted her down the center aisle and assisted her onto the stage. Following immediately behind Teri was another woman, who extended her hand to Lawrence for the same assistance.

"Oh, my lord, is that who I think it is?" Rita whispered.

"I'd say so," I responded.

"What's Teri gonna do with the boy's momma up there? What's his daddy gonna do?"

"We'll find out," I said with trepidation.

"We should've got that wine when we had the chance," Rita muttered. "I could use it right about now."

"Is the boy on his feet yet?" asked Mary.

"It's hard to tell with everybody around him, but I don't think so," I said.

Lawrence looked bewildered as he returned to his seat. In the short time I'd known him, he'd seemed unflappable. When risking his neck to save a chubby cat or facing down a boozy loudmouth or fearing for his life on the pontoon, he'd emerged remarkably cool and calm. But he was noticeably upset about the fate of a boy he barely knew. This touched my heart.

A Noblesville Police car pulled up to the stage followed by a shrieking ambulance. Officer Martin Hines and another young officer sprang from their car and took the situation in hand. The actors yielded center stage to the emergency medical team. After several anxious minutes, Teddy could be seen sitting up. "Thank God he's alive" went the whispers. The EMTs soon placed Teddy on a stretcher and lifted him into the ambulance.

A moment of truth was bearing down on Teri. Who would ride to the hospital in the ambulance with Teddy? It looked like Teri was heading for heartache as she, Jerry, and the woman we assumed to be Teddy's mother followed the stretcher to the ambulance. I could see Teri taking a few steps backward. Somehow it was settled. Jerry and the mystery woman hopped into the ambulance with Teddy and the EMTs. Teri, looking stunned, stood perfectly still for several seconds. Mr. Silvio exchanged a few words with the driver and the ambulance shrieked away with Martin Hines's car as an escort.

Teri's humiliation had played out in full view. Jerry had left her standing alone. I was upset with myself. If only I hadn't encouraged her to go to Teddy, her ordeal might have been avoided. I feared she'd bolt for her car immediately. Instead, she returned to our little tribe. Lawrence gave her his seat in the aisle and stood behind her as if to shield her. Even from a distance, I could see she was fighting back tears. Her heartbreak was on full display, and I wanted to thrash Jerry Bennett for his coldness.

The actors shuffled off to their makeshift dressing rooms. The woodwind trio gathered their music by the light of the moon and disappeared. The footlights were dimmed, and there was barely enough light to guide our footsteps to the parking lot. This had all been a jolting end to an otherwise successful dress rehearsal. I was disappointed for Lauren and Chickie; they would surely need consolation.

Pink, who had been unusually quiet during the evening, blurted, "What the hell's Silvio thinkin' makin' us walk outta here in the dark? Don't move. I'll get some light." He pushed through the crowd and disappeared. I suspected poor Mr. Silvio would soon be dealing with Pink in addition to Teddy's situation, but my real concern was for Teri. Since she was several seats away, I called her cell phone.

"Teri, we're all going back to my house for a nightcap. Please join us."

"I don't know, Jill. I think I'd rather be alone, and Jerry will be calling me, I'm sure."

"I'm not taking no for an answer. You shouldn't be alone tonight," I said, gambling that she would accept my pushy tone. "Besides, we're worried about Teddy, too. We can worry together. Please come."

Teri paused and exhaled. "Alright," she said, "see you in a little while."

The scene was surreal. The delightful, raucous comedy had turned into a somber retreat. Audience members picked their way silently toward the exits. Bright lights suddenly flooded the seating area from all directions. In only a few seconds, Pink had organized a shower of car headlights to guide our footsteps. Lawrence and I assisted Mary slowly toward the exit while Stephanie, Robert, Rita, and Teri crept patiently behind us. As expected, Mort had already bolted for home.

CHAPTER 23

Tangled Web

Though it was late, Mary wasn't ready to go home after the play. She didn't want to miss our little nightcap party, which delighted me. And, like the rest of us, she was worried about Teddy's condition. Once she was settled comfortably on my porch, I hurried into the kitchen to prepare snacks and drinks. I had a large charcuterie board waiting in the fridge. With the addition of some crackers, the board was ready to serve. Robert and Steph could serve the chilled wines. I made a highball for Pink and set up a little "help yourself" bar on the counter for others wanting a touch of hard liquor.

It had been years since Mary and I sat together on my porch. I was glad she was with me. The yard light cast a fair amount of dappled light inside the porch, and earthy-sweet scents were carried on the night breeze. This would set the mood for what I hoped would calm everyone after our topsy-turvy evening. I assumed Lauren and Chickie would join us, since a gathering of the *Much Ado* cast was unlikely that evening.

A car crept silently in the driveway. I wasn't counting on Teri showing up, but she arrived first. She was followed immediately by

Pink and Rita then Steph and Robert. Lawrence's rental car was the last to pull into the driveway. Before he arrived, I wondered if he might vanish again into the bowels of an all-night library or take another hiatus from the Merrick family circus.

Soon we were all decompressing in my rockers. The conversation was awkward since we knew Teri would be feeling fragile. After some small talk, Robert tackled the events of the evening, "The brats didn't do too bad," he said, balancing a pile of cheese and meat on a cracker. "Chickie Baby was definitely typecast, though. She just played herself in iambic pentameter."

"Whatever that is," said Pink. He took a long pull on his highball. We all chuckled, uneasily.

"And now that we know Lauren can act sweet and innocent, let's hope she'll do it more often," said Stephanie. A few more chuckles.

"My butt started hurtin' 'bout halfway through," said Pink. "I couldn't get comfortable no matter how I turned. Silvio's gotta do somethin' 'bout those damn chairs, and if he ever leaves us stumblin' in the dark again, he'll hear from me."

"I thought you were gonna put your feet on me there for a while," Rita quipped. "They shoulda had more breaks. I can't sit that long."

"You sit for hours at the beauty parlor, Honey," said Pink.

"That's different. I can understand what they're sayin'."

"More breaks?" Robert said. "Ye gods, we'd still be there. Did anybody besides me taste the wine? It was watered down. Silvio's getting cheap in his old age."

"We tried, but we were too slow," said Rita. "Just as well, I reckon."

"You're being hard on Ronaldo," said Mary. "He works like a mad dog with those kids. I don't think you're being fair."

"You're right, Miss Mary," said Rita. "We're bein' rotten. I thought the girls did great, Jilly, and your Teddy was so funny, Teri. I 'bout split a gut laughin' at those two. I didn't understand anything they said, but they were funny, anyway. I sure hope he's gonna be okay, Honey." Teri forced a smile.

"We all hope the boy will be just fine," said Pink. "I think they have to put people on stretchers when they go to the hospital. He probably coulda walked by himself."

"That's right. I'll bet he'll be up and around in no time flat," said Rita.

"The professor is quiet tonight," said Mary, looking in Lawrence's direction. "So, Mr. Milner, did you enjoy the play?"

"Very much," Lawrence said. "Couldn't believe they were high school and college students. I think most of them actually understood their lines. I'm sure you're proud of Lauren, Jill."

Yes, I was proud of Lauren and Chickie for their performances. Their triumph made up for some of their antics that week. Well, they were young, I thought, and harmless on the whole.

Mary was right; the professor was unusually quiet. I wondered what he was thinking. Was he thinking of me as I was thinking of him? Even in the dim light Lawrence looked handsome. The shadows enhanced his chiseled facial features. His muscular form was terribly distracting. How exciting it would be to kiss his lips. But how could such a man ever belong to one woman? His letter to me was sweet and oddly boyish. How could I not be flattered? When would I get to speak with him alone? Would I become tongue-tied? He must be waiting for the chance to talk with me, too. But the next day would be sheep shearing, and then he'd be leaving. A slight thrill of anticipation made me tingle, but I did my best to shake it off.

Teri's cell phone rang. She sprang out of her chair and hurried down the porch steps in search of privacy. The rest of us attempted more small talk, but the suspense made it difficult. She returned to the porch shortly with relief showing on her face. "He's okay," she said. "That was Jerry. They think Teddy got overheated. They couldn't find anything wrong with him. They're on their way home." I feared Rita might ask Teri if Teddy's mother was with Jerry, but thankfully, she kept quiet. Of course, I also wanted to know.

My pickup pulled into the driveway and lurched to a stop under the yard light. Lauren and Chickie emerged and made their way to the porch. They were met by a round of applause and sweet accolades, even from Steph and Robert. Chickie curtsied and Lauren smiled demurely. Their pancake makeup, thick eyeliner, and mascara made their faces look grotesque in the dappled light. They said they were tired and hungry, which was to be expected. But they were also subdued, which was unexpected. I supposed that Teddy's collapse had hit them hard, and they'd been through an exhausting evening. Surely, they had every reason to be subdued.

The girls didn't brighten when they learned that Teddy was homeward-bound. I reminded them of the left-over chicken in the fridge since only a few olives and cracker bits remained on the charcuterie board. They excused themselves abruptly.

"Let's all have one quick drink to celebrate a happy endin','" said Pink. "The girls did great and the boy is okay. Rita and me gotta scoot then. Big deal comin' down in the mornin'."

"It's way past my bedtime," Mary said, yawning. "If I have more wine, you'll have to carry me to the car."

I headed to the kitchen. "Just a short highball?" I asked Pink.

"You bet," he affirmed.

"Looks like I'll be drivin' us home, so no more for me," said Rita, rolling her eyes.

"How about you, Lawrence? Teri?" I asked. Teri declined. Lawrence lifted his glass for more wine. Robert obliged.

I decided to check in quickly with Chickie and Lauren before making Pink's highball. My instincts told me that something was amiss, and they might need help processing Teddy's collapse. Before going upstairs to the girls' room, I arranged a ride home for Mary with Robert and Stephanie. As I reached the top of the stairs, I heard Lauren and Chickie whispering—a clear indication to any mother that she'd better listen in.

"But what if he tells?" Lauren whispered.

"I keep telling you, he won't tell because he was in on it, too. He'd be in as much trouble as us," Chickie replied.

"He told me she was coming on Saturday night. Why did she have to show up tonight?" Lauren whined.

"Are you gonna keep asking that?" Chickie snapped. "You've asked that a hundred times. I don't know the woman."

"I guess he didn't see her," Lauren said. "I peeked at the audience before we started, but how was I supposed to know what she looks like?"

"It was packed. He couldn't have seen her with the footlights blasting his eyes," said Chickie. "He faked it well, though; I'll give him that much. Did you see him fall? I did. He's good. Looked almost dead. You do know the little weasel owns us now, right?"

A shock rippled through my body from head to toe. I had to think fast. Charging into their room and blowing open their secret would have been crazy since everybody—especially Teri—was downstairs. I was enraged and found it hard to breathe. I couldn't believe what I'd heard, but there was no misunderstanding. Teddy had faked his collapse on stage. My own daughter had taken part in a scam in front of a hundred people. Why would they do such a thing? What kind of mother raises children who don't know right from wrong? What possible excuse could they offer for concocting such a deception? Was it my fault somehow? Had my mothering been that bad?

My hands were shaking as I mixed Pink's whiskey and seltzer water and plopped in the ice. My mind raced with thoughts of the fallout from such a scam. I composed myself and stepped onto the porch. "Sorry for taking so long," I told Pink.

"No problem, Lambie. I'm gonna sip this quick and we'll be gone. We're rolling out new trucks tomorrow, and my guys'll need help."

"Your guys know exactly what to do," said Rita. "You just can't stand not directing everybody." Rita studied my expression. "Are you okay, Honey?" She'd read me like a book.

"I'm fine," I said. "It's been a big night. Just a little tired." I was gripped by an urge to tell all of them what I had just heard upstairs. Perhaps spreading the burden around would diminish the pain in my own heart. But that would end in disaster. This had to be handled strategically. I had to hear the whole story from Lauren and Chickie before making any moves.

Minutes earlier, I'd been relieved to kick back and relax with everyone. Now, I was anxious for everyone to leave. Rita gave me an inquisitive look as she and Pink said goodnight, but she had the good grace not to press me at that moment.

Lawrence gave Mary an especially warm goodbye and headed to his guest room. My lust had gone stone cold, and I was glad to see him retire. I accompanied Mary to the Jeep and helped her navigate the step up to the passenger seat. She expressed her joy at spending the evening with us. Robert and Steph said they'd stay with her until she was settled at home. I wondered if she would feel the same about us when she heard the news about the con artists.

Only Teri remained. Facing her while burdened with this new revelation was almost more than I could bear. My daughter and her friend had been partially responsible for Teri's embarrassment in front of a hundred people. She had been all but ignored by her ex-husband and overshadowed by his first wife—again. Anything I said to her at that moment would be a lie of omission, but how could I possibly share the truth until I confronted the girls? I wasn't ready to seek her forgiveness before understanding their motives. But should their motives even matter? I had excused their shenanigans too many times already. They must answer for themselves. Also, I wasn't ready to go public with news that would reflect so badly on me, my family, and my business. Juicy news travels at the speed of light in Noblesville.

"Teri, I'm so sorry for what you went through tonight," I said. "It wasn't right. I wish I hadn't encouraged you to go to Teddy. There wasn't time to think it through."

"It's alright. I would have gone to him anyway," Teri said. "You were right; Teddy needed me, and I needed to be there for him." She sat back in a rocker and gazed into the darkness. Clearly, she had even more on her mind. "I'm glad we're alone, Jill. I want to tell you something. Miss Lillian asked me something that has changed everything. She asked me if the reason I'm lost without Jerry is because I've lost myself. It made me mad at first. I didn't think she had any right to ask me that. She doesn't know me. But, isn't that the reason people go to see her? We went there to hear the truth, right?"

"What did you say to her?"

"I said I'd think about it, so I have been, and she's right. I lost myself when I met Jerry. We did everything he wanted to do. We went where he wanted to go with his friends, never with mine. He didn't like my favorite restaurants, so we never went there. I don't even like Chinese food that much. I like Mexican, but he doesn't, so I never ate it. I wouldn't even order it for lunch at work because

I felt guilty. Is that stupid or what? He didn't get along with my family, so I didn't see them very much. I had to sneak off to see my mom. Crazy! He made all the decisions about Teddy, and I kept my mouth shut." Teri's sudden self-awareness amazed me. "Tonight was the last straw. I don't think he even noticed I was there. He jumped in the ambulance and barely looked back at me. I'm surprised he called me."

"Do you think he was just caught up in the moment and worried about Teddy?" I asked. Teri gave me a look that challenged my question.

"No, I'm not lying to myself anymore. Miss Lillian asked the right question. I'm gonna dig myself out of the trash and clean myself up. First thing tomorrow, I'm gonna call my mom and invite her to El Rancherita for burritos and refried beans." We both managed a laugh. "I have you and Rita to thank, Jill. I wouldn't have met Miss Lillian without you." In light of what I had just overheard upstairs, Teri's gratitude was the last thing I wanted.

"Don't thank me. Thank Rita," I said. "I didn't want to go; she practically dragged me. Lillian gave me plenty to think about, too."

"It's getting late; I'd better go," Teri said, gathering her things. "Can I help you clean up?"

"No thanks. I'll clean up in the morning. Too tired to care about it now."

"Thanks for inviting me tonight," said Teri, "and thanks for all you've done for Teddy and me. You're a very special person. This week has changed my life all because you gave me a tissue at the deli. Life is funny, isn't it." A regular riot, I thought. Teri hugged me and headed away.

Juggling empty wine glasses and cocktail napkins on the charcuterie board, I made my way to the kitchen. The moment of truth was at hand. I was exhausted but determined that Lauren and

Chickie would answer for their deception that night. Luckily, they were awake and plundering the fridge as I walked into the kitchen. I sat down somberly at the kitchen table. "So, you had quite the triumph this evening," I said. "I was so proud of you."

Lauren had her head in the fridge to avoid eye contact with me. "I was nervous when we started," she said, "but after we got rolling, I was fine."

Chickie munched nonchalantly on a piece of chicken. "Deluca muffed a few lines," she said, "but I pulled him out of the fire. He owes me."

"Oh, really?" I said, "But everything else went according to plan?"

"Yep, perfectly for an opening performance," said Chickie.

"Teddy and Tom did a fantastic job," I said. "I had no idea they were so talented. Sure was a shame about Teddy collapsing like that. I wonder what happened. Did you have any idea that he was having trouble?"

"No, he seemed just fine all night," said Chickie, "but, wow, at the end. I mean, just boom!"

"We're awfully tired, Mom," said Lauren. "Do you mind if we take this stuff to our room?" She hurried toward the living room with a tray of food. Chickie followed her so closely that they nearly collided.

"Yes, it's lucky for you that Teddy's a good actor," I said, "or his fake collapse might have looked very fishy." There was silence for a few seconds before Lauren returned to the kitchen and placed the tray on the counter. Chickie followed her but remained in the doorway between the rooms.

"You know?" asked Lauren.

"I was on my way to your room a while ago. Had a feeling something wasn't quite right. Overheard."

"We were trying to help Teddy get his dad and Teri back together," said Lauren, pitifully. "We thought if it looked like Teddy was sick and had to go to the hospital they might get together and work things out. His real mom wasn't supposed to be there tonight."

"Yeah, she spoiled everything," said Chickie. "Some people just can't stick to a plan."

"Wait, wait. She spoiled everything?" I asked, incredulously. "You came up with a plan to deceive Teddy's parents, Mr. Silvio, the other actors, the police, the EMTs, and an entire audience, and now you're blaming Teddy's mother. I don't believe what I'm hearing."

"Well, it was Teddy's idea, really," said Chickie. "He was brainstorming about how he could get his dad and Teri together, and we listened mostly."

"You didn't think to say that his scheme was dishonest and stupid?" I asked.

"It seemed like a good idea at the time," said Lauren. "It made sense when we talked about it, but when he went through with it, it felt awful."

"Well, thank heaven for that," I said. "At least I know you have a conscience. I was beginning to wonder. Do you have any idea how awkward and humiliating it was for Teri to be left standing there as Teddy's mother and father rode away in that ambulance? There she stood in front of all those people she knows."

"It wasn't our fault that Teddy's dad left her behind," Chickie protested.

Lauren rolled her eyes at Chickie and said, "Seriously, though, if you were his dad, would you want to sit in an ambulance with both of your ex-wives?"

"You're missing the point entirely!" I said, exasperated. "The whole thing should never have happened, and you were complicit in that craziness—again. You went along with it. You were messing with other people's lives. In this case, people you barely know."

"Did you tell Teri what we did, Mom?"

"No, I haven't told anyone yet. It's not my news. You two and Teddy will have to tell everybody. At the very least, you'll tell Teddy's parents, Mr. Silvio, and Teri."

"I don't see why we should have to tell them," Chickie said. "We didn't do anything but listen to that little creep's idea."

"That's not true," said Lauren. "Teddy asked us for help, and we gave him the idea. We're as guilty as he is. But we were trying to help."

"You'll have to get up early tomorrow morning and call Teddy," I said. "Ask him to meet us here at one o'clock. I wonder how Teddy will explain all of this to his mother. According to Teri, his mom has been trying to win his dad back. And Teddy's dad and Teri had a dinner date planned for Saturday night. Teri's been hoping for a reconciliation. Now that's in jeopardy. This is a lovely mess."

"And Mr. Silvio will never trust us again," said Lauren.

"He'll forgive us when he finds out we were trying to help," said Chickie. "Besides, he loves us."

"I'd haul you to Mr. Silvio's house tonight if I thought it made sense," I said, "but we'd better play it cool until the play is over so the audience doesn't throw rotten fruit at you. Word gets around fast. You'll have to tell him after the matinee on Sunday."

"Uh, we have to go back to school on Sunday," said Chickie. "My parents won't like it if we miss classes on Monday." I found her sudden zeal for class attendance and for pleasing her parents exasperating.

"Which reminds me, you'll also have to tell your parents about this, Chickie," I said. She looked at me blankly and said nothing. She had enough sense to stifle open defiance. Her expression turned to worry. Perhaps she was already in trouble with her parents. I was not sympathetic. "So, I'll call Teri in the morning and ask her to meet us after sheep shearing. You'll apologize to her. Teddy can take responsibility for telling his parents. If he doesn't, I will. Let's get some sleep."

Sleep was a lovely notion, but it wouldn't come easily. My mind was crowded with dire thoughts. My aching legs and back gratefully embraced the coolness of the sheets, and I sighed with relief. Moonlight streamed through my window and onto the carpet. I considered getting up to close the blinds but was too tired. The moonlight offered a sweet cheerfulness. It assured me that dawn was hours away and that I could hole up a while before facing the circus to come.

I was seized by irrational night thinking. News of the girls' involvement in Teddy's fraud would travel fast. *Much Ado* cast members would spread the tale and on it would go. Lesser news finds its way into the local newspaper on a daily basis. What if reporters showed up at my door? Would I give them Lauren and Chickie's contact information? No, but it would be tempting. Thank heaven my guests are mostly from out of town; they would be unaware of the episode.

Other slings and arrows were sure to follow. Mort would lecture me about being too lenient with Lauren and too tolerant of Chickie. Rita and Pink would remain loyal, but they would give Lauren the cold shoulder indefinitely. Mary Porter would sigh, pity me, and chalk it up to my being an overburdened single parent, a tiresome stereotype. Stephanie and Robert were sure to use the incident as a cudgel. The thought of Bea and Carolyn Mawbrey's pontifications upon hearing the news was too aggravating to think about. I'd have to water the geraniums at night.

What would Lawrence think of us when he heard that my daughter had plotted to deceive all those people? First impressions are lasting. He'd already witnessed unusual behavior while residing with us that week. I wanted him to know that his nephew had married a girl from decent, principled people. After our perilous episodes and Lauren's lack of good judgment, Lawrence was sure to have misgivings about Robert's new family. I consoled myself by thinking that as a college professor he would be acquainted with the erratic behavior of young adults. Perhaps he'd make allowances.

Lawrence and I still hadn't spoken about his note. He wrote that I'd captured his attention at the wedding. Was it possible for Lawrence and me to make a life together? Again, I wavered in my thinking about him. His arms around me would feel so good, so consoling. His eyes held such a magical connection, and his skin was so inviting. He was undoubtedly a tender lover; I needed tenderness. Ah, damn that night thinking.

My anxiety fest was interrupted by a knock at my door. Since it was one o'clock a.m., the knock was alarming. I hopped out of bed, grabbed my robe, and raked a comb through my hair. Adrenaline surged through my tired body to the point of pain and heat rose in my cheeks. The knock came again, this time prompting my anger. How dare he? I knew he was too good to be true.

"Who is it?" I inquired, sharply.

"Lauren," came the response. Greatly relieved, I opened the door.

"Are you okay?" I asked, softening my tone.

"No. I can't sleep. Chickie fell asleep, but I can't. Can we talk?"

"Come in," I said. We made ourselves comfortable on my bed.

"Why is your face so red, Mom?"

"I couldn't sleep either, and it's warm in here."

"You're awake because you're upset with me, aren't you? I'm ashamed of what we did. It was so juvenile. I felt sorry for Teddy. As soon as I saw him on the floor like that, I knew it was a mistake. It was like a bad dream. I wanted to make him get up."

"Glad you didn't do that," I said.

"I don't know how I'm gonna show my face around here for a long time. Chickie says she isn't worried about it. She says what we did will make us folk heroes."

"Folk heroes?" I inquired.

"Yeah, like when people get a reputation for doing something outrageous or a little crazy and other people start telling tall tales about them."

"So, your goal in life is to be like Paul Bunyan or Johnny Appleseed?"

"Not really. Sometimes Chickie has stupid ideas. She also thought that if Teddy had to go to the hospital that cute police officer might show up, and maybe she could get a date with him. He showed up, but there wasn't time for that."

"So, she was less concerned about Teddy and his family than about getting a date with Officer Hines?"

"Something like that. Oh, I don't know. I just wish the whole stupid thing hadn't happened. I didn't want to hurt anyone, especially Teri. She seems like a nice lady."

"She may take your apology better than you think, but you must apologize."

"I get that."

"Good," I said firmly.

"There's something else."

"What?" I braced myself.

"Can I tell you tomorrow?"

"Better tell me now."

"I'm too tired. Tomorrow, okay? Please?"

"You and Chickie didn't kill anybody, did you?"

"Mom!"

"Okay, then I suppose it can wait."

"Good night, Mom."

"Good night."

"Love you."

I hesitated in order to convey my disappointment. "Love you, too."

"By the way, Paul Bunyan wasn't a real person."

"Good night, Lauren."

I was shot and past caring about Paul Bunyan or even about the other thing Lauren wanted to tell me. Her sincere contrition affected me like a sedative. I breathed a sigh of relief and slept until the alarm rang.

CHAPTER 24

Shearing Day

The night had been all too short; I wasn't rested. My cell phone rang as I headed for the shower. "Hi, Honey. Sorry for callin' so early," said Rita. "I had to catch you before your sheep man shows up. What happened last night? Somethin' shook you up. And don't tell me it was nothin' 'cause I won't believe it."

Rita would find out soon, anyway, and I needed to unload. "Lauren and Chickie did something that's got me really rattled. I can hardly bring myself to talk about it."

"Did they snatch off Mr. Silvio's hairpiece?"

"No, but it's gonna be the talk of the town anyway," I said, dialing the water in the shower to hot.

"I warned you about Chickie Stampler, didn't I?" Rita said.

"Rita, when kids grow up, they choose their own friends. Besides, Lauren's just as guilty as Chickie."

"What'd they do?"

"They were in on Teddy Bennett's collapse at the play last night. It was all a fake."

Rita paused. "No way! Ya mean he did that on purpose? Why?"

"I guess they thought it would help get Teri and Jerry together if they rode to the hospital together."

"Backfired big time, didn't it? Too bad they got Jerry back with his first wife, though I'm not sure Teri's missin' much."

"Well, that's not our call. I guess she loves him."

"Now, you can't let those girls go back to Muncie and leave you here to face all the talk. What are you gonna do?"

"We're gonna meet with Teri and Teddy this afternoon and get everything out in the open. Let the chips fall where they may. You can't tell anybody about this for a couple of days—not even Pink. Promise me."

"You know I can't keep secrets from Pinky, Honey."

"Promise!"

"Okay. Okay."

"I've gotta go. Gotta get the sheep ready."

"Wait, Honey. What about your other problem? What are you gonna do about the hunk and his little note? Isn't he waitin' for some kind of an answer?"

"I'm working on it," I said.

"Better work fast."

"I know. Gotta run." I pulled on old jeans and a long-sleeved cotton work shirt. The aroma of coffee filled the air as I made my way to the kitchen. Lawrence was at the kitchen table again pecking away at his tablet

"Morning," he said, quite chipper. "Sleep well?"

"Sure." I cheerfully lied. "How about you?" Making eye contact was uncomfortable since I'd been thinking about him in the night, and the *Much Ado* deception was clinging to me like a leech. Lawrence would find out about the deception in due time, but at that moment I was in a hurry and too ashamed to talk about it.

"Not bad. Thought I'd get an early start," said Lawrence. "The book is finally coming together. The coffee is great; better have some. No cream now." He gave me a wink and a charming smile.

"Thanks," I said, pulling two thermoses from the cupboard. "I'll take some out to the barn for Mort, too. He's gonna meet me in a few minutes. Have to separate the lambs from the ewes and comb the ewes before the shearer gets here."

"How come you shear sheep in July? Don't they need the wool for protection?"

"Harlowe Barnes, my shearer, usually comes in the spring before the ewes drop their lambs, but his wife got sick, so it didn't happen. I did a rough shear myself to help with lambing, but the wool's gotta go now."

"They're Merinos, aren't they?"

"How did you know?"

Lawrence nodded toward his computer. "Looked 'em up. What do you do with the wool?"

"Harlowe buys the fleeces from me and sells them to crafters," I said. I poured the steaming coffee and brazenly added a splash of cream. "Wish I had a Danish to go with this."

"Merino wool must be valuable. Do you make much money on it?"

I chuckled. "Harlowe pays for the fleeces, but by the time I pay for his services . . . well, let's just say I'm not getting rich off wool. In the long run, after feeding them and paying vet bills, I usually lose money. A small herd is an expensive hobby, an indulgence you could say."

"I see," Lawrence said. "We all need indulgences. I have a couple myself."

"Like coffee for example?" I asked.

"Yep, coffee and collecting first-edition books. That's become an obsession, I'm afraid. And I spend too much on my old sports car. I'm a terrible mechanic. I break stuff and then take the car to a real mechanic." If those were Lawrence's only indulgences, he truly was a marvel.

"I own two hundred cookbooks," I said. "I get it about books."

"Want help this morning?"

"With the sheep? Oh, well, it's a dirty job," I replied, genuinely surprised that he would offer. You'll be cleaning sheep's backends and picking stuff out of the wool. Harlowe pays less if the fleeces are dirty."

"So, you think I've never done dirty jobs?"

"Sorry, but you always look squeaky clean," I said. Lawrence laughed.

"Robert might have some old clothes with him. I'll wake him up."

"At this hour? You're kidding?"

"Nope. Don't want him to get lazy."

"I'll ask Mort to bring a pair of boots for you. He'll have something that will do," I said in a loud voice since Lawrence had already left the kitchen.

I could have raised the topic of Lawrence's note then and there, but time was short and after talking about wool prices, indulgences, and sheep's rear ends, a more serious and delicate discussion seemed out of place. It also appeared that Lawrence had little interest in talking seriously about anything. I should also have told him about the *Much Ado* disaster, but it was so early, and that topic was still stuck in my throat.

Mort had already penned the ewes and lambs in the barn when Lawrence and I entered. He'd opened the big track doors to admit the morning light. The ewes and lambs examined us suspiciously as if they knew something was up. Mort supplied Lawrence with fairly clean coveralls and overshoes. The getup looked all wrong on Lawrence. I laughed when he struck a Superman pose.

We set up a configuration of four pens. Mort had gathered the fifteen ewes and twenty lambs in the largest pen. From that pen we would pull the ewes as needed to a second pen for combing. Harlowe could then pull them to a shearing pen. Once sheared, the ewes would be held in a fourth pen where they would be sprayed for insects and for any infection caused by nicks from the shearing blade. Finally, the ewes would be returned to their lambs.

Lawrence took to combing wool like it was his life's work. Mort pulled the ewes away from their bleating lambs, and Lawrence and I dislodged litter from the fleeces. It wasn't long before our knees and backs ached. I handle my sheep often, so they are generally unafraid and docile.

"I suppose you've been doing this since you were a kid," said Lawrence.

"No, my father didn't like sheep. Black Angus cattle were his thing. They were beautiful, but cattle are too much for me to handle. I bought my first flock of Merinos when I opened the inn. Guests love feeding them, and I don't have to worry about anybody getting hurt."

"Do you compete with other sheep people for the best wool?"

"No," I said, smiling. "I'm not the competitive type—well, not anymore. I consider it a win to keep them alive and healthy." Lawrence continued working with few words between us. It was as if his note and his touch had never happened. While transferring sheep, our hands touched frequently. I tried to concentrate on the job, but it wasn't easy. Combing wool is monotonous and leaves plenty of space for the mind to wander. At least the smell of sheep overpowered Lawrence's musky after-shave lotion.

I excused myself and stepped outside to call Teri; her line was busy. Fearing that the tone of my voice might be alarming, I didn't leave a message but resolved to try her number again shortly.

It was nearly ten o'clock when we heard the sound of an engine roar up to the barn and cut off. I assumed Harlowe Barnes had finally arrived in his noisy diesel pickup and would soon join us in the barn. After several minutes, I found him leaning against his truck and casually gliding his shearing blades over a sharpening stone. His tall, lank body was dressed in what appeared to be the same coveralls he'd worn for the past several shearing sessions. I've never seen him without his faded Cincinnati Reds cap. Though probably sixty, Harlowe is still physically powerful and has the largest hands I've ever seen. "They ready?" he asked. He sacrificed no word of greeting or small talk as he entered the barn, blades in hand.

"They're ready," I replied. "I have some help this morning. This is Lawrence Milner. He's my son-in-law's uncle. He's staying with us this week."

"Uh-huh," Harlowe muttered. His eyes scanned the sheep. "Look pretty good." He tipped his cap slightly in Mort's direction. Mort returned a quick nod but kept a poker face.

"Thanks," said Lawrence with an exaggerated smile. "Do you like my coveralls?"

"The sheep, ah mean," said Harlowe. "Looks like you got 'em cleaner 'n last time."

"Well, Lawrence is helping," I said. "You can get started. We only have three more to comb out," I wedged the gate open slightly to admit Harlowe to the combing pen. The process began without further discussion. He grabbed the first ewe and set her upright on her rear end with her back resting on his legs.

"I'd like to watch if you don't mind," said Lawrence. "Is there a routine to shearing? I mean, do you shear each one exactly the same way? And may I ask why you use those hand clippers instead of electric ones?"

"What these? They're not clippers," Harlowe scoffed. "They're shearin' blades. Keep 'em sharp. Those 'lectric jobs cut too close. Ya want some wool left on 'em." Lawrence was unaffected by Harlowe's brusque manners. He had no fear of Harlowe and appeared to be annoying him with questions on purpose.

"Mind if I watch?" Lawrence asked again. By now, Mort was savoring their exchange.

"Don't care. Just stay out o' mah way." Harlowe grabbed the shears.

"Sure thing. So, what's your method?" Lawrence reiterated with all seriousness.

Cradling the subdued ewe's head between his legs and hunching over her, Harlowe began narrating each blow of his shears for Lawrence. Mort and I stood by in amazed silence. In all the years we'd known Harlowe, he'd barely spoken to us. I'd long since given up trying to get to know him, perhaps wrongfully assuming that he didn't like me or my sheep. And being a man of few words himself, Mort was not inclined to waste talk on unreceptive ears.

"Clear her belly off first thing, see," Harlowe said. "Then ah work 'em easy like 'round her teats and privates. Ya gotta be careful there. Easy to cut 'em there. Use your left hand to pull the skin taut away from 'er belly, see." He demonstrated each blow until throwing an intact fleece to the floor.

"Very impressive. How long have you been shearing?" asked Lawrence.

"Learned from mah dad as a kid," Harlowe said. "Been doin' it myself for 'bout fifty years."

Lawrence continued his interrogation. "You work fast. I suppose you've been in shearing contests."

"Did all time 'n mah twenties. Could han' shear a sheep quick as ya please. Went to New Zealand once 'n' got in a contest. Couldn't hold a candle to them boys. They could hand shear off a sheep in no time. Never seen nothin' like it."

"So, what happens to the fleeces now?" asked Lawrence.

"I take some to mah wife and her knittin' 'n' weavin' friends. Sell a lot of it on the wool market though. Good market for it 'round here. You'd be surprised."

With only a few more ewes to comb, I was anxious to finish my part of the job. Lawrence pelted Harlowe with questions about his southern Indiana roots for several minutes and then climbed the fence back into the combing pen with me to finish.

"Interesting guy," Lawrence muttered.

"I've never heard him talk so much," I said. "He must like you."

"Maybe he's in a good mood today."

The exchange between Lawrence and Harlowe had nothing to do with Harlowe's mood. It was due to Lawrence's remarkable gift for people; I admired him for it. Again, my mind wandered into the territory of extending time in his company.

The barn had grown warm and stuffy despite Mort's strategically positioned box fans. Harlowe was sweating as much as he was drinking. He'd removed his coveralls and was stripped to a t-shirt and baggy shorts. I felt guilty for asking a man of his age to shear sheep in such heat and couldn't wait for him to finish. Even in the heat, he pulled the skittish ewes away from us one after another, toiling with incredible stamina.

The morning was nearly gone, and I still hadn't reached Teri. I tried calling her again, but the call went to voicemail. Panic was setting in. I was desperate for the girls to meet with her before the play that night. Teddy was sure to leak the details of his trickery to someone, probably Tom Laughlin, and the story would take wings.

Teri would be hurt. I wanted her to hear about the grand deception from Teddy and the girls before anyone else.

Harlowe maneuvered the last ewe into place and lightened her woolly burden. I promised myself that next time I would not leave the choice of shearers to Mort. I would find a less eccentric shearer who believes in electric shears.

Harlowe rested on a hay bale while Mort watered the flock. Lawrence and I gathered the fleeces from the floor and bundled them according to Harlowe's exacting directions. We loaded them into his truck and secured them with a tarp. The process felt endless. Harlowe stepped to the pump and plunged his head under the cold stream. He then walked laboriously to his truck and climbed into the cab. "Rough one," he said, through the open cab window. "Next year, Feb'rary. Give 'em shade 'n' plenty o' water the next couple weeks. Ya might lose some of 'em if you're not watchin' out for 'em. Awful bad heat."

"I'll be careful," I said.

"Enjoyed talkin' to ya," Harlowe said to Lawrence. "Got somethin' for ya. Mah wife makes 'em." He handed Lawrence a lovely multicolored woolen stocking cap. Lawrence thanked him and made a fuss over the softness. Turning to me, he said, "I'll weigh this lot and send you a check by the end of the week. Remember, Feb'rary next time." His truck left the barnyard and chugged down the lane.

"Well, I guess you rate," Mort told Lawrence. "Never given us anything but a hard time."

"Nice fella," Lawrence said. Mort shook his head in wonder.

Robert came sprinting to us and announced that he and Stephanie had prepared lunch. I was hungry enough to take my chances with whatever they were serving. Mort and I could put the barn and the sheep back in order after lunch. For now, the sheep were watered and out of the sun. I tried Teri's number again. No answer.

The menu of grilled cheese sandwiches and canned tomato soup was a feast to my growling stomach. Steph was stirring and Robert was grilling as Lawrence and I passed through the kitchen. "Whoa!" exploded Robert. "Who let the sheep in here?"

"Did you think we'd smell like roses?" asked Lawrence. "You could have helped, you know."

"You should take your clothes off outside," said Robert, ignoring Lawrence's remark. Stephanie, Lawrence, and I stopped in our tracks and stared at Robert for the ludicrous remark, although his suggestion did have its merits on some levels.

"Is there any iced tea left?" I shouted to Robert on my way to a shower.

"Would like some, too. Lots of ice. No sugar!" Lawrence exclaimed, tossing the remark over his shoulder as he hurried toward his guest room.

"What about Uncle Mort?" called Stephanie.

"He went home to clean up," I replied. "He'll be back in a few minutes."

"What about the brats?" Robert yelled. "Shouldn't they be awake by now?"

I wasn't ready to answer Robert's question, so I shut my bedroom door without responding. Soon a cooling stream of water and my favorite French milled soap washed the sheep scent from my body. But what about the brats? Why were they still sleeping? Why weren't they awake and grappling with the mess they'd created? And why was I trying to untangle it for them? My mother's sage words when I was twenty years old flowed back to me along with the shower spray, "Jill, to be treated like an adult, you must act like one."

"Thank you, Mona," I muttered aloud. That was the backup I needed. Lauren and Chickie were soon to be awakened.

CHAPTER 25

Coming Clean

Robert had already called Lauren and Chickie to lunch when I arrived in the kitchen. As I suspected, they balked at eating tomato soup for breakfast, but Robert refused to pacify them. "Soup not good enough for divas?" he asked.

"Well, I'm not a fan of soup for breakfast," said Chickie.

"Sorry to say, we're fresh out of Eggs Benedict," said Robert, "and it's lunchtime for civilized people. Maybe you should try your parents' house. You might get something more to your liking there." Chickie ignored Robert's remark.

"Can't we have some coffee first," asked Lauren.

"Sure," said Robert. "Make yourself a cup and bring it to the table. We've gone to the trouble, so you can eat with us and be sociable. Besides, for some odd reason, Steph wants a final meal with you. We're leaving tomorrow morning, remember?" Robert plated enough sandwiches for an army. It distressed me that Stephanie communicated with Lauren consistently through him. Again, I blamed myself that the girls were distant. Had to be my fault.

"There's a strawberry pie in the fridge for dessert," I interjected cheerfully as if strawberry pie would produce *détente.*

The sandwiches were nearly cold and the soup slightly scorched by the time Lawrence and Mort joined us at the table. As with most family meals, the diners' moods varied widely. Mort and Lawrence were pleased with themselves over the shearing. Stephanie and Robert were broody, perhaps due to her nagging dissertation and his ungraded freshman themes. Lauren and Chickie, with their matted hair and rumpled lounge wear, were glum.

It was time to broach the subject of the *Much Ado* deception with everyone. Keeping Stephanie, Robert, Lawrence, and Mort in the dark was unfair and would surely lead to more trouble. Rita had undoubtedly leaked the news to Pink already. The time was right for the girls to come clean.

"I've had a great week," Lawrence announced. "Parade, fireworks, boat ride, Shakespeare, and sheep. Thought I'd be holed up with the New Deal, but look at all that's happened." He didn't know the half of it.

"It's been a pleasure to have you here, Lawrence," I said. "Now we know you better. The door is always open for you to come back." I lifted my iced tea tumbler in a toasting gesture to which Lawrence alone reciprocated. I changed my mind again suddenly and thought it might be best to forget about Lawrence's love note altogether, to chalk it up as a whim. Maybe he'd had too much wine when he wrote it and had forgotten his own words. Maybe I'd misinterpreted his advances in the barn, or maybe my chilly reaction had put him off the idea of "something more" for us. My relief was blunted by a twinge of disappointment.

Robert's cell phone rang. He stepped away from the table but stayed within earshot. "Hey, Pink," he said. "Tonight? Yeah, sounds good. Gonna be nice weather. What time? Can we bring anything? They're all right here; I'll invite them, too. I don't have any fishing gear with me. Should I pick up bait? Okay. Okay. Sure, I'll ask him. Sure. Sounds good. Yeah. See you then."

"Fishing?" I inquired.

"Tonight," said Robert. "Pink's keyed up. We're all invited. He's got all the gear and bait. He wants to go out at dusk."

The kitchen doorbell rang. I stiffened, sure that it wouldn't be a brown truck with a nice package. I opened the door and stared into the unsmiling faces of Teri and Teddy Bennett. To say they looked aggrieved, wouldn't cover it.

"Come in," I said, resigned. "Have a seat." Suspicious of this surprise visit but wanting to be polite, Lawrence and Robert fetched extra chairs. Teri and Teddy sat down somberly. Tension filled the air. Lauren and Chickie sat up straight in anticipation of what was coming.

"Has there been a death?" Robert inquired.

"What's going on, Mom?" asked Stephanie. She drilled me and then Teri with her eyes like a committed inquisitor. Mort sighed deeply and folded his arms as if asking "Now what?" Lawrence pushed his chair back from the table.

"I came to tell Lauren and Chickie that I'm not mad at them," said Teri, sweetly. She shifted her gaze timidly from me to the girls. "Teddy told me that it was your idea, and I thank you for trying to help."

"Wait a minute!" Chickie protested to Teddy. "You told her it was our idea? You little weasel! We didn't make you play dead. You did it on your own. You asked us to help, and we came up with some creative ideas, that's all!"

"You guys were the masterminds," said Teddy.

"Masterminds!" exclaimed Lauren. "You came to us all pathetic and got us involved. Don't you dare blame us."

"Okay, okay. You didn't actually make me do it," said Teddy.

"Let's get this straight," said Robert. "Are you talking about last night? Do you mean you all staged his freaky fall? He faked it? Oh, this is rich! This is a whole new level of crazy for you. Congratulations!"

"Jill, I think Teddy and the girls should tell Mr. Silvio and the cast the truth right away, don't you?" asked Teri.

"We've talked about that," I responded. "They certainly should, but they should apologize to you first."

"We do, Mrs. Bennett. We're sorry. It was a dumb idea," said Lauren. Teri smiled weakly.

"You knew about this, Mother?" asked Stephanie. "Did you try to stop them?"

"Good heavens!" I blurted. "I wasn't in on it. I found out by accident."

"Why would you do such a thing?" Stephanie asked Lauren.

"It's a long story," said Lauren, scowling at Teddy.

"Maybe after the Sunday matinee?" Teri suggested, trying to keep the conversation on track.

"That should start the cast party off with a bang," Robert said, gleefully.

"The cast party is tonight. We're not going," said Lauren.

"We're not?" asked Chickie.

"Good idea if you'd like to keep your skin," said Stephanie.

"The cast probably knows already. Did you tell anybody else about this?" Robert asked Teddy.

"I told Laughlin, but I made him promise to keep his trap shut." Teddy shook his fist.

Eyes rolled in unison. "They all know," Robert concluded, "and I'll bet they know who helped you with the creative idea."

"I don't care if the cast knows," said Chickie. "It's none of their business."

"It's kind of their business when another actor has a heart attack on stage," said Robert.

"It was during the curtain call," said Chickie. "It didn't mess up anybody's lines."

"It was supposed to be like a seizure, not a heart attack," said Teddy. "I had some seizures when I was a kid."

"Oh, I beg your pardon, a seizure," said Robert.

"What about Mr. Silvio?" Lauren asked Chickie. "We've got to explain it to him."

"If I were you, I'd go to his house right now," said Stephanie. "He needs to know the truth before the play tonight. If he hears it from somebody else, you'll be toast."

It was finally decided that Teri would drive Teddy, Lauren, and Chickie to Mr. Silvio's house with all haste in hopes of catching him before he left for the set in the park. Lauren and Chickie jumped into shorts and put on baseball caps to hide their bedheads and rushed away with Teri and Teddy. Though Lauren pleaded with me to come along, I refused. I wasn't going to rescue them or make excuses for them. There were no excuses.

Stephanie, Robert, Mort, Lawrence, and I remained at the table without speaking for several awkward seconds before Stephanie piped up. "Uncle Lawrence, you must wonder about my family. Apparently, my sister has lost her marbles."

"I hope it's not genetic," said Robert. Stephanie rolled her eyes again.

"She's gonna find her way," said Mort. "She's a good kid." His words warmed my heart.

"I can tell you both take after your mother, Steph," said Lawrence, "so I know your sister will be okay." I was embarrassed by Lawrence's patronizing remark. In reality, he knew very little about me.

"Strawberry pie, anyone?" I asked. I went to the refrigerator without waiting for responses. Lawrence chuckled in response to my diversion. While serving pie, I changed my mind again and was seized by an urge to talk with him about his note as soon as possible. Time was growing short, and I had nothing to lose now. He had been exposed to Merrick family trials and tribulations since his arrival. If I made a fool of myself, what difference would it make? I had to be honest with him if we were even to become friends, much less "something more." I would ask him to take a walk with me after lunch. The trouble was that I still didn't know exactly what I wanted to say to him.

With a mouth full of pie, Mort announced, "I'm thinkin' 'bout the sheep. Barnes is right. They can get sunburnt and sunstroke. I'm thinkin' they'd be better off in my woods for a couple of weeks for the shade."

"I thought you were letting the trees grow back in your woods," I said. "The sheep will strip the undergrowth, and what about the fence? It probably needs work?"

"The trees can come back after that," said Mort. "They can forage, and you can feed 'em, too. The fence needs some mendin', but it'll hold 'em. There's no 'lectric waterer out there, but we can rig up hoses that'll do in a pinch. Let's get 'em shifted this afternoon.

"This afternoon?" I asked with objection in my voice.

"Yep. Let's do it while we've got Lawrence captive. You'll help, won't you, Lawrence?" Mort was banking on a positive response.

"That's asking too much," I said. "We've already taken up Lawrence's entire morning with the sheep. He's supposed to be on vacation."

"I volunteered to help and enjoyed it," said Lawrence. "I'm at your service this afternoon, so point me in the right direction."

"Do you need us for this little exercise?" Robert asked.

Resistant but resigned, I asked Mort, "Will we drive them down the lane or haul them in your trailer?"

"It depends," he replied. "Do you want to chase 'em in the fields all afternoon or get 'em all there together? We'll load 'em up."

"How can we help?" Robert persisted.

Looking around, I said, "How about cleaning up the kitchen?" Robert and Stephanie acquiesced.

CHAPTER 26

Lawrence, Hero Once More

Hauling sheep was the last thing I wanted to do that afternoon, but I learned long ago not to cross Mort when he's set on a plan. Besides, he was probably right about the sheep. I didn't want to lose any of them due to negligence.

I'd been hoping to stop the world and talk with Lawrence alone and uninterrupted—not on the fly and not while moving sheep. I had rebuffed his advances and for some reason that I couldn't justify even to myself, I needed to explain. As I pulled another set of work clothes out of the drawers, I began to rehearse the spiel I would give him at the right moment. I would tell him how much I liked him and express my gratitude for the many ways he'd come to my aid. The words in my head became muddled after that. How would I end the conversation? Did I really want to say goodbye . . . have a nice life? Thoughts of him had infested my brain; his essence had leached into my heart. I remembered the feeling from when I first met Phil at college. Saying goodbye to Phil for even a few days was physically painful. The situation with Lawrence seemed almost as dire yet ludicrous at the same time.

The shearing and the visit from Teri and Teddy had been exhausting, and now we were going to round up sheep in 90-degree weather. Lawrence, in fresh blue jeans and a faded Colts t-shirt, walked to the barn with me. Everywhere, my gardens called out for attention. The boxwoods along the driveway screamed for trimming; herbs yelled for harvesting; rose bushes begged for spraying, and the weeds among the vegetables mocked me with perverse joy. I narrated these concerns to Lawrence as we walked. "We'll be out of your hair tomorrow," he said, cheerfully, "so you'll be able to catch up."

"I'm not anxious for you to leave," I said. "The place just gets away from me so fast in the summer, and now I'm not sure if Teri will still want to help me. The girls have made a mess of things."

"I have friends with kids. Parenting makes my job seem like a piece of cake."

"Did you ever want to have children?" I ventured to ask.

"I was married for a short time about twenty years ago. We talked about having children, but we were both selfish and focused on our careers. We thought our research would set the world on fire I suppose. She's a biologist and has done well for herself."

"Are you still friends?" I asked. We rolled open the front door of the barn. Mort's truck and stock trailer were already kicking up dust in the lane between our farms. He was wasting no time.

"Nah, she remarried and lives in Boston," said Lawrence. "She never had children either. I envy you for your family. Sometimes I wish I'd had kids. I suppose I should tell you that I haven't always been the most reliable guy in the world, but I've changed a lot of things about myself. It's taken work, I'll tell you."

I had no idea why Lawrence was confiding in me to the point of confessing his faults, but I appreciated his little disclosure. He was far from the tell-all type. "Well, we all have stuff to work on," I replied.

"I hear you've had a couple of goes at marriage."

"Yes, I have," I said. I wondered what else Lawrence had heard about me from Steph and Robert. "I'll tell you about my life sometime when you need a good snooze."

"I'll hold you to that," he said, gazing at me intently.

The ewes and lambs had had a stressful morning also, so they were lethargic and easy to handle. Our gloves lay on hay bales where we'd tossed them earlier. Mort backed the trailer to the front of the barn and let down the ramp. "I'm gonna walk the fence line in the woods and check for breaks," he informed us while unhitching the trailer. "Let's take 'em in two loads. You can start loading half of 'em now. I'll be back shortly."

I was not enthusiastic. "Maybe we should walk the fence line today and move them tomorrow," I suggested. "Walking the fence will take time, and breaks will have to be mended." Mort gave me an unhappy look—the kind of look Jimmy the Monster dished out when I contradicted him. I resented the look, but this was Mort not Jimmy.

"Okay, tell ya what, Lawrence can walk half the fence, and I'll walk the other half while you load the first bunch. Can ya do it?" asked Mort.

"Of course I can," I replied, in a tone bordering on snotty. I was irritated by Mort's condescension. He was pushing me for no good reason. "But I don't know if Lawrence will want to get his clothes full of burs and bull thistles out there."

"I'll be fine," said Lawrence, gamely and with a wink. "But can you handle the sheep by yourself?"

"Yes!" I said, icily. Mort and Lawrence climbed into the truck and headed toward the little woods between our homes. Dust rose from the washboard ruts. There was no hurry to load sheep into the trailer since they would be gone for some time. I jammed a couple of hay bales together, stretched out and closed my eyes. It was probably uncouth for a woman to nap on hay, but I was exhausted and beyond caring.

The hay smelled sweet. The barn was cozy, breezy, and warm. I could hear the sheep stirring, breathing, munching. As I drifted into slumber, strange notions came and went. Maybe I would stop inviting my daughters to stay with me at the same time. I would give up being the mediator and let them work out their relationship. The weeds in the gardens waved to me and laughed, Lawrence's face and forearms appeared and disappeared. I fantasized that he could move to Noblesville and teach at a university in Indianapolis. Maybe we could build a sheep empire together. I don't like to iron, so he'd have to iron his own clothes. Our guests would love him and his coffee. Pink would give us a good deal on a new pickup truck—a red truck would be nice. I had told the wise woman that I was a whole person, but was I?

I'm not sure how long the delirium lasted before I was awakened by a shadowy figure standing over me and repeating, "Mrs. Merrick, Mrs. Merrick." Overheated and sluggish, I managed to sit upright and bring my mind into consciousness. I was startled to realize that I was staring at the face of Jerry Bennett. His face was red, and he was shifting unsteadily from one foot to the other.

"Mr. Bennett?" I asked.

"Yeah, Jerry Bennett," he slurred. His eyes were bloodshot. "I'm looking for your daughter and her friend. My son said they put him up to that stunt last night; I wanna talk to them about it."

As I got to my feet, blood rushed to my head and anger rose in my chest and throat. How did he have the nerve to confront me in my own barn? And though I could understand Jerry's upset with the girls, they should not take the blame alone. It was Teddy who took the fall, so scapegoating Lauren and Chickie was unacceptable. It was also extremely aggravating that he'd approach me in his current state. How dare he come on my property intoxicated!

My thoughts flashed back to Jimmy the Monster's drinking and bullying. I had grown to despise Jimmy by the time we parted. My contempt transferred easily to Jerry. Given the chance, I would have dumped a bucket of cold water over his head, but that would have escalated the situation. I thought it best to be careful under the present circumstance, but Jerry had better watch his step.

"The girls aren't here," I said, mustering all possible composure. "Teri and Teddy were here earlier. They all went to find Mr. Silvio and let him know what happened. The girls meant no harm, Mr. Bennett. In their naive way, they thought they were helping Teddy. They were in the wrong, and they know it."

"How could they help Teddy by making him a laughing stock?" said Jerry. "The whole town knows he faked that fall last night. It puts me in a bind. You can see that, right?" Jerry's voice was growing louder. He stepped a bit closer to me and wagged his finger in my face. "The boy already has a reputation in town. We've been trying to keep him out of trouble and now this. When this kind of stuff gets around, people don't want to deal with you. What about my business?"

"That's not Jill's problem," came a voice from out of nowhere. Lawrence suddenly stood between Jerry and me. Good heavens, I thought, can this be happening again?

Jerry took a wide stance to steady himself. "I don't know you, do I?" he asked.

"I'm a friend of Jill's, and I'm not going to let you threaten her."

"I wasn't threatening her," said Jerry. "I'm upset about last night. Just trying to get to the bottom of what happened."

"What happened is that two young ladies thought they were helping your son by getting his parents back together," said Lawrence. "Their idea was unorthodox, but their hearts were in the right place. They meant no harm, and I believe they learned a tough lesson."

Jerry plopped down on a bale of hay totally dejected. "Which parents?" he asked.

"They were trying to get you and Teri back together," I said. "That's what Teddy wants you know. Teddy told the girls that his mother was coming to the play on a different night, but she must have changed her plans. They don't know her, so they didn't know she was there until she got into the ambulance. They thought Teri would ride with you."

"Does Teri want me back?" Jerry asked in a clueless manner.

I threw my arms in the air. "You'd have to ask her yourself, but I think so. Although she's pretty hurt about last night."

"Do you have any idea how crappy that was for me?" Jerry asked. "Both women standing there. My lord."

"I can't imagine," I said, projecting as little sympathy as possible.

"I'm gonna go," Jerry said. "I shouldn't have bothered you, Mrs. Merrick, and your friend. I need to find Teri and Ted. Maybe I've been an ass."

"Maybe you have," I said. I was glad Lawrence was still standing between us.

"You'd better stick your head under that pump before you go," said Lawrence. "Shouldn't drive in your condition. You could kill somebody."

"Yeah, yeah, you're right," said Jerry. I beat Jerry to the pump and lifted the handle. He stuck his head under the cold-water stream for as long as he could stand it. I wished it would have been longer. His hair and shirt were dripping wet, but I didn't offer to fetch a towel. Soon he looked steadier on his feet and seemed to be sobering up. "I'm gonna call Teri. Maybe she'll forgive me."

"I suggest you call Teddy, too. He needs you," I added.

"Yeah," he repeated as he squeezed into his sports car. He was soon out of sight, and I said a prayer for him and for others on the road. My anger at Jerry Bennett welled in my throat. He'd straightened up quickly when Lawrence intervened. What would have happened if Lawrence hadn't been there? Jerry thought it was fine to bully me, but he wouldn't try to bully Lawrence. I didn't like Jerry Bennett.

"You just can't stay out of trouble, can you?" said a smirking Lawrence. "How am I gonna leave you on your own?"

I shrugged, sighed, and sat back down on the hay bale, still trying to clear my head from an overheated sleep. "Where's Mort? Why did you come back here?" I asked.

"Forgot my gloves. It's a pretty rough patch out there. Looks like you were having a rough patch here, too. Did he scare you?"

"No," I said, but that wasn't exactly the truth. "I suppose he has a right to be upset, and I suppose the girls will have to apologize to him, too."

"Mort and I can finish this job, Jill. Why don't you take a break."

"Oh, no," I said. "If Mort thinks this place is too much for me, he'll want me to sell the flock. He already thinks the sheep are an unnecessary expense."

"Have it your way then," said Lawrence. "I'm gonna get back." He pulled on the gloves as he walked toward the big open door.

"Lawrence," I said. He looked back with a slightly self-satisfied grin. "Thanks . . . again."

"You're welcome. Better get those sheep loaded," he said in a slightly bossy tone.

Was Lawrence really telling me what to do or was he kidding? The last thing I wanted was another man giving me orders. I wasn't going to load the sheep. It was rare that I went against Mort's wishes, but forcing my sheep to stand in a hot trailer made no sense. I decided not to make a move until Mort and Lawrence returned. They soon reported that tree branches lay on the fence, and repairs were needed before the sheep could be moved. I felt vindicated and relieved that Lawrence, as my guest, would no longer be pressed into service. I also felt vindicated that I'd been right. Mort grumbled and drove off toward his place. Lawrence and I stood alone, and I knew I must seize the moment. It was time to go over the wall!

"Lawrence, it's time for us to talk," I said.

"Yeah. I've been meaning to talk with you about something, too, but it never seems to be the right time," he said, pulling up a bale next to mine and sitting. His expression was intent as he settled in.

I took a deep breath and said, "I'm not sure how to start this."

"Just start. I'm listening. Just start," he said, looking into my eyes.

I struggled for the right words. "I want to thank you for all the ways you've helped us out this week."

"The pleasure has been all mine. Seems like there's never a dull moment around here. Is that what you wanted to say?"

"Well, not exactly. I wanted . . . I wanted to know if you have some of the same feelings that I have when we're together. I mean, do you feel a chemistry between us?" I was suddenly out on a very skinny limb.

"I do feel a chemistry, and it's strong," he said. "It's funny, but it seems like we've known each other for a long time. Can't believe that we just met."

"That's exactly how I feel," I said. As I struggled to bring up the topic of Lawrence's note, Pink's pickup truck roared up to the barn door. Rita and Pink sprang out of the cab. I sighed.

"Ready to go fishin'?" Pink bellowed.

"Not me," I said, masking my frustration. "But I think Lawrence and Robert and maybe Steph are going."

"Well, the day's awastin' and so are the fish," said Pink, clapping his hands. "Rita's gonna stay here and keep you company, Sugar. I've got everythin' we need. Ready, Lawrence?"

"Sure, I'll grab a few things," Lawrence said. He gave me a sideways smile. "I'll catch up with you later, Jill." I nodded. We'd missed our chance again. This time, I wondered if God or the universe was trying to tell me something. Maybe Lawrence and I were never supposed to talk about his note. Maybe this was a sign to back off and leave it in literary limbo.

The Show Must Go On

The day was wearing on. The overhead fans pushed warm air around the porch as Rita and I made ourselves comfortable on rockers. I gulped iced tea while she sipped wine. I brought her up to speed on the events of the day. Lauren and Chickie were incommunicado since leaving with Teri and Teddy after lunch. They hadn't answered my texts, and I was getting worried. In just a few hours, they would report to the *Much Ado* set for a performance. Given the circumstances, their transition from 21st Century reality to 17th Century comedy would require some real acting.

I'd planned Margherita and Mexicali pizzas for our last family dinner, but that idea was blown to smithereens by the fishing expedition and the uncertainty of Lauren and Chickie's fate. Stephanie texted several photos from the fishing expedition. Lawrence had made the first catch of the afternoon—a large-mouth bass—and displayed it proudly. Mercifully, Pink has a catch-and-release philosophy, so no one would be bringing fish home.

"Relax, Honey," said Rita. "You'll hear from the girls soon. They probably stopped at the drugstore for makeup or shavin' cream or somethin'."

"Shaving cream?" I asked.

"Young girls are obsessed with shavin' their legs, and today they shave everywhere if you know what I mean."

"They're with Teri and Teddy," I said. "I doubt they stopped for shaving cream."

"I hope Ronaldo Silvio wasn't too hard on 'em, but ya have to admit that stunt last night was a humdinger. We were a little crazy at nineteen, but we didn't have that kind of nerve. Remember the night we got your daddy's car stuck on the railroad tracks? If those boys hadn't lifted the car off the tracks, we could have been smashed up. Served us right for thinkin' we could hold our liquor."

"Well, I was the one driving that night," I said. "Lauren probably inherited her foolishness from me."

We watched an unfamiliar car pull into the driveway. "I wonder if it's Ronaldo come to skin your hide," said Rita.

"Thanks for the pep talk," I muttered.

Craig Deluca emerged from his car first, followed by Chickie and Lauren. They ambled up the sidewalk, entered the porch, and sat on rocking chairs in silence. Lauren's eyes were red from crying. She turned her face away from us. Chickie sat with her arms folded defiantly and stared at the floor. Craig stared at the porch ceiling. This continued for several seconds.

"Well?" I inquired. "We were getting worried about you. What happened?" Silence. "Well?" I repeated, searching the girls' faces for answers. "Are you okay?"

"Mr. Silvio's pretty upset," said Craig.

"He's not just upset; he's furious with us," said Lauren. "I've never seen so mad."

"Actually, I have seen him that mad," said Craig. "During a performance of *A Midsummer Night's Dream,* his toupee was kind of off to the side of his head, and none of us told him about it.

He went on stage to introduce the play and then saw himself in a mirror later. Nobody had the nerve to tell him his rug was twisted. He went off on us like a Roman candle after the curtain call."

"Makes sense. He is Italian," Rita said.

"He told us that we'd ruined the play by getting everybody out of character during the curtain call," Lauren continued. "Then he lectured us for fifteen minutes about how important it is to stay in character, no matter what. How were we supposed to do that with Dogberry lying there?"

"He said it was a 'premeditated attempt to break the illusion, which is forbidden in the theatre,'" said Chickie. "He made us feel like criminals. It was a lot of bull."

"Did you explain that you were trying to help Teddy?" I asked.

"Teddy! I don't ever want to hear his name again," said Chickie. "Teddy . . . Dogberry . . . Dingleberry . . . that's what he is. He sat right there with Teri and Silvio and said we'd put him up to it. I hope Big Sue sits on those little creeps. To think we actually went to bat for them."

"I still don't get why you guys just didn't deny it," said Craig, offhandedly. Lauren and Chickie glanced at each other with expressions of hopelessness.

"Because we did help him!" Lauren exclaimed. "But we didn't know his real mother would be there. We told you this."

I sighed and turned to Craig, "How did you get into the act?"

"I was working on the set with Silvio when they showed up. As I see it, there's another problem, too. Verges told Don Pedro that Dogberry faked the dive, so I'd say most of the cast knows already."

"And most of the town," said Chickie.

"And I hate to heap on more trouble," I said, "but Teddy's father was here looking for you earlier. I told him that you were trying to help. Not sure he bought it, but at least he left."

"Sounds like a lynch mob is forming," said Craig.

"That does it!" Chickie blurted. "I'll fix all of them. I won't show up tonight. Silvio will have to beg me to come. The show can't run without me." We gazed at her in disbelief.

"That's the dumbest thing I've ever heard," said Craig. "You wouldn't do that . . . would you? What about the rest of us? We've worked hard."

"You didn't even know your lines until last week," said Chickie. "I knew them better than you."

"Honey, you don't mean it," said Rita. "You're just upset. You know this town; people love somethin' to flap their jaws about. Next week somethin' else will happen, and they'll forget all about this little ruckus. You wouldn't let everybody down like that."

Chickie folded her arms and coldly replied, "Watch me."

"That would be a big mistake," I said. "This thing with Teddy will blow over, but if you don't show up, you'll be labeled. Remember that Mr. Silvio knows the theatre faculty at Ball State."

Lauren jumped to her feet. "We're going tonight, and we're gonna give 'em a great performance," she said. We all stared at her, amazed. "We're gonna go on stage with our heads held high and do exactly what Shakespeare hired us to do. Nobody's running away." She was on fire. My timid daughter had found conviction. We waited for Chickie's response.

Chickie turned to Craig and said, "You wanna run lines with us for a while?"

"Sure, but we have to get something straight first."

"What's that?" Lauren asked.

"Shakespeare didn't employ women as actors . . . only men."

"Oh, shut up!" the girls snapped in unison.

A few moments later, Lauren gave me a pleading look and said, "Mom, will you come to the performance tonight? We need a friendly face in the audience."

"Sure, I'll go," I said, "and Rita will go with me."

"Wouldn't miss it, Darlin'," Rita said in a silky voice. When the thespians retreated to the kitchen, she turned to me, "Are you gonna make me sit through that again?"

"Wouldn't want you to miss it, Darlin'," I said.

Rita phoned Pink and asked him to prepare the pontoon and chill some wine for a cruise after the play. Pink told us not to take any "bullshit" from anybody at the theatre. "Take names and I'll whip butt if anybody gives ya grief," he instructed. "And tell the girls to break a leg." As always, I was thankful to have him in my corner.

Lauren and Chickie were understandably nervous about going to the theatre that evening. The rumor mill was surely grinding away. I pitied them to an extent but hoped they were learning some lessons.

"How will we know who knows?" Lauren asked.

"Trust me. Everybody knows," said Craig.

"If Dogberry tries to speak to me, he's gonna be out cold for real this time," Chickie threatened.

"Remember, you're going to give a great performance," I said. "Shoulders back, heads held high, chests out." Craig gave Rita and me a sweeping bow.

Rita and I drove separately to the theatre. I wanted my own wheels for the evening because I wasn't sure if Robert and Steph would stay for the pontoon ride or take off after fishing. Rita and I met at the park. My stomach was in knots. We arrived early and chose seats near the stage so the majority of the audience wouldn't see our faces. I hoped Lauren and Chickie would see us despite the glaring footlights. In sitting up front, however, we were spotted quickly by Ronaldo Silvio in tux and tails. "Good evening, my dear Mrs. Merrick," he said. He clutched my hands in his soft hands and gave me an uneasy caress. "I'm delighted to see you. The show will be marvelous tonight, so hang on to your hat!"

"I'm glad to see you, too, Ronaldo," I said. "Do you know my friend Rita Restin?"

Mr. Silvio turned to Rita and grasped her hand. "Certainly, I do. Isn't it excellent, Mrs. Restin, that you've come to see our budding stars in action?" Rita smiled politely.

"Ronaldo, I can't tell you how sorry I am for Lauren's involvement in last night's ... eh ... thing," I said, keeping my voice low. "I'd just like to say ... "

"No, no," he interrupted, placing two fingers to his lips. "Say no more, my dear. I came down hard on Charlotte and Lauren this afternoon. Did they tell you?"

"Yes, they did, but ...."

"I did it for their own good. They're young and maybe this play has given them false ideas about deception. I was shocked that they would take part in such a trick. It was my duty to set them straight. They have talent, you know. They also represent our theatre."

"Yes, I know," I interjected, quickly, "but did they give you the reason ... "

"Ah, there's our superintendent. I must go say hello," said Mr. Silvio. He waved and smiled toward a fixed point behind us.

"Ronaldo, I just wanted to say ..."

"Mrs. Merrick, I assure you all is well," he said. He placed a hand on my shoulder. "Charlotte and Lauren will apologize to the cast after the matinee. All will be forgotten." With that, he hurried away.

"Well, that was hopeless," I told Rita.

"Nice try anyway, Honey. Ya know, I couldn't think 'bout anythin' but his toupee. He needs to give it up. There's nothin' wrong with bein' bald. It's time for a new tux, too."

"I hope they're practicing what they'll say to cast," I said.

"I wouldn't ask 'em 'bout it. Better let the chips fall where they may."

The minutes dragged as we waited for opening lines. The footlights were on, but time was standing still. I was afraid to see familiar faces. I was afraid people would look away in disgust or embarrassment when our eyes met. I wanted to be supportive of Lauren and Chickie, but I regretted coming to the play. What a difference one day had made. The night before, I had held my head high and scanned the audience for friendly faces. Now I didn't want to say hello to the person seated next to me.

"Let's get out of here!" I told Rita. "I can't breathe."

"No way," she said, grasping my hand. "We're gonna stay right here and watch the show. We promised Lauren, so we will. Calm down, Honey."

"People are staring."

"Let 'em stare." Rita squeezed my hand again, sat back in her chair, took a deep breath, and looked straight ahead in anticipation of the opening line. She was immovable. I thanked my lucky stars for her.

Mr. Silvio was right; the play was terrific that night. Lauren and Chickie gave it their all. Craig charmed the audience, and Dogberry and Verges scored even more laughs than the night before. After the curtain call, I received a text from Lauren that read, "Thx for coming, Mom. Thx for being my #1 fan. Pls thank Rita too. Love you! Chickie and I r going out w/ Craig and Friar F tonight. Don't wait up." My suffering was rewarded, and life would go on. Maybe there would be gossip, but we would weather it. Buck Bray's catchphrase, "And this, too, shall pass," came back to me. Perhaps I was the one making much ado about nothing. I hoped so.

CHAPTER 28

Where's Harrisburg Anyway?

It was late in the evening by the time our party glided away from shore. I was feeling glum because the week was coming to an end. Steph, Robert, and Lawrence were leaving in the morning. Lawrence and I would part with unfinished business. It hurt, and I feared the hurt would last a while.

The water was glassy. A night breeze blew pleasantly as the pontoon sputtered into deeper water. Lights from homes, piers, and boats shimmered on all sides, casting long reflections. Pink was in the captain's chair. Lawrence sat on a cushioned bench seat near Pink while Robert and Stephanie cuddled on another bench.

I melted into a rear bench seat near Rita; my thoughts drifted inward. I thought about our frightening pontoon ride a few nights before and about Tim Johnson, the guy who never grew up. No one had mentioned that frightening encounter since it happened. I thought about Jerry Bennett's selfishness, drinking, and bullying. Teri was surely in for more heartache.

Involvement with Lawrence Milner seemed just as doomed. He was undeniably charming and smart, but he was bound to be complicated. He said that he hadn't "always been the most reliable guy in the world." Did I want to know what was going on behind that gentlemanly façade? Did I want another intimate relationship with all the complications of physical and emotional closeness? I closed my eyes and consulted my gut.

The gang was chattering away about their fishing excursion that afternoon. They had had an exciting time and were eager to share the details with Rita and me. Rita showed little interest in the fish stories and occupied herself by tidying cargo boxes.

"Lawrence caught the biggest one," said Robert. "It was a bass about yay long." He sized up the imaginary fish with arms extended.

"What do you mean yay long?" I inquired. "Didn't you measure it? You always measure, don't you, Pink?"

"I didn't measure today 'cause I didn't want Lawrence to get a big head about it," Pink said. "I only measure when I catch a big one!" He roared with laughter at his own joke.

"I had a handicap," Robert insisted. "Pink gave me a bent rod. Have you ever tried to cast with a bent rod? I couldn't get the hook more than ten feet from the boat."

"I doubt it mattered much," said Lawrence. "Your trolling technique was less than impressive."

"I also had to bait Stephanie's hook twelve times, which slowed down my action," Robert continued.

"Action!" Pink mimicked the word and laughed again.

"I can't help it if I don't like touching worms," Stephanie protested.

"They were rubber worms. Did you think they would poop on you?" Robert asked.

"My bait box is full of jigs and lures. Nobody had to use worms," Pink insisted. "Lawrence, you should fly up to Canada with me next spring and do some real fishin'. Ever been up there?"

"No. Sounds great," Lawrence replied.

"What about me?" asked Robert.

"You can come, too," said Pink. "We can fly into Winnipeg and take a small plane up to Lake Manitoba. The pike and trout just 'bout jump in your boat."

"You'd probably make me use the bent rod again," Robert whined.

Rita handed sweatshirts to Steph and me. The cool breeze made for chilly boating but kept down the mosquitoes. Rita settled next to me again and whispered, "So, you haven't talked with Lawrence, have you? Tick tock, Honey." I shrugged. "Well, whatcha gonna do 'bout it?"

"Nothing. Absolutely nothing," I whisperer. "He's the one who wrote the note, so he should be the one to open the topic."

"I can't figure out why he hasn't said somethin' to you by now," said Rita, resting her head on the soft seat cushion and folding her arms in dismay. "Makes no sense. Maybe Pinky could say somethin' to him. You know, like . . ."

"Rita, don't you dare mention anything to Pink about this," I said, impatiently.

"Okay, okay, Honey."

Lawrence made his way to me. "Pink wants to know if you'd like to stop at Wolfman's for a nightcap or something to eat. Interested?" he asked. I could smell his aftershave and feel his body heat as he leaned in my direction.

We soon pulled alongside the pier at Wolfman's. Once inside, the bartender informed us that the tavern would soon close for the night, so Pink ordered a few appetizers and a pitcher of beer. Neither appealed to me that late. Lawrence asked for espresso and the bartender gave him a dirty look and pointed to a clock on the wall. Rita ordered a whiskey sour. Stephanie and I ordered the house Chardonnay to be sociable.

The conversation wandered from topic to topic, sprinkled with laughs and more silly banter. After a couple of beers, Lawrence put his baseball cap on backward and launched into an impersonation of some baseball announcer. It was charming and made Pink and Robert laugh until our table shook. It pleased me greatly that Lawrence could relax and let down his guard with us. I felt sure that we were getting a rare glimpse of the professor.

"So, when can you guys get away and go fishin' with me?" Pink asked. "How 'bout next spring? Let's lock it in. Easter time? Steph, you're invited, too, but the quarters are a little rough up there." Robert, Stephanie, and Lawrence's expressions changed suddenly; their smiles disappeared. Pink looked confused. "Did I say somethin' wrong? I won't take the bent rod."

Stephanie looked at me somberly. "We need to tell you something, Mom," she said. Rita jumped off her chair and stood behind me with her hand on my shoulder. I sat on the edge of my chair in anticipation of baby news, but that's not what I received. "Robert and I are moving. He got an offer for a tenure track position in the English Department at Penn State, Harrisburg. He'll start in January. We started to tell you this morning, but there was all that stuff with Lauren and Chickie. We couldn't hit you with it then. I hope you'll be happy for us."

My heart sank. My mind went in all directions. What would happen if Stephanie and Robert did have a baby? How could I help them if they lived in Pennsylvania? Could Stephanie manage the trials of motherhood without my help? I felt a twinge of jealousy for Pennsylvania and the university there, no matter how ridiculous the emotion. Steph had told me at Easter that Robert was shopping for other university positions. Her warning didn't soften the blow. That was hypothetical; this was real.

I thought of Stephanie's childhood. Phil and I never had to push her to be successful in school. She was bright and loved reading as a six-year-old. Now, because of their brains and ambition, they were leaving. What had it all been for? Was it so I could get phone calls at Christmas and talk to a baby on FaceTime?

Rita gripped both of my shoulders to steady me. I managed a smile. "Of course I'm happy for you," I said. "Congratulations, Robert. What an accomplishment." Pink and Rita added their congratulations.

It was obvious that Lawrence was aware of Robert's new position. "It's a good contract and says a lot about how much they value his talent," he said.

"He'll be teaching British literature, exactly what he wants," said Stephanie. "We don't want to move far away, but we can't pass it up. It's what we've been working toward."

"I know," I said, placidly. "What about your PhD?"

"I can finish the PhD from just about anywhere, but I'll come back to IU to defend the dissertation," said Stephanie. "I have a lot of work to do before then."

"Where is Harrisburg anyway?" I asked.

"About a hundred miles west of Philadelphia," said Robert. "You and Lawrence will love all the history out there. We can explore together."

"I'll hold you to that," I said, buoyed slightly.

"I know this comes as a surprise," Robert continued, "but I guarantee we'll work our way back to Indiana at some point. You won't have to go without Steph forever." His attempt at making me feel better failed. The words "at some point" and "forever" invoked too much uncertainty.

"What about your parents? Do they know?" I asked.

"Yeah, we told them earlier this week," Robert replied.

"So, looks like I'm the last to know . . . again," I said, glancing at Stephanie.

"Only because we knew it would upset you," Stephanie said.

"I wish you two the very best always. You know that." I was getting a grip.

The bartender pointed to the clock again. As we stepped out of the tavern and into the cool night air, Lawrence extended his arm to me. He knew I was reeling from Steph and Robert's news. We walked along the pier and boarded the pontoon in relative silence—each of us lost in thought. Rita sat up front near Pink; Lawrence sat beside me. His face took on the dim blue glow of the pontoon's safety lights. "I guess we'd better look out for *Tim's Titan*," he said, softly.

"That's all I need tonight," I said. "Running into him again would be a fitting end to the week."

"It's been a good week, Jill. I feel like part of the family."

"You are part of my family."

"Listen, do you want to do something a little crazy tonight?"

"Like what?" I asked, intrigued.

"How much gas is in the truck?"

"Plenty, I think."

"Let's go for a drive. There's something I want to talk with you about."

"It's pretty late."

"Okay, if you'd rather not."

"I'm in. Let's do it." Lawrence and I leaned back on the cushy seat. I was as drawn to Lawrence as ever, but I knew what had to be done. I was nervous. We gazed at the stars and didn't say another word until we reached Pink and Rita's pier. They invited us in for a "final nightcap." We politely declined but helped tidy the pontoon and secure it to the dock. We soon stood in Pink and Rita's driveway in the shadows trying to get in a few last words. Goodbyes were especially difficult that night. A sense of endings hung in the air like a pall. Stephanie and Robert gave extra hugs before heading off. Robert vowed to stay in touch with Pink regarding the Canada fishing trip, and we all promised a trip to Harrisburg, PA. We watched the Jeep swing around the circular drive, pull onto the street, and zip away.

Rita hugged me tight. "It's gonna be okay, Honey," she said. "Robert says they'll move back here, and I just know they will. Before you know it, they'll be livin' next door to ya and you'll get stuck watchin' their kids all the time."

"I hope so," I said. "Thanks for going to the play with me tonight and for the boat ride and for everything. I love you guys," I said.

Pink turned to Lawrence. "Hey, you better take her home before the two of 'em start cryin' and make me cry."

CHAPTER 29

We've Been Had

Instead of driving toward home, Lawrence headed in the opposite direction. We were soon traveling quiet back roads in northern Hamilton County. Since he was at the wheel, we glided along without lurching between gears. The truck windows were down and air blew freely through the cab. Fireflies glowed over the soybean and corn fields. I was reminded of the exhilaration I'd felt as a teenager on summertime dates. Had I been out at such an hour then, however, I would have been grounded by Buck and Mona. Lawrence tossed his cap on the seat of the truck and ran his fingers through his hair as if cutting loose for the first time in ages. Maybe he hoped the wind would blow off years of sitting in libraries, grading term papers, and lecturing classes—if only for a few moments on a starry night. I knew I was lucky to be along for the ride, but I also knew that my mild euphoria couldn't last. It was time to explain myself.

"How about pulling over someplace," I suggested. It was hard to breathe with a stomach full of butterflies. Lawrence pulled the truck onto a sandy road that led to a stand of trees in the middle of soybean fields. The truck rolled to a halt at the edge of the trees. Lawrence killed the engine and cut the lights. Though it was dark, still, and eerie, I felt safe with him. "If this thing doesn't start up again, we're in big trouble. I'm not exactly sure where we are, but I'm sure we're trespassing."

"It's okay," he said. He patted the cell phone in his pocket. "GPS will get us home, and no one is watching us. Better roll up the windows before the bugs find us. I know you have something on your mind, so why don't you go first."

I fixed my gaze on the dark woods. It was time to get this conversation behind us. "Okay, here goes," I said. "After giving this a lot of thought, I don't want to get involved . . . with anyone, I mean. I've finally figured out who I am and my purpose in life. You might say that I've become selfish or you might say that I've become wiser. I'm finally able to take care of myself. The bottom line is that I'm happy as I am. I have my farm and a business, and I'm in control. I don't have to consult anybody but Mort on farm business. I don't have to constantly answer to anyone. I've been married twice. My first marriage ended in grief, and my second marriage ended in . . . well . . . grief of a different kind. I won't risk anything like that again. It's time for me to say uncle. No more. I feel whole for the first time in my life. It's hard to explain. I'd be very pleased to be your friend, Lawrence, but friendship is all I can offer. I hope you understand. I certainly don't want to hurt you. I truly appreciated your note; it was sweet. It made me feel so . . . so good. Do you understand?"

Lawrence was silent. In the dark cab, it was hard to see his expression, and his face was turned slightly toward the driver's side window. I feared that I had crushed him. Was he actually crying? After a pause, he turned his face toward me. "I think I'm beginning to understand. I didn't write you a note," he said.

"But there was a note on my dresser. I still have it," I demanded. How could he have forgotten?

"I don't know what you have, but it's not a note from me. What does it say?"

"I don't have it with me, but it says . . . don't you know what it says? It says you've been thinking of me since Robert and Stephanie's wedding, and you hope we'll become more than friends or something like that."

Lawrence chuckled and leaned his head on the headrest. "Oh, we've been had. Seems like your little tricksters were working overtime this week."

"Ugh," I uttered. "I don't believe it. I've raised a monster." I felt sick inside and angry.

"I wouldn't say that, but they are quite inventive." Lawrence pulled a piece of folded paper from his pocket and offered it to me. "Then you didn't write this?" he asked.

"What's that?" I inquired. I was quite sure of the answer.

"It's the note you wrote me. Don't you recognize it?"

"Good lord, I'm afraid to read it."

"Oh, it's a gem. Do you have a flashlight in here?" I pulled a flashlight from the glove box, took the note from his hand, and read.

Dear Lawrence,

When I heard that you were coming with Stephanie and Robert, I was so glad. I have thought of you many times since we met at the wedding. I have planned alot of activities for us this week so I hope you'll join us in everything. I hope you find your room comfortable since I prepared it specially for you. It's my best room. Lauren and Chickie wanted the room this week but I saved it for you. I've enjoyed our time together so far and hope you enjoy being with me. I look forward to us becoming good friends and maybe more than friends.

Sincerely,
Jill

"What a ridiculous note," I said. "Didn't they think we'd talk about it and discover the truth right away?"

"Well, we didn't, did we?"

"You actually thought I wrote this?"

"What was I supposed to think?" asked Lawrence. "You could be illiterate for all I know."

"This isn't far from it. Good thing they'll be taking more English classes. How did you get this?"

"Found it Wednesday morning. Slid under my door."

"I found your note Wednesday morning also—I mean, the note supposedly from you. Is this why you wanted to talk with me tonight?"

"Yeah. I've been working on a little speech of my own."

"Go ahead. I'm listening," I said and sighed.

Lawrence ran a hand through his hair. "I was prepared to say what you just said to me. It's not by accident that I've been a bachelor for twenty years. My reasons are much the same as yours. The freedom makes me happy. I come and go as I please, spend as I want, and travel as I want. I don't have to meet anyone else's expectations. Don't get me wrong; there have been women in my life. But when my marriage ended, I didn't want to commit again. Maybe it will catch up with me someday and I'll regret the way I live. We'll see."

I was stunned. I'd been a fool for thinking Lawrence was heartsick over me when all the while he was trying to figure out how to let me down. I was glad for the darkness as my emotions surged. I was furious with Lauren and Chickie for playing such a nasty trick and presuming to orchestrate our lives. They had put Lawrence and me through days of turmoil. I should have been more suspicious after the *Much Ado* deception, but my ego led me to believe that Lawrence was falling for me. I'd been a willing victim of the girls' game, and maybe Lawrence had been just as willing.

"I'm so embarrassed I could die," I said. "Think I'll walk home."

Lawrence chuckled. "Hey, one of us had to go first."

"You took my hand when we were in the barn watching the rain. What was that all about?" I asked.

"I told you there have been women in my life. I'm not a stone. You're an attractive woman. After that happened, I thought I'd better cool off for a couple of days; hence, the trip to Notre Dame. I was a coward for disappearing, but I had to get my head on straight."

"I can't apologize enough for what you've been put through," I said. "I'll find a way to punish the girls for this."

"You have nothing to apologize for. They have to take the rap, and I think I know a way to make an impression. Leave it to me."

"Okay," I said. I had complete confidence in Lawrence. "Are you tired?" By now, I was struggling to keep my eyes open.

"Yeah. Guess it's time to go." Lawrence fired up the truck; we rolled down the windows and headed for home. His phone stayed in his pocket. He knew exactly how to get back to the inn. We traveled mostly in silence. I suppose we were both thinking about the notes and wondering how we could have allowed ourselves to be deceived. I suppose we were also thinking about retribution. I wondered what lesson the professor had in mind for Lauren and Chickie. They were about to be schooled.

CHAPTER 30

Lawrence Milner, Friend

Mort rang my cell phone at seven o'clock on Saturday morning. His arthritis had flared, so I should feed the chickens and sheep. I asked if he needed help at his place. He would let me know. Knowing he is a proud man who doesn't like a fuss, I'd have to approach him carefully with offers of help. I'd also have to deal with his sons at some point, but that was more than I could think about that morning. He loves my chicken 'n' dumplings, so I'd make him a batch that afternoon—following a trip to Wilson's market for more chicken.

Lawrence was already up and making his nectar of the gods coffee as I walked into the kitchen. He looked just as handsome as he had the day before, but my feelings toward him had undergone an involuntary transformation. He was no longer the intimidating Howie Leonard from my high school typing class. He was Lawrence Milner, my friend. I felt jubilant over my unexpected change of heart. Our little conversation the night before had changed everything. If only we hadn't waited so long. He insisted on helping me with chores, so I grabbed the egg basket. As we passed the gardens, the weeds mocked me. I'd have my revenge soon enough.

Lawrence and I rolled back the barn track door and drove the flock into their pasture. The ewes and lambs bounded out happily to browse. Lawrence checked the electric waterer. The hens were also happy to be admitted into the daylight. Lawrence untied the ground corn sack and filled the feeder while I raided the nests and inspected the flock. All were present and accounted for and looked fat and glossy. I was glad that Lawrence seemed at home and knew what to do. "I'm gonna miss this place," he said.

"You're welcome anytime," I said, as I tied the mouth of the corn sack.

"This is none of my business, Jill, but how will you manage the place when Mort retires?"

"Good question. I'll manage. I'm more worried about how he'll take it when he can't work his place anymore."

"How 'bout meeting me in Harrisburg over the holidays, and we'll do some sightseeing. I haven't been there in years. Would you enjoy that?"

"I would," I said. "I'll need plenty of planning time since the inn gets booked months ahead."

Lawrence looked deeply into my eyes and smiled. "Okay, I'll remember that."

"What time will you be leaving?" I asked.

"As soon as Robert and Stephanie are packed, but how about breakfast first? I'd like the matchmakers to join us. I have a little surprise for them. Just play along with whatever I say, and bring the forgery with you."

I had Eggs Benedict in mind for breakfast but was missing Canadian bacon and English muffins, so I added these items to my shopping list along with a stewing hen for Mort's chicken 'n' dumplings. I hopped into the truck and drove downtown, leaving Lawrence to wake Robert and Stephanie and pack. As usual, the trip to Wilson's Market nourished my senses and lifted my spirits. Nona Wilson waited on me this time, and we agreed that Canadian bacon is superior to ham in Eggs Benedict. I was eager to get back home and see what Lawrence had in mind for Lauren and Chickie. Revenge is not a nice concept on any level and when perpetrated on one's children, it's especially diabolical. However, the girls had it coming.

When I arrived home, Lauren and Chickie were sitting on the porch still in disheveled sleep attire. They looked ragged around the edges with tousled hair and slits for eyes. It was clear they'd been out late, and they bitterly resented the wake-up call.

"Mom, why did Lawrence wake us up?" Lauren asked. "We didn't get home until three."

"Serves you right for being out that late," I said. "Where did you go, anyway?"

"We went to a party in Indianapolis with Craig and Friar Francis. I don't know exactly where it was," Lauren said.

"Most of the crowd was gay so there wasn't much point," said Chickie.

Lauren persisted, "Why did Lawrence wake us up? What's going on?"

"Have you forgotten that Steph and Robert and Lawrence are leaving this morning? They would like a final breakfast with you," I replied.

"We had a final breakfast with them yesterday," said Lauren. "So, is this the last final breakfast?"

"You're big on final breakfasts around here," said Chickie. "My parents didn't ask me to have a final breakfast with them."

"Have your parents even seen you this week?" I asked.

"I saw them on Tuesday. My mother and I had a slight disagreement, so I haven't been back home. I'll see them at the matinee tomorrow."

I picked up the groceries and moved on to the kitchen. Since I had a ton of green tomatoes in the garden, I decided to try a *Joy of Cooking* variation and place Eggs Benedict over fried green tomatoes. The ingredients would all be placed on one large warm platter. I'd need help with this, so I called everyone together and made assignments. Lawrence was in charge of the coffee and poached eggs. I fried the tomatoes and made a velvety hollandaise.

Breakfast preparation included grumbling and objections. Lauren and Chickie complained of being "too exhausted to move." Stephanie and Robert were "terribly busy with packing." Lawrence was the only agreeable soul, so he and I worked cheerfully despite the children. My suggestion to Lauren and Chickie that they dress properly for breakfast was met with more grumbling. Their deportment had changed noticeably in the past year and not for the better. I found myself regretting Lauren's choice of a roommate.

After a fraught thirty minutes, we assembled at the table. Realizing that our time together was short, Robert sought to lighten the mood. "Steph and I both like to cook now," he said, "and we're using the cookbooks that people gave us for the wedding. I'll bet there'll be some great farmer's markets in Harrisburg, and we can't wait to check out the local restaurants."

"You're welcome to take some of my cookbooks," I said. "There are only a few I won't part with. I believe I have a cookbook on Pennsylvania Dutch cookery. Help yourselves."

"I can use all the help I can get," said Stephanie.

"You'd better take them soon since your mother and I will be downsizing right away," said Lawrence, offhandedly. Lauren,

Chickie, Stephanie, and Robert stopped eating and stared at Lawrence and then at me.

"Downsizing what?" asked Lauren.

"I suppose this is as good a time as any to share our news. Your mother and I are getting married," Lawrence announced. He placed his hand on mine and smiled at me. "Soon." Though my blood pressure probably soared, I returned a smile and took on the demeanor of a blissful bride-to-be.

Stephanie gasped. "What? Mother!"

"That's why we gathered you together this morning," I said, earnestly. "We figured we'd better tell you right away. I know this is a shock, but I'm sure you'll all be happy for us when you make the adjustment."

"A shock? That doesn't quite cover it!" Stephanie exclaimed.

"I don't believe this! How could you do this? I mean, how would this work?" Lauren asked. She went pale.

"We've worked it out," said Lawrence. "Your mother has decided that since Mort is getting up in years, it's time to sell the farm and the inn. It's tough keeping up this big place on her own. She'll move to Bloomington with me. We've already talked it over with Mort. He's been thinking about retiring from farming, so he's on board."

"Mom, is this true?" Lauren asked, desperately. "You're selling the place? How could you?"

"Oh, I'm not doing it lightly," I insisted. "Lawrence and I have spent a lot of time talking about it."

"A lot of time!" Lauren blurted. "You just met him a week ago and now you're going to marry him?"

"No, no, actually, we met at the wedding. We've thought of each other very fondly ever since," I said, batting my eyelashes at Lawrence.

"We also thought we'd better tell you right away because you'll need to take whatever belongs to you so we don't garage sale it or pitch it by mistake," said Lawrence. I marveled at his acting ability. In fact, I began to wonder if he was acting.

"Pitch it?" Stephanie questioned. "You mean, you'd just throw away our stuff?"

"Well, we'd try to be careful, but we can't take it all with us," I said. "My storeroom is full of your clothes and books and dolls and band instruments. Lawrence and I can't take all of that to his house. There won't be room."

"You'd sell the farm, Mrs. Merrick?" asked a stunned Chickie. "But I thought you loved this place. It's the coolest place ever. Where will I go when I come home?"

"I suppose you'll have to go to your house . . . you know . . . that place where your parents live," I replied.

"Oh, there," said Chickie.

"We plan to get married soon," said Lawrence, between bites, "so we can get settled before the semester begins in August. It'll take a while to sell the farm and the inn, but we'll work it out. Your mom will sell the sheep right away. The chicken will be easy." The girls cringed. Robert sat very still and wide-eyed. Lawrence projected a side of his personality that I'd not seen. I knew now that he could be a bit nasty if provoked—and he was provoked.

"Just like that," said Stephanie. "Everything you've worked for, Mother. Everything you love. Our farm. Grandma and Grandpa's farm." Her eyes searched mine for answers and filled with tears. "How can this be?"

My heart ached for the girls. I wasn't sure why Lawrence was allowing Steph and Robert to become collateral damage in our prank, but I hoped he had a good reason.

"We thought you'd be happy for us," said Lawrence. "Isn't this what you wanted?" His question was followed by silence and a revealing exchange of glances. He then pulled from his shirt pocket the note supposedly written by me. "I'm sure that someone here left this note for me. Now is a good time to thank the author and say how much I appreciated this little push. I did enjoy meeting Jill at the wedding, and she's been on my mind. After spending time with her this week, I can't wait to marry her. No need to dream about it any longer." The words were charming and romantic. I almost regretted that we were lying through our teeth.

"And I feel the same about Lawrence," I said. I gave him a sticky sweet gaze and forced the words off my tongue. "So, there's no sense in waiting." I produced the note supposedly from him to me. "Who do we have to thank for this charming note?"

"It was Steph and Robert's idea," Lauren blurted.

"It was our idea to get them together," Stephanie responded, defensively. "We had nothing to do with leaving any notes. The notes were another one of your dumb ideas. How could you? Oh, let me guess, you were only trying to help."

"We had no idea these two would pull such a stunt," Robert said. "We just wanted you to meet again."

"Robert thought Uncle Lawrence might be lonely," said Stephanie.

"And Steph thought Jill might be lonely," said Robert.

"Have I ever indicated that I'm lonely?" I asked.

"So, what's the problem?" interrupted Lawrence. "You're all getting what you want."

"Well, we never thought you'd just run off and get married after one week," said Stephanie, "and we certainly didn't think Mother would sell the farm. I can't imagine life without this place."

"Don't worry," said Lawrence, in a conciliatory tone. "We're not going to run off and get married."

"You're not?" Lauren asked, hopefully.

"The wedding will be right here. You're all invited," Lawrence announced. But moods had turned somber. We finished breakfast in silence. Lauren and Stephanie cleared the table, sulking. They clanked my china service around until I feared every piece would be chipped. Robert shuffled bags to the Jeep in silence. Wisely, Chickie kept her opinions to herself for perhaps the first time in her life. I was feeling guilty and wondered how long Lawrence meant to keep up the charade. I gave him an inquiring glance, and he gave me a sly smile in return.

After Robert's third or fourth trip to the Jeep, he stopped in the center of the kitchen floor and announced, "I'm not buying it."

"Buying what?" asked Lawrence, coolly.

"I'm not buying this stuff about you and Jill getting married just like that. It's not your style at all. I think you're making it up, so I called Mort, and he's coming over here now. We'll see what he knows about this." My heart sank. I absolutely did not want poor, unsuspecting Mort involved in our lie. We had told the children that the farm would be sold, and I'd be moving away. He would be shocked and hurt. I decided that our deception, though justified, had gone far enough. Moreover, it irked me that our lie might backfire and Robert would prove too clever for us.

"Okay, okay," I said. "It's time to tell the truth . . ." Lauren, Chickie, and Stephanie were all ears. They sat at the kitchen table eyeing Lawrence and me suspiciously.

"Yep, I agree," Lawrence interrupted. "Let's tell them the truth. We may have to get married sooner because I'd like to take Jill on a honeymoon before fall semester. This means we may be getting married next weekend. Hope you can all come back." I continued doing the dishes as if this bizarre conversation wasn't happening. But I was beginning to fear that Lawrence had either lost his mind or was serious about marrying me—a problem in either case.

Mort knocked at the kitchen door and was quickly admitted by Robert. I froze, horrified by what might happen next. "Thanks for coming, Mort," said Robert. "Do you mind if we ask you a question?"

"If you're gonna ask me if Jill and Lawrence have my blessing to get married, the answer is yep," said Mort. "Never saw two people better suited." I managed a poker face. Could I possibly have heard his words correctly? What was happening?

"Uncle Mort, they want to get married right away, and Mother wants to sell the farm," Stephanie said, fighting tears again. "Did you know this?" Robert stood behind her and massaged her shoulders.

"Well, that's your mother's business," Mort replied sternly. "She can do as she pleases. I'm getting on and will be doin' the same thing one o' these days."

"Well, yeah, one of these days, but we never thought . . ." Robert paused. He was at a rare loss for words.

"What about us?" Lauren said, angrily. "Did you stop to think what all of this is going to do to Steph and Robert and me?" At least she was thinking about her sister's welfare, too.

"And me?" Chickie chimed in.

"Did you stop to think about your mother and me when you left those forged notes?" Lawrence asked, abruptly. "Do you know how your notes affected us and what the week's been like because of them? Did you think it through at all?" Lauren and Chickie exchanged glances but made no reply. Lawrence had sprung the trap like a courtroom lawyer. The girls were amateurs in comparison.

"You made this up," Robert said, dryly. "So, you aren't getting married?"

"No!" Lawrence responded, flatly. He said no more but helped himself to another cup of coffee and began clearing away breakfast dishes.

"Got chores to do," said Mort. "Gotta go. Good seein' you all." He returned his cap to his head and stepped to the door.

"Can I fix you some eggs?" I called after him.

"Not ready to eat," he said. "Too much to do. Glad to help, Lawrence."

"Much obliged," Lawrence replied. It was obvious that he and Mort were in league on the setup, but I wondered how they'd managed it.

We were all reeling from the events of the past few minutes. After cleaning up, I retreated to the porch to finish a cup of Lawrence's Sumatra and French Roast blend. It seemed like a month since he had made that first cup for me. Stephanie and Robert resumed packing. Lauren and Chickie fled to their guest room. We all needed some space. Lawrence brought his bags to the porch and sat down in a rocker beside me. "That may have been a little harsh," he said. "Guess I was more upset than I'd realized, but I hate being manipulated."

"They had it coming," I said, "but in their own silly way, they were trying to be helpful. Sorry, sympathy is an occupational hazard."

"They weren't thinking about you and me. They were thinking about what they wanted," Lawrence insisted. "Robert and Stephanie had matchmaking in mind all along. I see that now."

"It wasn't such a bad week I suppose," I said.

Lawrence smiled. "Well, it was great seeing you again, and I enjoyed rescuing you."

"How did you get Mort to play along?"

"I dropped in on him this morning while you were shopping. I know my nephew well. Figured he'd ask Mort to verify."

"You're amazing," I said.

"I'm not proud of the deception. It worked well for Shakespeare, but it doesn't work out well in real life. Maybe that's another reason I haven't remarried. Honesty's hard to come by."

"Yeah," I replied.

"Listen, I'm gonna slip outta here now since I still have the rental. I've decided to go back up to Notre Dame. Maybe I can concentrate this time."

"Will you say goodbye to the kids?"

"Nah, I think it's best to take off. More dramatic this way." Lawrence winked at me.

"Thanks for everything," I said. "Good luck with the New Deal. Hope FDR gets what he wants."

"I'm pretty sure he will."

"By the way, don't forget your coffee," I said.

"I left it for you. Consider it a thank-you gift, but do me a favor and don't pollute it with cream and sugar." Lawrence stood and held out his arms. I melted into them, and he gave me a bear hug. It was strange that tears should be welling in my eyes since I'd only known him a few days, but it felt good.

"Don't be a stranger," I said.

"I'll call you about our Harrisburg trip. And one more thing, call me any time you need a rescue. Can't wait to climb another tree." He lifted his bags and pushed open the screen door with his foot. Our eyes met, and I was no longer uncomfortable meeting his gaze—at least for a few seconds.

"Sounds good," I said. Something told me that Lawrence's offer was sincere. I watched him drive away and hesitated to walk back inside the inn. It would feel very different without him, and it would hurt for a while.

CHAPTER 31

Guardians All Around

The Jeep was loaded once again with suitcases and bookbags. Stephanie and Robert made a sweep through the inn to be sure cell phones, chargers, computers, books, and favorite t-shirts wouldn't be left behind. I was more concerned about all the opportunities we'd left behind that week. My plans for a cozy time with the girls had gone up in smoke like the fireworks. A sense of change was also in the air. Steph and Robert would be moving to Harrisburg. The distance would challenge all of us. I was sure that Lauren felt the change, too, since she carried Stephanie's luggage to the Jeep voluntarily.

I preparing a "care package" for Steph and Robert, including homemade bread, eggs, fresh-cut flowers, a few bottles of wine, some of Mort's premium beef packed in ice, cookies, and jars of my homemade strawberry and peach jam. We sat on the porch and talked about fall semester schedules, holiday plans, and the move to Harrisburg. I was proud of myself for projecting an optimistic attitude.

"I hope Lawrence won't stay mad at us for long," said Robert, broaching the subject.

"You have every right to be angry with us," said Stephanie. "Our good intentions feel pretty lame now."

"I'm sure we'll get over it," I said, "but you need to realize that Lawrence and I are not sad, lonely people. I know it's hard to believe, but it's possible to live a good life without a mate. Apart from not being able to solve world hunger, I'm generally a happy person. I've found my sweet spot. There is this thing called contentment, you know. It does exist."

"We didn't know for sure that you were happy," said Stephanie.

"You could have asked me," I replied. Stephanie sighed.

"We made some dumb moves this week," Lauren said, running her hands through her hair uneasily.

"Yeah, like having a crush on a gay guy," Chickie lamented. "That was a big mistake."

"You're not getting the message, are you?" Lauren said. "You can't think about anybody but yourself."

"Well, excuse me," Chickie snapped. "When did you become Dr. Phil?" She left the porch abruptly.

"I think a lot of us might be better on our own," said Stephanie, glancing in Lauren's direction.

I had heard what I needed to hear from my daughters. My heart was at peace, and I could let them go again. The week hadn't gone as planned, but maybe it went as the universe desired. New faces were woven into the tapestry of my life, and the fabric was richer for it. Come Monday, if the citizens of Noblesville were gossiping about us, I'd deal with it.

It seemed like a good time to give Stephanie the gift I'd been saving for a special occasion—Mona's Spode Chinese Rose tea set. Mona had been very protective of the beautiful set of eight cups and saucers, exquisite teapot, sugar bowl, and creamer. I was grateful she'd been stingy with the set all those years. Stephanie and I packed each piece with great care, and Robert positioned the box strategically in the Jeep. After hugs, they drove away silently. Lauren and I pulled a few weeds away from the tomatoes as a diversion. She picked up the little calico cat and carried her to the porch, where they rocked together. It was good therapy for both of them.

It was time to start the chicken 'n' dumplings for Mort, and my cleaning and laundry services were due to arrive shortly. But I was craving solace of my own. I loaded the truck bed with several buckets of water and rumbled off to the Bray Cemetery. My stomach was knotted for fear Carolyn Mawbrey's prediction about the pink geraniums would be correct. I was sure to find dead flowers beside the headstones. Letting the gardens at the inn languish for the week was bad enough, but letting the geraniums at the cemetery die was intolerable. I consoled myself by thinking that the rain may have saved them. I braced myself for guilt and grief.

To my great relief, the geraniums had not only survived but were blooming like crazy. Masses of pink petals stood out cheerfully against the gray granite headstones. It quickly became evident that the hard, clay soil in which I'd buried the roots had been replaced by dark, fertile soil. I was stunned. It wasn't Mort's style to "fiddle with flowers" on the graves, even Aunt Geneva's. I thought of Lawrence and sighed. The magnitude of my erroneous assumptions about him was sinking in. My imaginings had been ridiculous. All he'd wanted was a change of scenery for a week and to be with family. He wasn't looking for romance, just a room with a view and some quiet time with FDR. I thought about *Much Ado About Nothing* and how the characters deceived each other. Perhaps self-deception is the most destructive.

As I toted water to the flowers and watched it soak into the rich soil, tears rolled down my cheeks. I wasn't crying over departed souls. I realized with clarity that I'd been surrounded by guardian angels all my life, and Lawrence had joined their ranks. Even in death, Phil, Mona, Buck, and Aunt Geneva were watching me and guiding my footsteps. I owed so much to Mort, Rita, Pink, Mary, and others for carrying me over rocky shoals many times. My children, in their kooky way, had become my guardians also. I knew suddenly that I wasn't whole because I was a liberated woman or because I was making it financially. I was whole because I was never alone. My guardians, the visible and the invisible, surrounded me every day. The Wise Woman of Lapel had asked the right questions, but it took a crazy week and pink geraniums to guide me to the truth. I didn't know what the future held for me, but for the moment I felt wonderfully alive and complete. I couldn't wait to get home, grab my hoe, and restore my gardens.

CHAPTER 32

Equilibrium

On Sunday morning, I attended church and thanked God for his many blessings. Later that day, I attended the matinee of *Much Ado About Nothing*. The cast had hit their stride. The play was a big success, and Ronaldo Silvio was justifiably pleased. As promised, he assembled the cast after the curtain call so that Lauren, Chickie, and Teddy could apologize for plotting Teddy's deception. Chickie, however, was nowhere to be found. She had fled, leaving Lauren and Teddy to take the heat. She had also promised to give Lauren a ride back to Ball State, but that didn't pan out either. I drove Lauren back to school. She felt angry and betrayed, and I was sad for her. Though we traveled in near silence all the way to Muncie, I was able to clear up one little matter before we parted.

"You started to tell me something when you came to my room the other night. Were you going to tell me about the notes?" I asked.

"Yeah," she said, quietly.

"What stopped you?"

"I was in enough trouble," she said. "I'm sorry. I really am." I helped carry her luggage as far as the dorm lobby but declined to go to her room where I might see Chickie. Lauren would have to settle matters with Chickie on her own.

"When will I see you next?" I asked.

"I'll have a week between summer school and fall classes. Will you save me a room? It doesn't have to be the blue room."

"Of course," I said. "What will you do about Chickie?"

"The dorm has some single rooms open since it's summer. I'll move as fast as I can." We hugged goodbye.

Rita kept me company via cell phone on the drive home. It seemed she'd booked massages for us on Tuesday afternoon as a pick-me-up after my "hell of a week." Also, she and Pink "needed" new sofas, so she asked me to go shopping with her. And there was a big horse show coming up in Columbus, Indiana. Did I want to go? She and Pink were also planning a trip to Provence, France. They would stay in Avignon and swing down to St. Tropez. Would I like to go with them? "Sure thing," I said. "Might as well dream big. I need more lavender for the potpourri mix." We laughed. I'd heard similar travel plans from Rita many times. Who knew? Maybe it would work out this time.

"Thanks for being the best friend ever," I told Rita.

"Well, somebody's gotta keep you outta trouble," she said.

The weather turned blessedly cooler on Monday. I trimmed the boxwoods along the driveway, harvested herbs for drying, and weeded the vegetable garden. I was exhausted by four o'clock but elated by my progress. I sat on the porch with my little calico cat and made out a menu and grocery list in preparation for my next guests. Teri Bennett wheeled into my driveway unexpectedly. She was dressed for gardening and ready to get started. We talked a little about Jerry and Teddy, but she changed the subject. Since we hadn't gotten very far with *Flowers and Herbs vs. Weeds, 101*, I started over. I was thrilled to have Teri back and pleased that we could take our time.

Finale

Ayear has passed since that eventful week. In case you're wondering, Teri is now my right-hand helper at the inn. She and Jerry got back together in the spring after months of counseling. She demanded he sober up, and believe it or not, he has. Teddy Bennett and Tom Laughlin worked off their debt under Big Sue's direction and then wrote and directed a play at the high school called *Thrift Shop Murders*. I supposed they'd invented some bizarre end to Big Sue. Lauren found a new roommate, and they're on a mission trip in South America this summer. Rita, Pink, and I haven't made it to Provence yet, but we keep talking about it. Lawrence and I, however, did tour Harrisburg with Steph and Robert over the holidays and had great fun. After the trip, Lawrence sent me a note. No, it wasn't a love note. It came in a box with the woolen stocking cap he'd received from Harlowe Barnes. He thought the cap would look better on me. Seriously, Lawrence? Not a chance.

About the Author

Peggy Aylesworth Novotny grew up on a farm in Indiana and is well acquainted with the setting for this debut novel. She was a communication specialist at universities in Indiana and North Carolina for thirty years. Now retired from East Carolina University, she's bringing to life engaging fictional characters. She lives in Winterville, NC, treasures time with her children and grandchildren, and enjoys seeing the country by train.

Reviews are welcome on Amazon or wherever this book is purchased. Peggy may be contacted at novotnyp633@gmail.com.